One True Love

One True Love

Lisa Follett

An Original Press

2011

This is a work of fiction. Names, characters, places, and incidents are products of the author's imagination or are used fictitiously and are not to be construed as real. Any resemblance to actual events, locales, organizations, or persons, living or dead, is entire coincidental.

Published by *An Original Press*
Friendswood, Texas 77546
U.S.A.
Cover design by Kimberly Killion

Dedication

To my one true love—my husband. I love you forever.

A special thanks to Elizabeth, my dear friend and editor.

One True Love

Chapter One

ORD WILLIAM PRESCOTT touched the ring in his pocket. Another refused proposal to add to his list, yet, he refused to believe in a silly curse.

"William, why do you look so melancholy tonight?" Mary startled him out of his thoughts. The drawing room buzz went quiet. His siblings thought the curse particularly amusing. He had suffered their teasing since he was in leading strings, but he did not think he could bear it tonight.

"Did Miss Peterson refuse your suit?" asked Jane. He decided the real curse upon his head were his four pesky sisters.

"She refused." His hand slipped back into his pocket.

"Twelve rejections. I do not know how you bear it, dear William." Anne's eyes twinkled while she squeezed his arm in sympathy.

"The curse is your destiny—*your fate.* It is such a shame. You would make a wonderful husband and father." Elizabeth's smile reached her dark eyes. He knew she teased, but tonight it cut deep.

Simply because every woman he courted refused his suit, or managed to get themselves in a compromising position with someone else, did not prove the curse existed. Did it matter that Lady Charlotte Manvel ran off to Gretna Green with Viscount Martindale the same night she rejected his proposal of marriage? Surely, no one would believe such a thing, simply because Miss Martin fainted dead away when he appeared on her doorstep with a bundle of flowers in his hand. And really, how could anyone associate the curse with Lady Fiona Berkeley's tendency to run and hide whenever he came near?

"A man's lot in life, his fate, his destiny, is made by his own actions and reactions, not by some ancient tragic tale." William took a swallow of his brandy. "Just because every second son since the third Marquis of Camberley lived life alone, did not mean it was because of a curse. If anything, each of my predecessors used the curse as the perfect excuse to stay a bachelor."

"And you should follow in your predecessors footsteps if you ask me." James, his notorious rake of a brother chuckled in his brandy. At this rate, he would be in his cups before dinner was served.

"I did not ask you," said William.

"Tsk, tsk, no need to be so testy. I do not understand why you are so determined to marry," said James.

"Marriage is an honorable institution James," said Elizabeth.

"If it is so honorable then why are you so firmly upon the shelf, sister?"

Elizabeth paled. At nine and twenty, she much preferred her writing to finding a husband. His entire family, with the exception of himself, avoided the marriage shackles. The only one who needed to marry was Stephen, the heir to the Marquis of Camberley.

"James, really! Mind your manners," his mother, Lady Camberley scolded her youngest son. "I am sorry, William. I thought Miss Peterson would surely come up to scratch."

"At this rate England is going to run out of eligible young ladies, *and* widows, *and* spinsters. Perhaps you should go to the continent to find a wife, or America," said Stephen.

"Perhaps I might." William finished off his brandy and stood up. He felt restless and needed to move. He looked out the front window in time to see a carriage stop in front of the house. "It appears the new vicar and his family has arrived."

"About time, I am starving," said James.

He watched as an older balding man with a paunch belly and spectacles on his face stepped out of the carriage. The man's dour expression left little to recommend his Sunday sermons. He had yet to meet the new vicar since he recently moved into his own home over an hour away. The vicar turned and helped down an overlarge woman with curling gray hair and a jolly smile on her face. They seemed a rather odd pair. He could only assume the woman was the man's wife.

"Poor souls—to be thrust in the midst of a Prescott family supper. What will they think?" he muttered.

"What did you say, William?" asked his mother.

"Nothing."

Mary leaned against him to peer out the window, "I heard that." She piled her hair on top of her head tonight in waves of dark loose curls that matched her chocolate colored eyes. They shimmered with laughter. "Now you behave yourself, William."

"Me behave? Look who is calling the kettle black, you little hellion."

"I am not a hellion Lord William Spencer Prescott. I am independent!" Mary huffed and turned away from the window. He laughed at his twin, the mischief-maker of the family.

He turned back towards the window and froze. The air whooshed from his lungs as he watched an angel alight from the carriage. "Who is the young woman with the vicar and his wife?"

Elizabeth peered over his shoulder. "That would be Miss Cassandra Chambers, the vicar's eldest daughter." She gave him a quizzical look, as if trying to decide whether or not to say something more.

"She is quite a beauty," said Jane from across the room.

"Intelligent and witty as well," said Anne.

"Yes, too bad she is already betrothed William," said Mary.

Of all the damnable luck! He shook his head and peered into his empty glass. He needed a refill. He moved away from the window and waited for the vicar's family to enter the drawing room.

A few moments later William sucked in his breath when she came through the doorway. The candlelight bounced off her golden curls and shone like the fairy dust from one of Elizabeth's stories. Her lush pink lips curved up and the world melted away. *God, she was beautiful.*

"William, do come and meet our guests." His mother turned to the vicar. "I believe you have met everyone except my son, Lord William Prescott. William, this is Mr. Joseph Chambers."

He shook the vicar's hand. "I am pleased to meet you, sir."

"Lord William, may I present his wife, Mrs. Chambers."

"Mrs. Chambers." He took her gloved hand and raised it to his lips for a light and proper kiss of air, but his eyes strayed to her daughter.

"And this is my daughter, Miss Cassandra Chambers," said the vicar.

"*Miss* Chambers." He took her hand, and lifted his gaze to her eyes, large green pools in which he could simply drown. Perfect. Absolutely perfect. Her smile lit something inside of him. He kissed her hand, holding on a fraction too long. He did not want to let go. Their eyes locked for a brief moment before she spoke.

"My lord," her silky voice shivered down his spine to the lower regions of his body. When she curtsied, he caught a glimpse of her milky white skin against her properly cut bodice hiding what appeared to be delectable round breasts. He moved his eyes to her face before anyone noticed his brief moment of impropriety.

Her rose silk gown clung to her generous curves and gave her cheeks a pink glow. She had the face of an English rose, slightly round and angelic, and topped with a pert little nose. Something tugged at his heart, but alas, he did not have to feel the pain of her rejection. She could not be his.

The weight of the blasted curse crashed around him and roared inside his ears. He would find the perfect wife, his one true love, despite the curse, his family's infernal teasing, and the ton's vicious harpy gossips. He would follow his parent's example and find happiness.

His parents enjoyed a marriage beyond the pale of polite Society. *They* actually loved each other. Six children later and they still acted as if they were in the first blush of love.

The butler announced that dinner was served. William offered Miss Chambers his arm. The warmth of her presence wrapped around him like a fur-lined coat on a winter night. He mentally scolded himself for acting like a besotted fool, but when he looked upon her face, he could not help but feel an attraction, which ran deep into the well of his soul.

He looked ahead and reminded himself of her betrothal, muttering under his breath, "Damn the curse!"

"I beg your pardon, Lord William?"

* * *

Cassie peered out the carriage window as it rumbled down the long drive to Nightingale Hall. The u-shaped mansion dwarfed the land with its sheer size, columns, and towers, like a castle she once read about in a book. The combination of wild nature, and perfectly manicured lawns of the surrounding park left her feeling as if she tumbled into a magical world.

The inside of the house did not disappoint her imagination. Cool white marble floors and painted cherubs on the rotund ceiling in the entryway delighted her senses, and the cozy round entrance surrounded by tall Roman Columns reminded her of a gazebo. The butler escorted her family down a wide hallway awash in candlelight from wall sconces, and graced with dozens of paintings from portraits to landscapes. She wished she could take the time to stop and study the masterful art, but she hardly caught her breath before they entered a drawing room like no other. Spacious and filled with members of one of the most elite families in all of England, she arched her neck to see the faces in a forest of towering Prescotts.

Cassie knew her sister would expect to hear every detail of the evening. Unfortunately, Jocelyn took to her bed, plagued with a head cold. How could she possibly describe how her slippers sank into the burgundy and gold Aubusson carpet in the drawing room, or how the soft tan colors of the walls trimmed in a green the color of the darkest forest made the room seem brilliant? The drawing room was filled with the finest furnishings, a grand piano she knew her mother would covet, a fireplace higher and deeper than the tallest Prescott, and dozens of candles. Perhaps she entered a dream rather than a drawing room.

Her pulse quickened and a frisson of awareness stirred inside her when Lord William bent over her hand during their introduction. "Miss Chambers," his deep masculine voice sent a shiver down her spine all the way to her toes.

She found herself drawn to his hard, angular face that softened into a boyish grin when he smiled—a grin that stole her breath away. Dark chocolate eyes collided with her own and she nearly melted from the heat. His thick brown hair with golden lights fell over his eyes, and she had the oddest desire to brush the locks away from his face.

The effect this man had on her startled her sensibilities. She prayed he did not notice the heat that surely crept up her neck and tinged her cheeks with a crimson glow. Why did a mere stranger unsettle her so?

Before she had a chance to ponder these disturbing thoughts, the butler announced that dinner was served, and Lord William offered his arm to escort her into the dining room. A warm, tingling sensation moved through her hand and pooled in her belly, *and below*. The oddest need to squeeze her thighs together and cut off an abrupt ache overcame her.

Cassie noticed the strength of Lord William's arm and his wide, muscular chest; not soft, like some men, like Mr. Parker. Why did she suddenly think of her betrothed as soft? What an odd mental image; after all, Mr. Parker was handsome, and charming, and utterly delightful. How fortunate for her to catch a future viscount who also made her positively giddy when he smiled at her. He even kissed her once when they took a walk in the gardens. She wanted him to kiss her again, or longer, or with more passion, but instead, he offered his arm and escorted her back inside the house.

How would Lord William's lips feel against hers? *Oh dear.* She really should not consider such a thing. She only just met Lord William, and to begin comparing him with her betrothed was surely the height of impropriety, even if the improper conduct was contained to her private thoughts. Perhaps she really should stop reading Mrs. Radcliff's novels.

She shifted her unsettling thoughts to her host and hostess. Lord and Lady Camberley were quite different from any married couple she knew. They actually appeared to be in love. She noticed the secret glances and small touches. She believed her own parents cared for each other, but never once did they appear to share a romantic love. She often wondered how they managed to conceive two children. If anything, they spoke to each other in the most redundant way, only speaking when necessary, and making small conversation at best. They never touched, or smiled, or caught each other's eye. They simply were.

Cassie's eyes widened as they entered a grand formal dining room. The entire first floor of her home could fit into this one room. She was fortunate to visit a few of the larger manors of aristocrats who sought her father's spiritual company, but never before had she experienced the grandeur of an estate like Nightingale Hall. Flower arrangements, candles, Sevres china, and crystal topped the formal cherry wood dining table. Tapestries hung from floor to ceiling, depicting scenes from medieval times, and low hanging crystal candelabras reflected prisms of color throughout the room. A fireplace burned at one end of the room, and a buffet of dishes with tangy and sweet aromas filled the air on the other end.

William's voice startled her out of her deep rambling thoughts as he pulled out her chair for her to sit. "It appears you are to sit next to me." She tried to sit gracefully and not plop, feeling the eyes of her mother watching her, expecting her to act every inch the lady. Her mother smiled and turned towards Lord Camberley. "Miss

Chambers," William started as he took his seat, "How do you like our quaint little village thus far?"

"It is positively charming." She smiled and thought of her new, but temporary home, since she was betrothed to Mr. Parker. The cottage was roomier than the family's former house in Cornwall. Indeed, her father took a step up when he agreed to take this position. His pay afforded them not only a housekeeper and cook, but a footman and butler as well. The countryside took her breath away, and so far, the neighbors were gracious and kind.

Cassie's only shame fell in her inability to see Mr. Parker until their wedding drew near. He went to London to speak to his uncle, the Viscount Winnington, about their upcoming nuptials. The disappointment of not seeing him until their wedding lodged in her stomach like coddled egg that sat too long. Her betrothed wanted to give her the wedding of her dreams. She only hoped the viscount would be biddable.

The conversation began with the usual pleasantries of weather and local gossip. She felt comfortable with Lord William, in an unnerving sort of way. Mr. Parker always made her feel nervous and as shy as a schoolgirl. How strange to fall into such contented talk with a man, a stranger, no less, as if they had known each other for an eternity.

"Now, I must warn you about developing too close of a relationship with Lady Mary. She will certainly lead you astray and ruin your reputation." William grinned across the table at his twin sister as he teased her.

"William dear, you are lucky indeed that four feet of table separates us, for if I were closer I would bean you on the head. Miss Chambers, you must completely ignore my obnoxious brother. He delights in my grief." Lady Mary eyed her brother with a look that spoke of a closeness only known and understood by two who were born of the same womb at the same time. The light manner in which they teased and played warmed Cassie's heart, and it caused her to wonder what it would be like to have such a large family. Of course, Lady Mary was a bit outspoken and rather outrageous, but she admired her courage to thumb her nose at Society and live as she pleased.

The amusing banter continued on all sides. Lady Elizabeth sat to her right, William on her left, with Lady Mary and Lady Anne across from her. The family chatted back and forth down the stretch of endless table. Her father seemed jollier than his usual somber self, and it was rather obvious mother enjoyed the company of such a prestigious group, but it was the gentleman to her left who kept her attention. She glanced at his aristocratic profile: strong chin, lush lips, straight nose, and large eyes. Her hand itched to reach up and touch a finger along the edge of his jaw. *Oh my!* She really did need to get control of her thoughts. She envisioned Mr. Parker's hair. Short. Straight. Thin.

Cassie pursed her lips. *Will Mr. Parker lose his hair early?* She thought he might and considered how she felt about being married to a man with a balding head. She nearly laughed aloud at her own silly ponderings. She loved Mr. Parker, and assumed she would love him still when he became bald and round in his old age. She only hoped he would still love her when she grew fat with their first child.

"So, you are to be married soon." William looked at her with such an intensity, she nearly spit out her wine. The cool February evening suddenly seemed as warm as a summer day. For the first time since Mr. Parker proposed, she did not want to discuss her upcoming nuptials.

"I...ah, yes, I am, my lord." The words jumbled in her mouth and made her feel quite ridiculous. "In June. I am to be married in June." Her reaction to his question stunned her. She laid a hand on her churning stomach. The sudden nausea could not be due to his question, *or could it?*

"I have never met Mr. Parker, although I did meet Lord Winnington once. He is rather old and crabby if you ask me." William took a bite of his dessert, raspberries and cream, then licked the remains from his lips. She should have been shocked by his comment. It *was* beyond the pale. Instead, she was fixated on his mouth and the sweep of his tongue across his lips. *What it would be like if he kissed her?*

Oh, dear, she should not think of such things. She was betrothed, and she loved Mr. Parker. He was everything she ever dreamed of in a man. Handsome, a few inches taller than herself, blond hair and blue eyes that reminded her of the turbulent ocean, and...*thin* lips. All of a sudden, Mr. Parker's lips no longer appealed to her, at least not in the way a certain lord's lips appealed to her. She swallowed. She must stop these errant and sinful thoughts from running amuck in her mind.

"Really, William. That was not a nice thing to say." Lady Anne scolded her older brother and gave him a look that would shrink anyone to a less than proper size. The conversation at the table stopped. Everyone turned and looked at William.

He glanced up, "What? Oh, good gracious, I do apologize Miss Chambers if I offended your, ah, future father-in-law."

"I do not see that he is here to offend, and according to Mr. Parker, you are quite correct in your assessment. Lord Winnington is rather old and crabby." Cassie watched as her mother's face drained of color. *Oh well.* She only had a few more months to offend her mother with her colorful words, and then she would be a married woman, living in her own house, and making her own rules.

William burst out laughing, as did the rest of the Prescott family, and she found herself caught up in their laughter. The rest of the meal went by without incident. The ladies left the men in the company of their port and smelly cigars. Her mother would have a fit if her usually staid father came home with his breath smelling of cigar. At least it would diffuse the fit her mother would most likely have about her comments during dinner.

Cassie sat in the drawing room on a sofa talking to Lady Anne when the men entered the room. Her eyes were immediately drawn to Lord William. Dressed in a coat of dark blue, a white shirt and finely starched cravat, completed with tan trousers on muscular legs, he looked every inch the aristocrat.

Lady Anne stopped mid sentence and looked at the men, then back to Cassandra with her brows drawn together. "Tell me about your Mr. Parker, Cassie."

She forced her gaze to leave Lord William's handsome face and turned toward his sister, "He is a fine gentleman; handsome, witty, and wealthy. Well, he will be wealthy when he inherits his uncle's title. Until then he must live under the man's thumb. I just hope we will be able to live in peace. Mr. Parker tells me Lord Winnington can be quite obnoxious." She glanced sideways and watched as Lord William moved about the room speaking to his brothers, sisters, and her parents. All the while his eyes were on *her.* His gaze unnerved her and made it difficult to pay attention to Lady Anne.

"He sounds delightful. However did you meet?" Lady Anne asked.

"Oh...I...uh...we met at a country dance. Mr. Parker was visiting his friend, Lord Sheldon, a nobleman in our former district." Cassie knew Mr. Parker had insisted on an introduction. Their association grew from the moment they first danced. The very next day Mr. Parker paid a call on her. He brought her a perfect yellow orchid along with chocolate from the finest confectionery in London. She fell in love without hesitation or thought.

A shadow moved over her and she glanced up, into *his* face. She shook her head as if she were trying to shake away an annoying fly. *This is his family home. I am here as a guest. He is simply acting polite.* Nevertheless, why did her heart thunder in her ears every time he came near her?

"Miss Chambers, your mother tells me you are an accomplished singer, and that you often sing for your father's congregation. Would it be too much to ask you to entertain us with a song?" asked William.

"Oh that would be lovely, Cassie. I am sure Jane or Elizabeth could play anything you asked. Unfortunately, I did not inherit the gift of music, but Jane is amazing. Would you be a dear and sing for us?" Lady Anne grasped her hand and smiled. She certainly could not deny Lady Anne's plea, even though her stomach churned like butter.

"I suppose I could," she replied and looked at Lady Jane, the youngest Prescott, who moved to stand next to Lord William.

"Do you know *Flow Gently Sweet Afton*, Miss Chambers?" asked Lady Jane.

"Yes."

Lady Jane turned to Lord William. "Please accompany Miss Chambers in song. It has been much too long since we have heard you sing."

Cassie swallowed a lump in her throat. She was to sing with Lord William?

"I would be honored sweet Jane. Miss Chambers." Lord William offered her his hand. She took it, and discovered the contact was no less shocking than before. A slow fire built inside of her and heated her entire body. She expected perspiration would break out on her face before the end of the song.

They stood near the piano while Lady Jane took her seat and began moving her fingers across the ivory keys. The exquisite tone sounded sweet to her ears. For a moment, she lost herself and almost missed her cue, but then she began, and when she did, a hush fell over the room. Her voice joined Lord William's in perfect union. Their voices carried and melded into one, like long lost lovers who just rediscovered one another.

When she glanced up, she was drawn into his eyes, into him. His voice flowed over her and touched her skin like a loving caress. Before she knew what happened, he took her hands in his. The world fell away, and left them alone in song and something else, something unexplainable.

The music wrapped them in a cocoon, and bound them together in a moment of sweet captivity, but soon, the song ended, the piano stopped playing, and the magic broke. The applause roared in her ears as they broke eye contact and turned towards their audience. She forced a smile while gripping her shaking hands together.

Lord William took her hand again and bowed, "Miss Chambers. Thank you for the pleasure of accompanying you. I enjoyed it immensely."

"Yes. No. I mean, thank you," Cassie whispered. He raised her gloved hand and did not kiss the air above it, but put his lips to her fingers, and in a movement only she could be aware of, he circled the underside of her wrist with his thumb. Her skin tingled. Her breasts swelled. Never before had she experienced such a strong sensation based on a mere touch. The flush of inner heat that crept up her neck surely burned her cheeks. She pulled her hand away, nodded, and turned towards her mother, who lifted her brow in question.

* * *

William sat in the library with his brothers, sipping a brandy and brooding. He did not believe in the damned curse, yet the strange occurrence of so many women rejecting him gave him pause. Of course, Miss Chambers did not exactly reject him. He simply met her too late.

He smiled as he thought of her hair arranged in a coiffure that framed her lovely face in ringlets of golden curls. He wanted to touch her hair, to remove the pins from each golden strand and run his fingers through sunshine. Her green eyes reminded him of spring. Her naturally pink tinged cheeks atop milky white skin, and her deep red lips, full and lush and kissable, affected him with more than just interest. The idea seemed ludicrous, but he knew it in his bones—she was born to be his. *His.*

He swallowed the rest of his brandy and struggled to contain the growing erection in his pants. He wanted another glass, but he did not dare get up from his chair and risk his brothers' noticing the hardened bulge. How is it that one woman, a woman he had only met this evening, could have such a powerful effect on him?

"Our new vicar will be good for the parishioners. He is a thoughtful man. His wife seems kind enough, and of course, his daughters are lovely." Stephen, the eldest Prescott brother stated his observation while taking William's glass and refilling it. "You look as if you could use a little more refreshment. You seem quite agitated William. Is something wrong?"

"Nothing more than usual. I find the woman of my dreams and she is taken." William drank deep from his glass and blew out a disgusted breath.

"Miss Chambers? I thought I saw a glint in your eyes. She is quite stunning," said Stephen.

"I do not understand why you are so determined to get yourself leg-shackled," said his younger brother James. "I would think you would enjoy sampling the feast rather than selecting the main dish."

"Samples alone cannot sustain a man," said William.

Both of his brothers laughed. They were determined to remain bachelors for as long as possible. Stephen would have to marry and produce an heir one day, but James could keep sampling into his old age, as long as one or both of his older brothers produced sons.

William wanted something more. He wanted the same kind of love and lasting companionship his parents had. If only he had met Miss Chambers before her Mr. Parker. He shuddered to think of her married to another man, in bed with with him, with her glorious golden hair spread across the man's pillows, and her body a naked feast for another man's eyes. *As if he had a right to think it.* Perhaps this last rejection from Miss Peterson affected him more than he realized. He was beginning to wonder if he would stay a bachelor forever or head to bedlam.

"Shall we go into town and find some sweet nectar?" James stood up, randy and ready to go as always.

"You two go on. I think I shall retire. I feel rather tired." In truth, he had no desire to sink between another woman's thighs tonight, or any night. He was positively ruined for any other woman, and he had only met Miss Chambers this very night. He shook his head and tried to make the image of her go away.

"What about you Stephen? Are you joining me?" asked James.

"No, not tonight, but you go ahead and enjoy yourself, and try to stay out of trouble." Stephen poured himself another brandy and sat across from William.

James rose and headed for the door. "Suit yourselves. Good night brothers."

"Good night," William and Stephen said in unison. They sat in comfortable silence, finishing off their brandies, each reflecting in their own personal thoughts.

William could not take his mind off Miss Chambers. The green of her eyes sat in his vision like a dream from which he could not wake. He tried to think of something else, but nothing would come. He could not recall a time when a woman attracted him this way.

"You do not seem heartbroken over Miss Peterson's rejection," said Stephen.

"Miss Peterson is a fine specimen of a woman. Lovely face and figure...raised quite proper with a decent sense of humor. She would have made a fine wife."

"Your disappointment amazes me. You are thinking more on Miss Chambers, a woman already betrothed when you met her, *only* this evening, than the woman you courted the past three months."

"Yes, well, I suppose I like Miss Peterson. I did offer for her after all, but she is not and never would be the love of my life. I think perhaps that I am allowing desperation to set in. After the last eleven rejections, I am beginning to believe I will never find a wife to take home to Rosehill Manor." He looked in his brandy, thinking he might like to drown in the dark liquid.

He thought himself in love once, when he was a youth, but his intended married a duke. After his first failed romance, he decided to search for a wife who would physically please him, then work at falling in love with her. *How do two people come to love each other?* If only he knew.

Somewhere deep down he truly believed he would know when he found "the one". The rejections frustrated him, but they did not leave him feeling hopeless or heartbroken. The women he courted and offered for in the past were not meant for him. He would continue his search for the perfect mate.

Then he met Miss Chambers. Deep in his gut, he experienced a tug he could not deny. She was his soul mate. She had to be, but how could she be? She was betrothed to another man. William made a fist and searched the room for something to punch. He could hit Stephen. Surely, his older brother would forgive him for pummeling his frustrations out on him. *Well...maybe not.*

It was no use dreaming of something he could not obtain, or of someone he could never touch, but oh, how he would love to take her in his arms and into his bed. He finished off the brandy and rose. "I am done for this night. I will see you tomorrow."

He startled Stephen out of his own thoughts. "Oh, yes, goodnight William. Try not to dream of her. It will only make matters harder." Stephen's smile indicated what he truly meant by *harder*.

William rolled his eyes. "I shall try to have nightmares of an old woman with shriveled tits. That should shrink my dreams well enough." He headed for the door with Stephen's laughter at his back.

* * *

The next morning, William walked to clear his head. Despite his best efforts, he could not shake Miss Chambers from his thoughts or his dreams. His erotic dreams woke him in the night so hard he had to use his hand to relieve himself. Why did he have to have such a powerful attraction to a woman who is betrothed? Perhaps he should have gone with James and found another woman who could relieve him of his misery. Somehow, he knew it would not be the same. Not even close.

How could one meeting with a woman torture him so? A lit flame, an attraction, an interest—connection he could understand; but, instead, he experienced an all-consuming fire that burned through his body, his dreams, and to his very soul. He wanted this woman like no other, and he could not for the life of him understand why. Why did "the one" have to be *her*?

He took off across the fields allowing the winter winds to cool his face and his lower region. A brisk walk would do him some good. After his obligatory family visit, since his mother would never forgive him if he did not stay a few days, he planned to head to London. He gave up his last mistress out of boredom, but now he thought it necessary to find another, *and fast.* Perhaps he would seek out Lady Quartermane. She was a beauty, an Incomparable in her first season, before she met and married the late Lord Quartermane, but now he was dead and she widowed. She flirted with him even when she was married, and more so since she shed her widow's weeds. Yes, a tumble with Lady Quartermane might be just the thing to clear his mind.

William walked down a winding path through the ancient skeleton trees leading to a quiet river. The echo of birdsongs and chirping crickets sang in sympathy to correspond with the changing colors of the sky. He snuggled deeper in his jacket and took a deep breath of crisp, clean country air. As soon as he rounded a corner, he ran straight into a body, a soft body, the same body he dreamed about all night.

She gasped and reeled backwards. Neither paid attention, so deep were they in their own thoughts. He grabbed her shoulders to steady her and fell into her eyes, not sure if he saw yearning or confusion, but knew what *he* felt—a yearning desire, and a roaring heat. He wanted her with every breath he took. Common sense edged itself into the corner of his mind and skittered across his vision. He let her go, "Miss Chambers, what a surprise!"

"Yes, this is quite a surprise. I thought perhaps I was the only soul awake at this uncommon hour," she said.

He followed her glance to where deep colors of red tinged with pink and purple and blue lit the sky. The sun just peeped over the horizon. It was an ungodly hour, even for the country.

"What on earth are you doing walking about at this hour?" he asked. Daylight just broke and here she was alone and trouncing about the countryside. Any manner of disasters might occur, and no one would be awake to hear her screams.

"I…uh…I could not sleep." She turned towards the winding river, but he did not miss her pinkened cheeks. Surely, she could not be having a tryst, *or could she?* He shook the thought away. She was betrothed and her fiancé was away in London, and really, she *was* an innocent vicar's daughter.

"It seems we are both afflicted with the same malady. I did not get a wink's slumber last night myself." He stifled a yawn, and wondered why she could not sleep. He certainly knew why *he* could not sleep. The reason stood in front of him. "Where are you going?"

"I was just taking a walk to clear my mind." Her lips trembled into a somber smile.

"A lady should not walk around alone without a proper escort. Since I happen to be taking a walk as well, may I escort you?" He offered his arm.

William noticed her brief hesitation before taking him up on his offer. "That would be lovely, my lord."

The simple contact of her hand on his arm sizzled beneath the material of his clothing. A woman never felt so perfect on his arm. He stole glances at her profile. Her lovely golden hair was pulled into a chignon at the nape of her neck. Her ears were tiny, delicate. He thought about circling his tongue around the outer edge before moving down her long neck, and swallowed.

They walked awhile in silence before she spoke, "What do you do for enjoyment, my lord?"

He knew what he wanted to do, but he decided he should not say such things, especially to her. "I have recently purchased an estate not an hour's drive from here. I have been up to my elbows in renovations."

"How exciting! Please tell me all about it."

Her lips were ripe as berries, *and oh,* how he wanted to taste.

Forcing himself to look away from her lips, he continued down the path, not for a moment forgetting how her hand on his arm affected his pulse. "I purchased the estate from the Duke of Wentworth. He once used it as a country diversion, but since his wife passed, he no longer had use for it. The house sits up on a hill overlooking a small lake." William loved his new home, Rosehill Manor, a home in need of a woman's touch. A home he hoped to fill someday soon with a wife and children.

A quiet pause passed between them. They walked across an old stone bridge covered in moss, and stopped in the middle to look out at the cerulean river flowing towards the sea. The songs of the nightingales and their breathing was the only interruption to the hush of the morning.

A small breeze whipped the loose curls around her face, and the skirts around her ankles. She wore a light green morning gown with a darker green velvet redingote. The colors matched her sparkling eyes which seemed to change shades from light to dark along with her mood. His heart sank to his stomach with a deep sense of regret squeezing his chest, plunging him into a melancholy moment. It was a useless emotion to lust after a woman he could not have—now or ever.

"Shall we continue our walk?" Offering his arm, he directed her across the bridge and down a well-worn path. He told her more about the house, his renovations, and his plans for furnishing and decorating his home. She listened and added intelligent comments. Cassie's strong sense of color and style, and her advice was well worth the pain of her company. Not that she was a pain, but that he was in pain, hard, throbbing pain. Even a dip in the cold river might not soothe his aching heat.

In order to see Miss Chamber's home, they had to cut across a wooded path. Surrounded by ancient trees and a mellow morning light, they continued on when she stilled and let go of his arm. She tiptoed a few steps, turned her head, and brought her finger to her mouth to indicate he should be quiet. He looked ahead where he saw a doe and her fawn standing in a copse of trees, and then turned to watch her expression change from surprise to delight. She reminded him of a child ogling a new toy on Christmas morn. Something churned deep inside of him, and settled in a tight ball over his heart.

The fawn stopped and stared at the intruders before disappearing into the woods.

Miss Chambers turned, beaming. "What a delightful treat! I love observing nature."

She started back toward him when her foot stumbled over a protruding rock, which caused her to tumble forward.

He wrapped his arms around her to catch her fall, and then drew her tight against him.

Their eyes met and held for a defining moment in time. The instant was too real, too intense, so he broke the contact, only to find himself drawn to her ripe, luscious, kissable lips. Last night he dreamed about her soft mouth, of tasting and exploring her depths. He forgot himself, forgot the circumstances, forgot his honor, and lowered his mouth to hers to taste her sweetness, but once was not enough. He touched his lips to hers repeatedly, and begged her with the pressure of his mouth to open for him—*and she did.*

When he pushed his tongue into her mouth, she moaned and

pressed further into him, and placed her hands against his chest. Heat burned through his clothes all the way to his skin.

Somewhere in the back of his mind, he brushed away the little voice telling him to stop, to set her aside and forget her existence. His control slipped in a whirlwind of need, and instead of pulling back, he went deeper into her mouth, tasting, taking, giving her inexperienced mouth a drink from the fountain of passion. She tasted like his favorite dessert of raspberries and cream. The need to over indulge, to probe his tongue deeper into her mouth, to feed his starving heart and soul, drew him into an oblivious state of arousal.

Her hands slid up his chest and around his neck, and then her fingers plunged into the thickness of his hair. He deepened the kiss.

Something tapped on the door of his mind. He pushed it away and tightly wrapped his arms around her, moving his hands up and down her back. His need for her overtook his soul, and kept the guilt at bay.

This woman did something to him, something he could not explain or deny. Helpless, he continued his pursuit of her, drugged by her mouth and her innocent responses.

The temptation to touch her, to lift her skirts, and feel her bare skin almost won out, until her deep moan broke through his passion filled fog. *What the hell was he doing?* Ravishing an innocent woman, a betrothed woman, a woman who belonged to another man, taking what was not his to take, in the woods where anyone could come across them and see. He wanted more, but alas, she was not his for the taking.

He lifted his mouth from hers, regret and guilt biting into his consciousness. "I am sorry. I do not know what came over me."

Cassie's eyes widened in astonishment, and her chest heaved as she struggled for air. She held her hand to her mouth, stared at him in bewilderment, confusion, and with obvious desire.

Then she picked up her skirts and ran.

Chapter Two

CASSIE STOOD AT JOCELYN'S WINDOW and peered out at the church's graveyard. Jocelyn slept, allowing her the luxury of being alone with her thoughts.

When she returned from her walk she learned her sister had a turn for the worse. Jocelyn's fever spiked during the night. Their exhausted mother spent the night pressing cool rags to her youngest daughter's forehead. Finally, sometime in the early morning, her fever broke. Cassie took over so her mother could go to bed.

Not for the first time since her walk, she touched her fingers to her tingling mouth. Like a wanton, she allowed a man who was not her husband to take liberties, but most disturbingly, she enjoyed his kiss as if it were the most natural thing in the world. Closing her eyes, she replayed the moment in her mind. He kissed her, and she kissed him back without a care for the consequences. She lost herself to the desire pulsing through her veins, and now the shame left her grappling with her conscience. She pulled her shawl tight around her shoulders. How could she have sinned so?

She bit her fist to stop the sob that swelled in her throat.

Mr. Parker.

Her one true love.

She betrayed the man she loved above all else, and this before they were married. What would Mr. Parker think or say or do if he learned what she had done? Surely he would cry off and leave her broken hearted.

Why did Lord William kiss her? More importantly, however, why did she kiss him back? Mr. Parker's one fleeting kiss left her tingling and wanting more, unlike Lord William's kisses which left her hot and achy and wanting something she could not comprehend.

The door opened, cracking the silence, intruding on her mood like a black veil lifted from a widow's face. Mrs. Hopkins, the housekeeper, stepped inside carrying a luncheon tray. She set it down on Jocelyn's desk and whispered across the room, "I thought you might be hungry."

Cassie attempted to answer. She was not the least bit hungry, in fact, her stomach churned, leaving her somewhat nauseated. Of course, she was not about to disclose her feelings to a servant.

"Thank you, Mrs. Hopkins," she said.

"Has she stirred at all?" asked the housekeeper.

"No, she has slept like a babe. I imagine she needs her rest." Cassie moved to the chair in front of the desk. She looked down at the roast beef, peas, and carrots. Her dry mouth and throat tightened.

She took a sip of water while Mrs. Hopkins touched Jocelyn's head and clucked, "Fever is broke. Good thing too. Your poor mother nearly had the vapors from worry. 'Tis nothing nature will not heal."

"Thank the Good Lord," murmured Cassie between dry bites of beef.

Mrs. Hopkins took her leave, once again leaving Cassie alone with her turbulent thoughts. She managed to swallow a few more bites before she shoved her tray away and laid her head in her arms. Hot, blinding tears came, soaking her sleeves with salty moisture. Would her soul burn in hell for eternity for her one indiscretion? "Oh, God, please forgive me...please forgive me..."

"Forgive you for what?" croaked a small voice from the bed.

Cassie's head snapped up as she turned toward her sister, "I...uh...was praying for forgiveness of my sins."

Jocelyn struggled, but managed to sit up in the bed, "You are perfect, dear sister. Whenever have you sinned?" Jocelyn's teasing smile reassured Cassie she would recover just fine.

"I am far from perfect. Just the other day I thought Mrs. Bloomingburg's hat made her look like a spotted ostrich." Cassie forced a smile for Jocelyn's sake.

Jocelyn laughed, but then she sobered and asked, "Why were you crying?"

"I was feeling sorry for myself. I suppose I miss Mr. Parker."

Another sin—*lying*. She did miss Mr. Parker, but that was not the reason for her tears. The shame crept up her neck and flushed her face. "How are you feeling?"

"Much better. My dreadful headache is finally gone." Jocelyn looked at her older sister with an assessing eye. "It must be terribly hard to be separated from Mr. Parker."

Cassie poured a glass of water and handed it to Jocelyn. "Here, drink up." She hesitated before continuing, "It is difficult. I wish he could at least visit before the wedding." *Five long months.* "It is not as if London is so very far away." If Mr. Parker were here she might not be so tempted by Lord William—at least that is what she told herself.

They spent several hours playing whist to pass the time. She described Nightingale Hall and the Prescott family while leaving out details of a *certain* Prescott. Jocelyn would know right away something was wrong if she were not careful.

Mrs. Chambers entered the room at mid-afternoon, gave Jocelyn a once over with her eyes, then turned to Cassie smiling and holding out a letter, "The post arrived. You have a letter from Mr. Parker."

Guilt washed through her, soaking her conscious like a thunderstorm would soak one's clothes. She covered her hot cheeks with her hands to hide her apparent shame. She jumped up and snatched the letter out of her mother's hand then turned towards the window to read it in privacy.

My Darling Miss Chambers,

I have arrived in London in good time. The air here is thick with a most unpleasant smell. Oh, how I miss the sweet scent of roses in the country. I can hardly wait to see you again, my dear.

I have met with my uncle, and must confess he is none too happy with our engagement, but I vow to bring him round in time. I can imagine no other woman as my wife but you. Your smile warms my heart. We will be together soon my love, as husband and wife. Give your dear family my love. Until we meet again, keep me in your dreams.

Your devoted fiancé,
Miles Parker

Cassie's eyes welled with a mix of guilt, shame, and love. She loved Mr. Parker, and missed him so very much.

She would *not* betray him again.

She squared her shoulders and stiffened her spine. "Lord Winnington is giving Mr. Parker some grief about our upcoming nuptials, just as we expected. However, my betrothed has everything in hand. He sends his love." She folded the letter and placed it in her pocket. "If you do not mind, I would like to take some air."

"Of course dear, you go on. I will keep Jocelyn company."

* * *

The local assembly room was already crowded when Cassie and Jocelyn arrived. They each wore their prettiest ball gowns. Jocelyn dressed in yellow to match her dark hair and Cassie in soft pink. Their mother went off to speak to a group of ladies, leaving the girls to their own devices. No one expected anything untoward to occur at a country event.

The sea of faces swam before Cassie's eyes, until she spotted a familiar one, Lady Anne. Then she braced herself in case she ran across Lord William. She would be polite, but she had no intention of letting him near her again. Over two weeks had passed since their morning walk, a walk she avoided at all costs, although she did feel closeted near home, constraining her movement to the gardens and graveyard. She thought perhaps he would attend Sunday church, but so far he did not come with the rest of his family. The last she heard he was in London. She hoped he stayed there, but more so, she wished he would stay out of her dreams.

"Cassie, I am so glad you came." Lady Anne hugged her. In the short time since they met, the two girls were on their way to becoming the best of friends.

"I would not have missed it. Of course, Jocelyn would sulk for days if we did not come, and neither mother nor I can abide her sulking." Cassie laughed as Jocelyn narrowed her eyes.

"You are right. I had to come; otherwise, I would never break free of *your* sulking over the absence of Mr. Parker." Cassie grimaced at Jocelyn's comment.

The girls chatted for awhile about the local ladies and gents. Lady Anne pointed out the most eligible bachelors, including Mr. Jones, a handsome and wealthy land-owner. Jocelyn's eyes widened when she saw him across the room. He turned their direction, and came over to address Lady Anne. After an introduction to Jocelyn, he whisked her away to the dance floor. Cassie's heart tugged with jealousy. She wished Mr. Parker was here.

"Oh, William is here." Lady Anne tugged on her sleeve. "Come, I must greet him. He must have just come in from London. He left the day after the dinner party."

Cassie froze. *Oh, dear heavens!* She did not expect to see him here. Granted, she knew it was possible, but she truly thought she would be safe. How could she possibly face him? Her insides quivered. She did not want to greet him, look into his face, his eyes; see his mouth. She instinctively covered her mouth with her hand. Her lips burned from the memory of their kiss. Why did he come tonight?

Cassie knew she would not be able to avoid him. She tried to imagine he would stay in London, or go back to his new home, and she assumed she would not see him before her wedding. Once she married Mr. Parker, she would be safe from Lord William, safe from his intrusion into her thoughts.

Lady Anne dragged her through the thrones of people across the room. The closer she came to Lord William the more ragged her breaths became. She struggled to compose herself. *He is so beautiful.*

Oh, what could she be thinking! She must smash these wayward and sinful thoughts. She could not think about Lord William, and how his kisses heated her from the inside out, how they melted her resistance, how they made her desire him above Mr. Parker. No! She loved Mr. Parker. Truly she did.

"William, I am so happy to see you here. When did you arrive?" Lady Anne reached out to hug him as he bent and kissed her cheek.

Heat rose in Cassie and warmed her entire being. His arms were around Lady Anne and his mouth kissed her cheek, but his eyes went directly to Cassie's soul. The look he gave her stripped her raw, burned through her, sending shockwaves through her body. She thought she might swoon.

Ridiculous! She never swooned in her life. She was not the swooning type. She had a strong and healthy constitution, and she certainly was not a milksop. She held herself erect and placed a cool mask of indifference across her features. She would not cow or waver or faint. She would be polite and move on.

"Miss Chambers, how do you do?" Lord William took her hand and kissed the air above it which she found disappointing. She mentally scolded herself. Lord William did not need to kiss her hand, or her lips...

"Fine, thank you, *my lord.*" She curtsied while considering a way out. She had to find a way to leave his presence. She desperately tried to create a mental image of Mr. Parker in her mind, but it came like a ghost haunting a house, fading away as soon as she conjured it up.

"May I have the honor of the next dance?" asked Lord William.

No. No you cannot.

"Yes, of course."

Lord William took her hand and escorted her onto the dance floor. She should have made up an excuse. She should have told him she was about to visit the lady's retiring room, anything to remove herself from this awkward situation, but the words left her mouth before her brain had time to process his request. Wonderful! The next set would last at least half an hour. She just placed herself in the company of the one man she should avoid.

She set her hand on his arm. Waves of tiny sparks moved across her skin. A heavy achiness spread to her most intimate regions. Her knee buckled slightly causing her to grasp his arm tighter. He turned and raised an eyebrow in question, but he did not say anything about her near misstep. She tried desperately to compose herself as they moved onto the dance floor, and stood across from each other until the music began. He was so handsome in his formal attire consisting of a dark blue coat, white shirt, and striped blue and gold knee breeches. He almost looked like a London dandy, but no, the way he carried himself and the lack of ornament made him seem more masculine somehow.

Mr. Parker was a dandy, perfectly groomed and dressed and sometimes ornamented to the point of being obnoxious and she loved it. She secretly thought his wardrobe hysterical. The bright colors suited his sanguine personality. He was always laughing and joking, and making everyone around him laugh. Mr. Parker made laugh, and oh, how she needed laughter in her life. Her staid and stoic existence bored her beyond belief.

The set began. They moved together and apart, at first quiet, but the contact of their hands caused the gooseflesh on her skin to rise. She pursed her lips in an attempt to mask the feelings bubbling from the surface.

"Miss Chambers, you must accept my apology for the...um...events that occurred recently." His voice startled her out of her own contemplations.

"I need no reminders Lord William of my one indiscretion in life. I prefer to sweep it away and forget about it. Please do not speak of it again." She watched his eyes lift in question. She surprised him with the coolness of her answer. Good. She had no choice.

"Of course," said Lord William.

They continued with the dance for a few more minutes before he spoke again. "It was not an indiscretion."

"What?" She nearly stopped in the middle of the dance floor upon his odd declaration.

"There is something between us, something we would be bound to explore if it were not for your betrothal. However, we cannot change our circumstances, so it is pointless to carry on."

She hissed between her teeth, "We are not carrying on. And you are right, my lord, I am betrothed. I love Mr. Parker." She raised her chin. She could be as haughty as any aristocrat if need be.

"I see." A shadow passed over his face and his jovial features were replaced with a face of cool stone. He tensed. And when their hands connected she noticed he withdrew his contact just enough to continue the dance, but not enough to touch her as if he held her.

It appeared she put an end to whatever stirred between them, except she felt a pain, a great pain of loss. How could she feel loss for something she never had? Not really. A small glimpse is all. One that created turmoil in her mind and heart. How could she possibly regret the loss of something that exhilarated and tormented her at the same time?

"Anne tells me you have joined her committee for raising funds for a local home for orphans." At least he changed the topic to something safe.

"Yes, I have already noticed a number of homeless street urchins running around the area, unchaperoned, or cared for, begging for food or scraps of cloth for clothing. It is shameful any child should be left on their own devices."

"It is a shame. I am in full support of the endeavor. I promised Anne to escort the committee on their search next week for a suitable location for a home." His eyes crinkled in the corners when he smiled and his straight white teeth gleamed in the candlelight.

Cassie might have sighed, except for the panic rising up within her. She also promised to go with Anne, and a few select members of the committee on their search. If she had know Lord William would act as their escort, she would have invented a reason to decline.

Her stomach churned at the thought of spending the day in Lord William's company. The unsettling feeling caused her to stumble and step on his foot. "Oh dear, how clumsy of me."

He braced her arm with his hand and gave her a questioning look. Surely, he did not think she stepped on him on purpose? Oh, but of course he did. She wished she had a fan to smack him over his head.

"Think nothing of it sweetings."

"I am not your sweetings!" Cassie spit out. How dare he? The man itched her last nerve.

He laughed. *Laughed.* A rich, warm, bold laugh that put her on the edge of a cliff where she felt herself tumbling heart first. How could she possibly spend an entire day with this man? Her strange and uncertain feelings reminded her of a trip she once took with her family on a sailing ship, and how the angry sea roared through her body causing her to be weak with nausea and rolling stomach cramps. Except this time the sea did not upset her constitution, but the man before her.

"I apologize if I offended you Miss Chambers."

The dance continued. How much longer would she have to endure this sweet torture? His eyes skimmed her face and landed briefly on her bosom. Her breasts throbbed like they had in her dreams at night, dreams that plagued her since meeting Lord William. The room suddenly grew hotter. Perspiration formed on her forehead and in the crevice between her breasts. She longed for the snapping cold of the February air.

The dance came to an end. He bowed; she curtsied. He took her arm and headed towards the punch table. "Perhaps you should escort me back to my mother."

"I thought perhaps you would like a drink."

"No. I want to return to my mother's side, now, if you please." She did not intend to sound snappish, but she was on edge, teetering on a line where panic poised to snatch her at her throat.

"Of course, Miss Chambers." A flicker of raw emotion passed over Lord William's face before turning back into cool, hard, stone. A mask. They both wore masks to disguise the growing frustrations between them. The man positively rattled her, and left her unsure of her own feelings. Would things have been different if she met Lord William before Mr. Parker?

No. She was merely a vicar's daughter, a commoner.

But he was a commoner too, despite his courtesy title. However, he was the son of a marquis, second in line for the title.

Mr. Parker was also in line for a title, and was assured he would become the next Viscount Winnington in his lifetime. The viscount was an old man, in his seventies, near his maker's door. Yes, her Mr. Parker would inherit the title and she would become a viscountess, the mother of the next Winnington heir. And yet, she was a vicar's daughter, her father the son of a fourth son, the grandson of an earl.

She never knew her grandfather. He died long before she was born. She only met her uncle twice before he cocked up his toes and left the earldom to his son. Granted, a little blue blood ran in her veins, but now it was far enough removed that she determined it did not count or matter.

She knew she was fortunate Mr. Parker overlooked such a thing as her common birth. He did not care. He loved her. He wanted to marry her, despite the obstacle of convincing his uncle of her worthiness as his bride. He did not wait for his uncle's approval, but instead, he proposed to her, promising her the moon and the stars and a lifetime of love.

She did not need the complication of Lord William. She had her Mr. Parker, and he was all she ever needed.

* * *

William watched Cassie dance with Lord John, a young buck barely out of knee breeches. The pink of her dress added a blushing glow to her porcelain skin and face. The dress flowed against her womanly curves, ripe breasts, and swaying hips. He groaned.

She tried to act cold to him during their dance, but only half succeeded. He felt her shivers and racing heartbeat through her hands and at the mere touch of her waist.

She wanted him. He knew it. She denied it.

He should turn away from his desire for her, but she was like a river of rushing water for a man dying of thirst. Miss Cassandra Chambers was his very own mirage. He wanted to drink, knowing it would never, could never, be enough.

He tried to shake her away; remove her from his thoughts, his dreams, and his every waking moment, but found it impossible. He journeyed to London to seek relief for his pain, but only found emptiness.

Lady Quartermane was happy to oblige him. He went to her bed, touched her body, kissed her lips, sank into her warm depths, but left feeling incomplete. Miss Chambers face never left his mind. It was her image he saw when he closed his eyes and thrust into Lady Quartermane's body. It was her voice he heard cry out when her body shattered into thousands pieces of light. Not Lady Quartermain. Miss Chambers. Cassandra. Cassie.

He quit the room and wandered out to the patio to find a quiet corner, and a cold stone bench to rest his heated body. The bitter winds whipped his face and through his clothes. Exactly what he needed. He heard a moaning sound in the nearby bushes. Great. A lover's tryst. The sound increased to panting and mewling. *Damn!* He only wanted a moment of peace. He rose and started down the steps to the gardens below. He walked the path, passing Mr. and Mrs. Brumsfield, nodded a good evening, and carried on. He came to a small resting area with a couple of benches and took a seat.

He had to remove Miss Chambers from his mind. He could not imagine how he would do that when he had to spend an entire day in her company next week. Why did he promise Anne to act as escort? Stephen should go. As the heir, the responsibilities of a local home for orphans will eventually fall onto brother's shoulders. Perhaps he should try to convince Stephen to take his place. He did not think he could endure an entire day Miss Chambers' company, knowing he could never touch her.

He thought back to their kiss in the woods. He had not meant to kiss her. He could not say what overcame him. He had no right to taste her lips, to run his hands down her arms and back, but he could not help himself. He dreamed of her, wanted her, needed her. Why *her*? Why did it have to be her?

Chapter Three

ASSIE WALKED THE SHORT DISTANCE from the parish to Nightingale Hall. The imposing structure still struck her with awe. The white stone mansion sat far behind a long stretch of green lawn with a few trees scattered about. Great windows ran along the front of the house, and met in the middle near double doors as high as two tall men standing on top of one another. A footman opened the ironwork gates to let her enter. She walked up the winding drive until she reached the steps that carried her up to the door.

"Good day, Randolph. I am here to meet with Lady Anne." She smiled at the old butler and handed him her coat and hat.

"Good day, miss. Everyone is in the drawing room. I will announce you."

Butterflies instantly fluttered in her tummy. Her mind tossed this encounter about since she danced with Lord William. She admitted she lied to herself, telling her heart she did not look forward to this day, when in truth, she did, and this fact disturbed her above all else.

Of course, her tossing and tumbling night dreams did not help matters in the least. Last night she woke in the middle of the night with her entire body drenched in perspiration. She felt hot, needy, wanting for something she did not understand, but the oddest thing she could not figure out was the throbbing wetness down *there*. Just the thought of her dreams caused her face to flush hot. Oh, how she wished she was not so prone to blushing.

As soon as Randolph announced her, Lady Anne came over to hug her. "I am so glad you could come. You have met Mrs. Bloomingburg and Lady Danforth?"

"Yes. Lady Danforth, I am pleased to see you again." She curtsied and then turned her attention to Mrs. Bloomingburg and nearly laughed aloud. The woman's outrageously large and floppy hat had an entire birds nest on top, complete with a stuffed bird and four ostrich feathers at least two feet high, and this with a pea green and yellow dress. "Mrs. Bloomingburg, how do you do?"

Both ladies greeted her with the customary greetings. She sat down on a settee across from the two local grand dames and took the cup of tea Lady Anne offered her.

"I must apologize for my cabbaged-headed brother. The man will probably be late to his own wedding. I should have told him we were leaving at eight-thirty instead of nine-thirty, and then we might possibly have a chance of him arriving on time." Lady Anne huffed and took a sip of her tea.

"Lord William is getting married?" asked Mrs. Bloomingburg.

Cassie's chest squeezed tight at the idea of Lord William married to another woman, a woman he would kiss, a woman who would become the mother of his children. A shadow of melancholy passed over her causing her heart to beat faster and her breathing to become shallow.

"Oh no, he is not engaged, as of yet that is. Out of all of the Prescotts, William is the only one of us who actively seeks a spouse. He has always dreamed of a house filled with children."

"That is mighty strange for a young bachelor of the *ton*. Most men run from the marriage minded mamas and young misses as if their life depended on it." Lady Danforth laughed as if she said the funniest thing in the world.

Cassie could not say if she giggled from seeing Lady Danforth laugh so, or from the sudden sense of relief. Not that it was her place or concern to worry about Lord William's future wife and children. She would soon be a wife and mother herself. Lord William had every right to find the same happiness. She simply could not figure out why it bothered her so.

This madness needs to stop! She must compose herself right now, before Lord William entered the room, before another blush warmed her cheeks, before she threw caution to the wind and begged him for another kiss.

Another kiss?

Surely she did not just think that.

"Good morning, ladies. Are you ready for the journey?"

Cassie melted at the sound of his voice, warm and deep, and in her case, *dangerous*. Their eyes met for the briefest of seconds, seconds that stayed with for an eternity. Oh, heavens, it was going to be another hot February day. How could she always feel so warm with such frigid temperatures outside?

"I saw Randolph in the hall. The carriage is ready with plenty of warm blankets. Shall we?" The ladies rose as one. Lord William hung back as he allowed his sister and the two ladies to pass in front of him. He held out his arm to her. "Miss Chambers."

She hesitated. Why did he have to single her out? He should have taken Lady Danforth's arm. She was the highest ranking lady in the room. Why did he force her to touch him? She did not want to touch him.

Not really.

Then she might feel that warm feeling wash through her and make her throb in her most secret place. She did not know what it meant, but thought perhaps it was desire. When she felt the wetness there, she sensed an emptiness so strong she knew it needed to be filled. But with what? Her reactions to Lord William were unsettling at best.

She took his arm. What else was she to do? She certainly could not give him the cut direct. She tried to smile, but her mouth wobbled, somewhat like her legs. She worked to arch her spine, lift her chin, school her features and look straight ahead.

Lord William leaned over and whispered in her ear, "Are you troubled about something Miss Chambers?"

"No, of course not, whatever would give you that idea?" She practically growled. She must pull herself together or she would not get through this day.

He was simply a man. A man who kissed her once. A man who entered her dreams and caused her to toss and turn in her bed with a wild, forbidden need she did not understand. A man who was *not* her betrothed.

"You seem agitated. I hope I am not the source of your agitation." Lord William's cheeky smile nearly did her in.

"You are quite sure of yourself, my lord, to believe you are the source of my distress. Not that I am distressed, mind you, because I am not."

"Tsk,tsk. Testy, too. I hope you are not so growly all day." His eyes crinkled up with suppressed laughter. Cassie was tempted to pop him on the head with her reticule.

The walk to the carriage seemed miles away. She let out a breath of relief when they arrived. She tried to set herself apart from Lord William, but somehow he managed to put himself between her and Lady Anne. Mrs. Bloomingburg and Lady Danforth sat in the seat across from them.

The close contact with Lord William was too much. Their upper arms touched, as well as their thighs, and despite their clothes, her skin burned. "How long is the drive out to Mulberry House?"

"Mulberry House is approximately ten minutes to the North. I have never been there myself, but from the description sent to me by Lord Dray's solicitor, the property sounds perfect for our needs. It was once a school for young ladies run by Lord Dray's late sister," said Lady Anne.

"I hope it will suit our needs. I would hate to continue dragging ourselves around the countryside looking for a property," said Mrs. Bloomingburg.

"How many bedchambers are in the house?" asked Lady Danforth.

"There were eight chambers for pupils. I believe they had two girls per room, but the solicitor wrote that four children would comfortably fit in each room. There are four additional bed chambers for staff and rooms for servants."

"The property sounds ideal," Cassie added, hoping to think on something besides Lord William's body wedged next to hers. The half hour passed with conversation about the orphans and Mulberry House. Lord William added little to the discussion, but she could have sworn the man kept glancing down at her in a way that could be called into question at any moment. She hoped no one else noticed.

* * *

What did he ever do in his life to deserve such torture? Granted, he spent a few of his youthful years gambling, drinking, and whoring like most young men, but really, he never gambled in high stakes games, only drank himself sick once (which was quite enough), and never touched an innocent, well...until recently, until he stole kisses from Miss Chambers in the woods. He thought himself an honorable and proper gentleman. He invested his funds wisely, bought a grand manor to make a home for his future wife and family, and made himself available to both his friends and family whenever they were in need.

After all, he *was* accompanying a group of ladies to search for property for a home for orphans. He could not think of too many gentlemen of his acquaintance who would do such a thing without proper persuasion.

He volunteered.

Well, perhaps he volunteered after Stephen turned Anne down, claiming he had a business meeting of sorts in London, and after he learned Miss Chambers would be joining the party.

Miss Chambers.

He closed his eyes and felt her arm and thigh against his. The contact was too much for him to bear.

However would he get through this day without touching her? She was everything he dreamed of in a wife. Lovely, caring, intelligent. He wanted her. He wanted her in his house and in his bed, but he could not have her.

He constantly reminded himself she belonged to another man. Something else swelled in his gut. He did not know this Mr. Parker, but he decided already he did not like him. He comes from the same family tree as his crabby old uncle, a man whose idea of pleasantry is barking at those around him. He had disliked Lord Winnington the moment they met, and he thought his nephew, his heir, the man who lived under his thumb and influence certainly could not be much better.

What attracted Miss Chambers to such a man? Mr. Parker must be handsome and charming, and really, a future viscount for a common vicar's daughter could be attraction enough. Perhaps it was the man's title or his fortune. Except she did claim she was in love with the man. He clinched his fists at the sudden need to punch something or someone.

Lord William's title was only a courtesy, and his fortune a gift from his father, but he was second in line for the title of marquis, which should account for something. Oh bother! This line of thought would get him nowhere. He glanced down at Miss Chambers. Her soft features begged to be kissed, and her bosom, ample and round, and heaving, begged for something more. Why was she breathing so hard?

He thought they would never arrive. He bounded out of the carriage to help the ladies down in order to escape the close knit quarters. Miss Chambers departed last. He took her hand as she descended the steps. The touch of their hands sent shockwaves to a certain part of his body. Thank God he had on a large overcoat.

"The solicitor said he would meet us here at ten. It does not appear he has arrived yet," said Lady Anne. They walked up to the front door. William soundly banged it with the knocker. They waited. No one came. He tried to open the door, but it was locked.

"It appears we will have to wait. The house is locked up and no one is about," said William.

"I suppose we could walk around the property." Anne pursed her lips. She obviously did not like this turn of events. She expected the solicitor to be here when they arrived. Unlike himself, Anne was never tardy.

"Humph," grunted Lady Danforth. "I will be quite put out if we came all this way for nothing."

"I am sure the solicitor will be here soon," said Miss Chambers.

"Yes, you are probably right. Shall we tour the grounds?" asked Anne.

The party walked around the gray stone manor house until they found a gate leading to the gardens. Overgrown flower, herb, and vegetable gardens stretched across the walkways. They had to pick their way through the weeds and vines. A lovely gazebo sat in the center of the gardens. Lady Danforth and Mrs. Bloomingburg climbed the short steps to make good use of the benches.

"Well, If we decide to purchase this property we will need to clean up the gardens, however, they are quite ideal," Anne spoke to the group as she followed the two older ladies up the steps. Miss Chambers bent down to study some vegetation.

"The children can help attend the gardens under the guidance of a gardener. This will help keep food costs down and teach skills some might find useful in their future employment," said Miss Chambers.

"The girls could learn to cook and sew as well. I also believe all of the children should learn to read, write, and do their figures. An education could substantially improve their lot in life," stated Mrs. Bloomingburg.

"Yes, we will need teachers and perhaps some of the local ladies could lend a hand at teaching various skills." Anne turned to William who was still contemplating Miss Chambers backside. "What do you think William?"

"Oh...I...yes, of course, whatever you say." He smiled but caught his sister's lifted brow. She knew he was not listening, but at least she did not accuse him of woolgathering in front of the ladies, especially considering where his thoughts had strayed.

"Hullo!" A short, round man with a balding head and spectacles came through the gate shouting and tripping over the vines winding across the path. William took him for the solicitor. The man stopped to remove a handkerchief from his pocket and wipe the sweat off his brow. William could not imagine how the man could sweat in this cool temperature. "My lord, ladies." His bow was awkward at best.

"You must be Mr. Henderson, Lord Dray's solicitor?" asked Anne.

"Yes indeed. I do apologize for my tardiness. I had a devil of a time getting out of London this morning."

Anne made the proper introductions and then everyone headed to the house.

The house was bare, stripped of furniture and wall hangings. The floors were dusty, and spiders made their homes in the corners along the ceiling. They toured the drawing room, kitchens, library, study, and ballroom. The library shelves were empty. They decided the ballroom could be divided into smaller rooms for lessons.

"Perhaps we could ask for donations of books and furniture?" asked Anne.

"We are certainly going to have our work cut out for us, but so far the property appears to be ideal. Why do not you all tour the rest of the house while Lady Anne and I discuss the details with Mr. Henderson?" Lady Danforth lifted her eyebrows as if her question were really more of a command.

"Yes, I agree. Mr. Henderson?" said Lady Anne.

"Of course, Lady Anne and Lady Danforth. I apologize there is not a place to sit," said Mr. Henderson.

"Nonsense. There was a table with benches left in the kitchen. We shall go there. Shall we meet in the entryway in half an hour?" Lady Anne asked.

"I am going to need to rest these old bones. No more stair climbing for me. Lord William, Miss Chambers, I am certain you can tour the rest of the house and give us a report of what you find. I will join Lady Anne and Lady Danforth," said Mrs. Bloomingburg.

William could not be sure if Mrs. Bloomingburg's large girth truly tired her out, or if she did not like being left out of the negotiations. He turned to Miss Chambers and saw the stricken look on her face.

"Miss Chambers, are you alright?" Her face had gone pale.

"I am not certain it is proper for Lord William and I to walk through the house unchaperoned. I am not yet married," said Miss Chambers.

"Psshaw. Lord William is an honorable gentleman and we are all right here. It is not as if he is going to ravish you dear." Lady Danforth's eyes twinkled mischievously.

"Yes, well, I suppose it would be alright."

"Of course it is alright. Do not be a silly nilly. Go on. We expect a full report." Lady Danforth turned towards the kitchens as if the discussion ended. Mr. Henderson and the other ladies followed.

Miss Chambers stared at him with wide eyes. She did not trust him, or perhaps she did not trust herself. He offered his arm. She took it and they began the descent up the stairs. They walked to the far end of the hall and entered the first bedchamber, empty, but surprisingly larger than either of them expected.

"I can see how four children could comfortably live in this room. It is larger than my own bedchamber."

The thought of Miss Chambers' bed did not help matters. He found being alone with her disturbing enough. They walked through the rest of the rooms, speaking only when necessary, until they reached the last room. "Oh my." Miss Chambers lay a hand across her heaving bosom. William gritted his teeth.

This room was furnished with a great mahogany four poster bed, side tables, a grouping of chairs, a wardrobe, and writing desk. The decor was soft and feminine, pink and white striped walls, deep burgundy carpet, and fine white linens on the bed. And it was clean, not a speck of dust or cobweb.

"This room must have belonged to Lord Dray's sister. I wonder why he left the furnishings in this one room and stripped the rest of the house," he said.

"Perhaps he could not bear to change this room. It is rather odd how clean this room is compared to the rest of the house." His gaze strayed from Miss Chambers to the large, imposing bed in the center of the room. She saw where his eyes went and walked over to the window. "The view of the countryside from this window is rather spectacular."

William walked over and stood behind Miss Chambers. He could feel her body heat only a few inches away. The sunshine lifted the lights from her golden hair. He was tempted to dig his hands deep in her hair and breathe in her lemony scent. He closed his eyes to try and gain control over his rising feelings when she suddenly turned around, her breasts a hair's breadth away from touching his chest.

"Oh." A tiny gasp escaped her lips. Her eyes were wide with a mix of wanting and fear.

He did not move. He could not move. They stood this way for several long seconds before his hand left his control and he cupped her face, then ran his thumb across her lips. All reason and sanity left the room as his lips came down on hers.

* * *

Cassie should have refused to tour the rest of the house alone with Lord William. Surely this could not be proper. She did not trust the man to keep his hands to himself.

Far worse, she did not trust herself to fight off his advances. If she were honest with herself she would admit she wanted him to kiss her, to touch her. No, no, no! She must shake these sinful thoughts from her mind. She turned from the window into a wall of chest, hard, male chest. Her breasts tightened, wanting desperately to brush against something, against him.

She looked into his eyes and saw something dark, something like desire. Did he want to kiss her again? They stood less than an inch apart, staring into each other's eyes, not daring to move, or speak, until finally his hand came up and cradled her face.

Hot. So hot. It was happening again. She wanted to strip her clothes and let the cold bite her bare skin. He ran his thumb across her mouth, the sensation tingled and burned, and she lost all rational thought. She wanted more. She wanted his lips on hers.

And then they were there.

His kiss was not soft and gentle and probing like it was in the woods. This time his mouth came crashing down on hers, possessing, claiming, opening her up and merging their tongues and hearts and souls into one. The intensity of his mouth on hers was more than she could bear. Her legs wobbled and she sagged against him. The contact of her breasts against his chest, even in full clothing sent her whirling into a sensational bliss.

Without a thought she reached up and wrapped her arms around his neck and plunged her hands into his soft hair, holding her to him.

His arms moved around her and brought her even closer, his hands running the length of her back and cupping her bottom, pulling her against something hard in his lower anatomy. She wondered for a small moment if he carried a pistol on his person. It seemed an odd place to keep it hidden. What if it accidently went off?

He broke the kiss, but not the contact. She gasped for air and moaned as his lips made a trail across her jaw and down her neck. The sensation warmed her between her legs. She felt a wetness there and wondered what it meant -*again*. This was the same sensation she felt when she woke from her dreams. She ached for something, but she could not imagine what.

His hand moved up her hip and side until it found her breast. The warmth of his hand across her breast nearly undid her. She held onto him for dear life less she slip and melt to the floor. He reached inside her dress and touched her bare skin. The shock should have brought her to her senses, but the neediness she felt caused her to press herself into his hand. He flicked his thumb over her delicate tip and she cried out, but he captured her sound with his mouth.

Her body caught on fire as he drew her into a deep well of mysterious sensations. She craved more of his exquisite touches, wanted more, needed more, but then the sounds of voices reached the edges of her mind. He broke his mouth from hers and put her dress back in order. He stepped back. They were both breathing hard, staring at each other as if they saw an apparition.

"I believe we are about to have company." Lord William turned and walked out of the room. She tried to control her breathing before she followed him out.

* * *

The ride back to Nightingale Hall proved the longest trip of her life. She managed to enter the carriage first and squeeze herself into the far corner. Lady Anne sat next to her, unwittingly sparing her of physical contact with Lord William. She kept her eyes glued to the window. The ladies were chattering like birds in the wind about the property. She contributed little, afraid she would give herself away with her shaky voice. She noticed that Lord William only spoke when spoken to, his voice clipped, his face drawn and his mouth taut.

Cassie fought the tears threatening to pour like a hard rainstorm. She sat in shock of her own actions and reactions. What was the matter with her? What could she have been thinking?

The truth—there was little thinking, only feeling, only want and sensation. She lost herself in Lord William. She wanted his kisses. Cassie physically shuttered away the thought, and tried to bring Mr. Parker's image to her mind. His shadow formed somewhere on the edge, but she could not make the picture complete.

The guilt tore at her heart. The shame ate at her soul. She reminded herself that she loved Mr. Parker. Yes, she loved him and she would marry him.

Would Mr. Parker kiss her like that? Would he touch her? Put his hand on her breast and circle his thumb across her throbbing nipple?

"Are you cold, Miss Chambers?" asked Lady Anne when a shudder ripped through Cassie.

"Yes. It is rather nippy out today." Cassie pulled a blanket around her shoulders despite the heat coursing through her body.

After what felt like hours, the carriage finally stopped in front of the vicarage on the way to Nightingale Hall. Lord William got out of the carriage to hand her down. She turned before exiting and said her goodbyes to the ladies and then she took his hand. His eyes met hers for a fleeting, intense moment as she alighted from the carriage and made her way down the steps. They did not speak, but she felt him, felt his warmth, smelled his scent, and knew his focus was on her as hers was on him. She nodded and walked as quick as she could to the front door without raising suspicion.

The moment she entered the house she felt her skin prickle. Berkley, their butler rushed to take her redingote, hat and gloves. "You have a visitor in drawing room Miss Chambers." A small smile escaped Berkley's usual tight lips.

"Oh. Who is it?" she asked. She did not want to talk to anyone, and could not imagine who it could be. She wanted to go upstairs and lie down. The day's events had worn her down.

"I have been instructed to tell you the visitor is a surprise," said Berkley.

A surprise? The last thing she wanted or needed was a surprise, but no matter, she could not stand in the entryway, she had to face this unknown visitor, and with any luck, find a way to get them to leave as soon as possible.

She entered the drawing room to see the back of a familiar man facing the window. He turned and she gasped, "Mr. Parker!"

Chapter Four

WILLIAM SAT IN HIS CARRIAGE with only his snoring valet, Briggs, for company. As soon as he returned to Nightingale Hall he ordered his bags packed and his carriage brought round. He had to get away from her. He could not explain to his family the real reason for his sudden departure, so he claimed he had business to attend to at his estate, *but he had to go.*

He closed his eyes and pressed his lips together. How could he be so foolish? He never before dallied with a young innocent miss, much less a betrothed one. A discreet affair with a widow, yes. A night in the arms of a courtesan, yes, *but not an innocent.* Never. Why did she tempt him so?

His restless nights were beginning to wear on him. He needed dreamless sleep. Since he met her she never left his mind. His imagination ran away with her, kissed her, touched her, made love to her. If the insanity of his thoughts did not come to an end, he would be a candidate for Bedlam.

He shifted. The constant state of his anatomy these days cried out for relief. He already attempted a toss between the sheets with Lady Quartermane, but left unsatisfied. He feared he might forever stay in this condition, especially considering he would never be able to indulge his carnal desires with the only woman who he believed could cure him.

The trip back to Rosehill Manor seemed like days instead of a mere hour. He was tempted to knock on the roof and demand his driver take up the reins as if giving chase. He tried to sleep, but sleep would not come, not that it mattered since his dreams most likely would include her.

He should not have touched her as he did. He had no right, but when she looked at him with those green eyes, he felt like a drowning man thrown a rope to save himself. He grabbed on and did not let go. He wanted to kiss her. He needed to touch her. The feel of her breast in his hand nearly made him explode his seed in his pants.

If the sound of the ladies nattering voices did not burn the edge of his consciousness no telling what he might have done. How easy it would have been to kiss her breast, to lick it with his tongue, to suckle on it as a babe might do.

These thoughts were not helping him one bit. He stayed in a constant state of hardness thinking of her. He could not continue on like this, and he needed to avoid her at all costs. He would stay away from Nightingale Hall until she married her Mr. Parker and left the area. He had plenty to keep him occupied at Rosehill Manor, and he could always take a trip to London to relieve himself of his pain.

The site of his new home made him smile. The white, three-story manor stood at the top of a hill, like a queen overlooking her subjects. Tall windows gleamed in the sunlight. The doors opened as if by magic as he headed up the steps.

"Welcome home, Lord William." Scott took his coat and hat. "You have a guest waiting in the drawing room for you."

"A guest? Who?"

"A Lady Quartermane, my lord."

* * *

"Miss Chambers." Mr. Parker came to her, took both her hands, and raised them to his lips. "I have missed you so much darling."

"And I you." Cassie felt the familiar giddiness rise within her whenever she saw him. Mr. Parker did not tower over her, but instead, met her face to face. His sparkling blue eyes held her captive. His lips curved into a brilliant smile, tickling her senses as always. Her reactions to him did not change, yet the shadow of what she had done, and her reactions to another, squeezed her from the inside out.

She bit her lip to keep from crying out the sordid truth of her sins. Her stomach clenched and unclenched. Despite her best efforts to get her emotions under control, a tear slipped out and streamed down her cheek.

"Miss Chambers, what is the matter dear?" Mr. Parker cupped her face with his cool hands and looked into her eyes. Surely he could read right through her, right into her heart and soul, and see the black marks of betrayal.

She turned her lips to his palm and dropped tiny kisses. She wanted him to kiss her, not a tiny tingling kiss, but a deep passionate kiss. "I have missed you so." He started to pull his hands away, but she grabbed his wrists. "No. Kiss me. Please kiss me."

Mr. Parker raised his brow and smiled. "If you wish, my love." He set his lips to hers. What happened to the tingle? One quick moment and he moved his mouth away.

"No. I want you to really kiss me," she pleaded.

"I did kiss you darling." Mr. Parker's brows creased together in confusion.

"Passion, Mr. Parker, I want passion." Cassie begged him with her eyes and her words and her heart.

"Passion is best reserved for the marriage bed, Miss Chambers." Mr. Parker pulled his hands away from her hold and stepped back.

"How can I know we will have passion in our marriage bed if you do not kiss me with passion before we marry? What if we do not suit in that way?"

"What do you know of passion? You are an innocent. This is not a proper conversation, and certainly not what I intended to discuss with you now."

Feeling admonished, Cassie walked over to a straight backed chair and matched her spine to it when she sat. "Then let us discuss whatever you intended."

Mr. Parker followed her and went down on bended knee. "You are angry now. Let us not start off this way. If you wish for a kiss, then I shall give it to you."

He reached up and took her face between his palms once more. This time he exerted more pressure on her mouth. She opened her lips, but he did not press his tongue into her. Instead he gave her a dozen soft, sweet kisses. She liked his kisses. They did not overwhelm her or frighten her the way Lord William's kisses did.

Cassie placed her hands on his shoulders for balance. His touch was gentle and slow, as if he wanted to adore her with his mouth, caress her with his touch. His lips left hers and found the path along her jaw, down her long throat, and across her clothed bosom. She did not burn, yet she yearned for him to continue. His hands reached up and grasped her breasts, kneading them gently until he had her panting for breath.

He suddenly pulled back. "I am sorry. I should not have taken such liberties. We are not married yet. I do not know what overcame me."

"Please, do not apologize. I wanted you to show me passion. I wanted to know what it would feel like between us."

Mr. Parker watched her a moment, his features changing a bit as he appeared to consider her words. "We will suit each other well." He rose, took her hand and guided her over to the settee where they could sit next to each other.

"I have come for a purpose Miss Chambers," he hesitated and looked away a moment before turning his eyes back to her and continuing, "My uncle refuses to approve our match."

She took in a small breath and held it. He just said they would suit, surely he did not intend to cry off. She bit her lip and drew her brows together. He must have seen the anxiety in her face.

"It does not matter. He is a stubborn old goat. I will not allow him to rule my...*our* lives." He took her hands and said with determination in his voice, "I am convinced once we are married he will come around, but I do not believe we should wait."

"Do you want to move up the date of our wedding?" Excitement and fear rumbled through Cassie's stomach at once. The sooner she married Mr. Parker, the sooner she could get on with her life and put Lord William behind her.

"Well, yes, in a way. I think we should elope tonight to Gretna Green."

She choked on a startled breath. Elope? To Gretna Green? How scandalous! Women were ruined and couples looked down upon for such sensational behavior. She thought about her parents, her father who would preside over the nuptials, her mother who already started planning her wedding, and Jocelyn who would stand up for her. She could see the disappointment and censure on their faces, and hear it in their broken voices. They would be hurt to be cut out of the most important day of her life. How could she do it?

"It is now or never Miss Chambers."

"What? Why?" She could not understand the rush. "We do not need to elope. My father could call the banns this Sunday. We could marry next month."

"No. My uncle has threatened to call on his solicitor and arrange to cut me off, but if we marry now, I know he would back down. He would not like the scandal he would induce if he turned his back on us, especially after the sensation of our visit to Scotland. We need to go now."

"Now? You cannot be serious." His tone told her he was dead serious. She never saw this side of him. She did not know what to do. Would he cry off if she refused to elope? Could she talk sense into him and make him see reason?

"I am quite serious Miss Chambers. If you love me you will go with me tonight. I will wait in the church graveyard for you at midnight." Something about meeting in a graveyard to embark on their lifelong journey together sent waves of foreboding through her.

"And if I do not?" She had to ask even though she knew the answer already.

"Then I will assume you wish to cry off. My heart will break, but it will mend." He looked away, catching a small tear with his hand. Her heart swelled. How could she resist him? Even in his yellow canary jacket and navy pants, ornamented with flashy diamond buttons and gold embroidery, and topped off with a snow white shirt and perfectly starched cravat, Mr. Parker was everything she dreamed about in a husband. Witty and charming and handsome, he made her feel special and important.

"What about my family? Running off and depriving them of our special day will break their hearts. How could we do that to them?"

"I realize they will not be happy, but they do love you, and they will forgive you. They may not forgive me, but they will forgive you. They will understand when they realize we had no choice."

"How can you be so sure?" Her sins of late were mounting up and choking her. How would running off to Gretna Green with her betrothed, a man approved of by her family, compare to entangling herself in a compromising position with Lord William. She shuddered to think of the repercussions if someone had found them embracing, kissing, touching. Shame crept up her neck and burned her cheeks like the hell fires of eternity.

"I can only be sure of our love. Pack a bag and meet me tonight. I will wait for you by the Prescott family crypt." He rose, took her chin in his hand, kissed her briefly, then he turned and left.

What was she going to do?

* * *

Lord William did not know whether he should turn her out or lift her over his shoulder and carry her to his bed. He needed relief in

such a way that his bed tempted him. Maybe he should lock the door
to the drawing room and take her here. For her audacity to show
herself at his home, he should lift her skirts, bend her over, and
pump into her until she screamed. Except her bottom is not the one
he wanted to see and touch. No, another bottom came to mind.
Bloody hell!

He pasted a smile on his face. "Lady Quartermane, what do I own
the honor of this visit to my home?"

She stood and breezed over to him, placed her arms around his
neck and kissed him thoroughly. Her lips were soft, but they did not
taste like raspberries and cream. He thought of mint tea. He sniffed.
She smelled and tasted like mint. It reminded him of the sprigs he
chewed on each morning to freshen his breath. He broke the kiss and
reached up to remove her hands from his person. He lifted a brow in
question and waited.

"William, darling, I missed you since our time in London. I was
passing by on the way to a house party and thought to stop in and
visit with you."

Her creamy breasts spilled over her burgundy gown. A long curl
of dark black hair fell from her coiffure to the tempting center of her
décolletage. Her lips were painted red and a touch of rouge
heightened her cheekbones. Large black eyes and long dark
eyelashes batted at him, offering herself up for his pleasure.

He should consider her a godsend, a wicked little nymph to
please him and relieve him, to take his mind off his true and most
sinful desires. He knew she could not cure him of this affliction, but
perhaps, she could make him forget for just a little while. He needed
to forget a certain pair of bright green eyes. This is the reason he cut
his visit short and returned home. Lady Quartermane offered him the
perfect opportunity.

He turned and locked the door. She purred like a kitten who just
polished off a bowl of cream. She started to come for him, but he
took her and turned her around. William reached around her and
kneaded her breasts. Her head fell back onto his shoulder. She
moaned. Another moan, one from an earlier encounter during the
day breached his consciousness. He shook it off and began
unbuttoning her dress.

He had her naked within moments. William wrapped his arms
around her, and reached down to her center. Her back pressed

against his chest and her bare bottom against his groin. He touched her tiny bud and watched her large breasts heave. His hardness pressed against her, thrusting slowly, tantalizing her with what was to come.

He wanted to pound his frustrations into her. He removed his hands and unbuttoned his breeches, relieving his swollen cock. He rubbed himself against her bottom, then bent her over a table, her breasts mashed against the cool wood, and took her. He pumped and pumped and pumped until she cried and screamed and shattered. He pulled out in time to spare her his seed and an unwanted pregnancy.

She stood and turned and slid her hands up his chest. "Oh my. I believe that was well worth the unplanned stop. Do you think we could find a bed and repeat the performance?"

They dressed and moved through the halls until they came to a guest room, not his bedchamber, no, he would not take her to *his* bed. As soon as they reached the room he closed the door and stripped her again of her clothes. They tumbled onto the bed and repeated their "performance" over and over again, well into the night. It wasn't until she fell asleep, exhausted and sated, that he stared at the ceiling and felt the guilt choke him.

What did he have to feel guilty about? Miss Chambers was betrothed to another man. Lady Quartermane was a widow, available, and willing. Why did he feel as if he betrayed someone? And why did he feel so deeply unsatisfied and empty? As if his pleasure were truly his pain.

* * *

Dinner at the Chambers table went on forever. Cassie pushed her potatoes around her plate, trying to listen to the conversation, and contribute, in vain. Her family did not know about Mr. Parker's arrival today. They were out visiting families in need when he came and left. Considering her fateful decision, she did not mention his visit, and certainly not their discussion. She even impressed on the staff that she wanted to surprise them tomorrow when Mr. Parker came to call, and to please not reveal her secret. Little did they know of her true intent.

She already made her decision. She packed her bag and stuffed it into her wardrobe. She would meet Mr. Parker at midnight, then run off to Gretna Green with him. By the time they returned, she would be a married woman. She would bear her family's disappointment, for she knew Mr. Parker was right, they loved her and would eventually forgive her. It would not be easy at first, but once they saw her happiness, they would relent. And she would be free of Lord William.

Once Mr. Parker took her to his bed and made her his wife, she was sure her mind would clear. In time, she would forget Lord William, and her guilt and shame would slowly disappear. She was sure of it.

"Cassie, is there something on your mind? You are quiet tonight," asked her mother.

She nearly dropped her fork. She looked up and saw her family looking at her as if she suddenly had spots on her face. Did they know? How could they possibly know? Surely the staff did not reveal her secret. "I am tired, that is all. Today's visit to Mulberry House wore me out. I think I will retire early tonight."

Her mother's brows creased together in concern. Her father turned back to his plate, and Jocelyn lifted her brow, showing her disbelief. Jocelyn always knew when something bothered Cassie. She would most likely come to her room later and hound her until she broke. Well, she would have to pretend sleep. She could not tell Jocelyn what she planned to do.

After dinner, she excused herself and went to her room. She took her time writing a letter, actually wasting several sheets of vellum before finding the right words to explain her decision to her parents. How could she possibly explain something she did not understand herself? She would go because Mr. Parker asked her to go, and she feared he would leave her if she did not. And then where would she be? Alone. Ashamed. Ruined.

She tried to imagine being married to Mr. Parker, if only that pesky image of a taller, darker man would get out of her way. She wanted to curse Lord William for intruding on her life, but why add another sin to her list? She imagined living in Mr. Parker's London town house during the season, attending parties and routs and balls, a dream denied to her due to her inconsequential birth. As the granddaughter of an earl, she could have had a season, but her parents lacked the funds, the connections, and the interest.

Each of her father's brothers were married, and perhaps one of their wives, her aunts, would sponsor her into Society, but they did not offer, and her parents did not ask. She never saw any of her father's family. She always wondered why. Her mother once told her they did not approve of his marriage. She could not imagine anyone not loving her mother, but apparently there were ghosts in her mother's closet, or her family's closet that is.

Her mother's father was a baronet, a town drunk who beat his wife and children. The shadows of his abuse never quite left her mother's eyes. She often thought her mother was haunted by her past, her memories of such an awful childhood. She never met her grandfather because he died of too much drink in the gutters of London's underworld. Her mother picked up the pieces of her life and married the new, young vicar in her local parish. She thought her mother needed rescued from her life, and her father needed to be someone's knight in shining armor. Perhaps they loved each other in their own strange way, but they never showed affection, or exchanged knowing glances, or smiles.

She wanted love; true, romantic, passionate love. And she believed she found it with Mr. Parker. If only Lord William did not appear in her life and shake the very foundation of belief she held so dear to her heart. She decided her feelings towards Lord William were carnal lust and sin. True love went beyond physical touches and passion. True love was like a warm cup of tea on a winter day; comforting, reliable, knowing.

Her love for Mr. Parker gave her the strength to go this night. The desperate need to escape Lord William spurned her on. She would go, she would marry Mr. Parker, and she would forget the man who made her insides melt.

Chapter Five

THE CARRIAGE ROLLED TOWARDS SCOTLAND. The night passed into day, and the day into night. Mr. Parker told Cassie about an inn only another half hour away. Darkness descended upon them, but they continued on to their destination. They would stop to rest, then complete the trip first thing in the morning. They would be Mr. and Mrs. Parker by noon tomorrow.

During the trip they played cards, read, and discussed their future life in London. Mr. Parker gave her a pillow and encouraged her to sleep during the night, but her mind buzzed and her heart pounded. She could not sleep when she just embarked on the adventure of her life. She was always a good girl, following the rules of propriety, minding her manners, respecting her elders, never causing a breath of scandal, until now, until recently. Her actions were proving more and more scandalous by the moment.

She could hardly believe what she was doing, what she was going to do, but she made her decision, and she knew it was the right one. If only something would stop nagging at the back of her mind. She could not put a finger on it, but there was an itch, a bother, something pulling at her and twisting her and imploring her to turn around and go home. She decided it was bridal nerves, and the guilt she felt for sneaking off and leaving only a note for her family. She forced herself to push those thoughts away. There was nothing that could be done about it. It was too late. What was done was done.

The carriage stopped at the Birdsong Inn. Lamplight glowed from within, lighting up the windows and illuminating the dark night. The innkeeper recognized gentry and came to them immediately. Her betrothed asked for two rooms, baths, and a private dining room to enjoy their evening meal. The innkeeper sent his sent his staff off to do their bidding, and ordered a maid to show Cassie her room.

The room was clean, bright, and warm with candles glowing and a fire roaring. Two maids brought water and filled the copper tub. She locked the door, pulled off her clothes, and slipped into its' heat. The bath eased the tension from her shoulders and washed away the dust of travel. She closed her eyes and tried to relax, but images of her wedding night crept into her mind.

Tomorrow night she would become a woman. She thought of Mr. Parker naked and could not help but giggle. She wondered if he would reveal himself to her. She wondered if he would want her to reveal herself to him. Cassie covered her breasts with her arms at the very thought.

Her mother explained what happened in the marriage bed right after she became engaged. She told her how it would hurt at first, and how she would see blood, but after the first time it could be enjoyable, even pleasurable. She could not imagine her mother and father coupling like that, touching and kissing, and joining together. She laughed at the ridiculous image, but knew they must have or she would not be here, and neither would her sister.

She washed her face to remove the images of her parents from her mind, and tried again to imagine Mr. Parker. He touched her breasts, kneaded them, made her squirm and pant in her family's drawing room. Would he do the same to her in their bed? Would he touch her naked breasts?

She laid her hands on her breasts and squeezed them the way Mr. Parker did. She closed her eyes and kneaded, and flicked her thumb over the stiff crests the way Lord William touched her. *Lord William.* Bright blue eyes changed to black, stormy eyes. Blond hair changed to dark chocolate. Mr. Parker's hands changed to Lord Williams. They moved down her body and touched her where no man had ever gone.

She stood up in the tub so fast water splashed over the sides and onto the floor. She wrapped her arms around her chest and shook not from the cold, but from her wayward thoughts. A sob rose up in her throat and threatened to rack her body. She stood this way for a long time, water dripping down her body, until the air chilled her skin and raised her gooseflesh.

Finally she stepped out of the tub, grabbed the towel and briskly dried herself and her thick curling hair. She donned her nightgown and sat by the fire, pulling a brush through her tangles. She had to stop these insane imaginings. What was wrong with her? She could not continue on like this. She braided her hair, slipped beneath the covers, and drew them up to her chin. She closed her eyes and attempted to will herself to sleep. Sleep finally came late in the night, a restless, dream filled sleep, a sleep that haunted her throughout the night, and snapped her eyes open before the first strands of light broke through the morning clouds.

* * *

The next morning Cassie dressed in a green silk gown, the very one she ordered made for her wedding day, and joined her future husband for breakfast. She tried to scrub away the shadows on her face and the dark circles beneath her eyes, but they remained. She finally resorted to a touch of powder and rouge. She hoped Mr. Parker did not notice either.

They sat in a private room next to a window facing a small pond with a family of ducks. She watched five baby ducks follow their mother across the water, onto the embankment, and march across a small bridge. She laughed at the delightful sight, and thought this little family of ducklings was a good sign.

Mr. Parker smiled at her amusement, his blue eyes light and crinkled at the corners, his mouth wide and white with straight, clean teeth. "I shall build a pond in our gardens and fetch a family of ducks so that I may watch your expression every morning from the breakfast room."

She chuckled, surprised at how it made her feel to think of watching a parade of ducks every morning at breakfast. "I would love that."

"Finances may be tight for awhile, at least until I can convince my uncle how wonderful you are and get him to release my allowance again. And I do have a few investments that are sure to pay off. Things will settle down soon. I just hope I can keep my creditors off my back for now." He put a forkful of egg into his mouth and chewed.

She nearly dropped her cup of tea. She was missing something here. "I thought your uncle only threatened to cut you off. Are you telling me he actually withdrew his support?"

"Do not worry your pretty little head about it. I should not have said anything. It is only temporary." He continued his breakfast as if he did not have a care in the world.

"But if you have no income, how will we live?" Her concerned deepened as she began to realize her error.

"I have a little money stashed away. We will manage for a couple of months, and by then, I am sure my uncle will change his mind. I am his only heir you know." A serving girl interrupted their conversation to refill their mugs. She shook her head trying to clear her mind and piece together this turn of events.

"And if he does not change his mind?"

"He will." He stated with an air of finality.

"What about your mother and sisters? Are they not dependent upon your support? And what of our children? What if you are wrong? What will happen to us?" Cassie could see the future as clearly as the pebbled bottom of the river running through Camberley. His crabby old uncle would turn his back on Mr. Parker. He would cut him off, therefore, cutting off his mother and sister's means of support. He would come to resent her. She would be the reason for his financial distress. He was not thinking. He was following his heart and not letting his head consider the ramifications.

Tears clouded over her eyes and fell down her cheek as she realized what she had to do.

* * *

William sat at his desk and went over his accounts for the fourth time this morning. He could not concentrate. He read and reread the same entries over and over again without comprehension. He shut the book and rubbed his hands across his face. He should take a walk to clear his head, but that only reminded him of another walk he took not long ago.

He gently sent Lady Quartermane on her way the next day, insisting she risked her reputation by staying in a bachelor's home. The truth was he wanted her to leave. He felt a disgust with himself for taking her pleasure and not offering anything in return, for using her to sake his lust, especially when he had no intention of seeing her again.

He started to rise when a knock sounded at his study door. "Come."

Scott entered, but before he could announce his visitors, Mary, Elizabeth, Anne, and Jane pushed themselves past the shocked butler and swarmed into his space. He laughed and met Stephen's eyes who followed his sisters in. Stephen shrugged. The girls obviously twisted his arm and insisted on his escort for this little unexpected visit.

"What brings half the Prescotts here? I am assuming it is half." He looked around Stephen to see if any other Prescotts, mainly his mother, appeared in the doorway, but the space behind Stephen remained empty.

"Just us." Stephen walked over to William's brandy and helped himself. He raised his glass in question, and William nodded yes. A good stiff drink is exactly what he needed at the moment.

"It was Mary's idea," said Anne.

"My curiosity overwhelms me. I wanted to see what my brother has done with Rosehill Manor." Mary cocked her chin daring anyone to question her motives.

He caught her eye. Something was afoot. He loved all of his sisters, no matter how pesky they could be at times, but he had a special connection to Mary, his twin, his better half as she often reminded him. She had something on her mind and could hardly wait to let her lips loose, and would if not for Elizabeth and Anne giving her a warning glance.

Jane walked over to William and kissed his cheek. "How are you doing William? You left in such a rush we wondered if something was wrong."

"I had paperwork to attend to, and I wanted to check on the third floor renovations. I do not like to be away for so long, leaving the carpenters unsupervised." Part truth. Part lie. How could he tell them he was running away from his desire for a woman he could not have? His answer would have to satisfy their insatiable curiosity, not to mention his sister's penchant for being nosy where their brothers were concerned.

"The house looks lovely William. You are doing a splendid job. I cannot wait to see the library." Elizabeth hugged him. His older sister with her ink stained fingers would probably last five minutes before she made her way to the library and pulled out her journal. He secretly smiled when he thought of the books he bought for his library. He thought of her when selecting each volume, and the smile it would bring to her face. It reminded him to ask Stephen if he found out the name of the "lady" writer of *Sense and Sensibility* and *Pride and Prejudice* yet. They were working to obtain an autographed copy of each book for Elizabeth.

"It is impressive William. When do you expect the renovations to be complete?" asked Stephen.

"A few more months. I recently added a bathroom and built in tub in the master suites. I am also expanding the third floor nursery." If only he had a wife to give reason to expand the nursery. He thought of Miss Chambers and took a quick, fortifying breath.

"Are you planning on filling the nursery soon, William?" asked Mary.

"He needs a wife first," said Anne.

"Do you have one in mind?" asked Jane.

"What is this? The Prescotts pushing for a wedding? I thought you were all immune to the idea of wedded bliss." William could not imagine what got into his sisters. Granted, he was the one who openly wanted a wife and family, who did not deny his willingness to marry when he found his bride, but the rest of the Prescott lot were the bane of his marriage-minded mother's existence.

"We were just wondering. That is all," said Elizabeth.

"You too?" He looked at Elizabeth with suspicion. She shrugged her shoulders.

"Speaking of weddings, it seems the poor vicar's daughter, Miss Chambers will not be marrying after all." Mary gave William a pointed look.

He did not move a muscle. He looked from one sister to the other until his gaze landed on Stephen. Each of them looked at him and waited for his reaction.

"What happened?" He was almost afraid to ask, to believe.

"It is quite the sordid affair, really," said Jane.

"The same day you left Miss Chambers went missing." Anne arched her eyebrows, but she looked bemused rather than shocked.

"Missing?"

"Yes, missing. Her parents found a letter. She ran off with her Mr. Parker to Gretna Green." Mary began to rattle off the tale, but she paused when she saw her brother's face drain of color. "She came back."

Anne filled in the gaps. "Unmarried. Ruined. Well, I do not know if she was truly *ruined*, but ruined in the eyes of Society."

"It seems she changed her mind. She cried off and asked Mr. Parker to return her home," said Elizabeth who was no doubt dreaming up a story based on this sordid turn of events.

"It is a shame, though. She is such a sweet dear, and we have become such good friends. I hate to see her packed up and sent off to Yorkshire." Anne chewed her bottom lip.

"Yorkshire? Why is she going to Yorkshire?" His gut churned. He could see the flickering light in the darkness, yet he failed to regain his composure from the shock of this outrageous story.

"She is disgraced, William. She ran off to Gretna Green and returned unmarried. Ruined. Humiliated. On the shelf. Done for." Mary looked as if she wanted to smack him across the face, and it would not be the first time.

"Her father is sending her to live with a great aunt," Anne sighed. "I shall miss her so."

"It is not fair that she must live in exile because she had the good sense to change her mind, to retreat before making an irrevocable mistake. I imagine her Mr. Parker will return to Society, select a new bride, and carry on. The way women are treated in this world..."

"Stop Mary!" William never hollered at her. Mary's eyes were wide with disbelief. He did not understand his reaction either. He was used to Mary's rants, to her modern ideas about women and their independence, but he did not want to hear those right now.

He needed time to think.

"So, what are you going to do about it?" asked Stephen.

Bloody hell! Did he read like an open book? They stared at him with clear expectation in their eyes. Of course, they knew him too well. Heaven forbid he ever hold a secret, a personal desire, something that was his alone. He was surrounded by a family of mind readers and tormenters.

What was he going to do about it? "Make yourselves at home." William walked out the door, ordered Scott to have his horse saddled, and within a quarter of an hour was headed on the road to Camberley.

* * *

Cassie blew her nose and pushed away the never-ending tears. She upset her family, but she never imagined her parents would send her away. The disgrace and scandal was too much for the new vicar to handle. His parishioners would look upon the family with disdain. Lord Camberley might send them away, force her father to find a new position. What would happen to them? Her actions could affect Jocelyn's chance to find happiness. She washed her face again for the hundredth time. Someone knocked at her door. *Not now.* She took a deep breath before answering, "Come in."

Jocelyn entered the room. Her eyes were as red rimmed as her own. She hated to leave Jocelyn. She hated what she had done to her sister. She only prayed Jocelyn would not suffer the repercussions of her actions. Once she was gone, she prayed the community would forgive and forget.

A fresh bucket of tears welled in Cassie's eyes. How long would she have to suffer this misery from her actions? Forever...yes, probably, forever.

"Mother says that maybe once things calm down you could return home. Once the dust is settled and the gossips move on to the next *on dit.* Consider this a temporary visit to see an aged aunt. That is all it is, truly."

"I only wish...I am so sorry, Jocelyn. I should have thought of you, the scandal, and how it would affect you. I confess I was selfish, only thinking of myself, my own feelings." Cassie turned away, so ashamed she thought she might retch from the pain. She could not look at Jocelyn's tear stained cheeks.

"I do not blame you. You are in love, and Mr. Parker is so charming, so convincing. You were betrothed after all. I am glad you did not marry him. How would you have lived? And what about his mother and sisters? They would have suffered, and I know you Cassie, you would have never forgiven yourself for causing their miseries."

Cassie clenched her teeth. "But what about you? What about father and mother? Look what I have done to the people I love most in the world."

Jocelyn took Cassie in her arms and let her cry until the tears dried up and her eyes stung. It was done. She could not turn back time.

Jocelyn helped Cassie pack her clothes in a trunk brought down from the attic. She picked up her green silk wedding dress, fingered the soft material, and handed it to her sister. "Burn this."

"What? But it is so beautiful," cried Jocelyn.

"I no longer need it, or want it. I suppose you could keep it. Change it up some. Save it for a dance or a ball."

Her mother knocked at the door, but did not wait for Cassie to call out for her to enter. She had a brilliant smile on her face. The sudden change in mood startled Cassie. Just this morning her mother burst into tears at the breakfast table. She shamed her mother, and she could not think how she would ever forgive herself for it.

"The most unbelievable thing has happened. You are saved Cassie!" Her mother beamed and hugged her to her heavy bosom.

"Whatever are you talking about?" she asked.

"Lord William Prescott just asked for your hand, and your father has given his approval. They are arranging a special license. You will be married in two days."

Cassie sat on the bed in shock. Lord William offered for her? But why? She was ruined. Her skin tingled and her heart thudded in her ears. *Marriage to Lord William?*

She closed her eyes and shivered from the memory of his touch. The man disturbed her sleep and interfered with her days. She half blamed him for her predicament. If he only had kept his hands to himself, if he had not kissed her senseless and left her confused, perhaps she could think straight.

Because she ran off with Mr. Parker in a rash moment after her indiscretion with Lord William, her entire life was in shambles. Out of fairness, she could not lay her sins at his door, no, not really, not when she embraced his kisses, dreamed of him, wanted him with every fiber of her being. The madness of her attraction to this man led her astray in her thoughts and actions.

Cassie looked into Jocelyn's eyes and saw hope. Perhaps she could redeem herself and save Jocelyn from the repercussions. Lord William provided her a way out of this impossible situation, but that would mean marriage, a lifetime bond with a man she barely knew. What other choice did she possibly have? She could continue her journey to Yorkshire and leave their fates in God's hands, or she could correct her mistakes.

Marriage to Lord William held potential. Their attraction to each other gave her assurance she would not suffer the indignities of the marriage bed with someone who did not appeal to her. At least, he was handsome and kind. Cassie braced herself to face Lord William, and to accept what he offered. This unexpected turn of events changed everything.

"He is waiting for you in the drawing room." Cassie's head

snapped around and she meet her mother's eyes. "Go on now. Do what must be done."

Cassie was reminded of the time when her mother scolded her for playing with her grandmother's finest china. She brooked no argument. She knew her mother expected her to accept this offer and make things right for *everyone, for Jocelyn.* She turned and caught Jocelyn's tentative smile. For Jocelyn, she would do this.

She washed her face again, stiffened her spine, and descended the stairs to face her future.

Chapter Six

WILLIAM WAITED IN THE SMALL, but well appointed drawing room of the vicarage. The soft mixture of blues, pinks, greens, and lavenders made him think of spring time, which turned his thoughts to sunshine, ultimately leading him to Miss Chambers' golden hair.

He could not wait to make her his. He dreamed of this moment, but never thought it could be a reality. He did not hesitate to come round and offer his suit once his family descended upon him, although he was surprised to learn his affections for Miss Chambers were so obvious.

He worried a bit that she might resist him and refuse his offer, but something inside him knew better. From the moment they met, something lay between them; something they were now free to explore.

His arrival shocked and pleased Cassie's parents. They thought her ruined, and he could tell they were truly devastated she was forced to go away, but they thought it best to save her and Jocelyn from Society's disdain.

He wondered what happened on the road to Scotland and back, but he would not press the issue now. It did not matter. The only thing that counted was making Miss Chambers *Lady William Prescott*. He wanted to show her Rosehill Manor, to let her have her way with the decor, not to mention the man of the house. He smiled at the taste of her lips, and the feel of her breast against his hand. Yes, married life would suit him well.

The door to the drawing room finally opened. Cassie's face was face drawn, and her eyes were red and puffy from crying. He wanted to go to her, wrap his arms around her, and reassure her everything would be fine. Time would heal all wounds, and once he wooed and seduced her, he felt certain she would put all of this in the past forever. He counted on their physical connection to get them through the first days of their marriage.

His smile reached her. She smiled back, shyly turning her eyes to the floor; a blush blooming on her cheeks. He knew she was embarrassed, but he vowed to wipe the pain away, for her. "Miss Chambers."

"My lord."

"Please, come and sit down. I have something I wish to discuss with you."

She appeared grateful for the opportunity to sit and fairly collapsed on the rose colored sofa. She twisted a handkerchief in her hands, kept her eyes in her lap, and chewed on her lower lip. He lowered himself beside her on bended knee, and took her hands then forced her to abandon her handkerchief. He lifted her chin with his index finger in order to meet her eyes.

And then he kissed her.

Her lips were sweet, succulent, like a fine wine after dinner. She was the dessert, and he wanted to taste her, all of her. He wanted to kiss and lick every inch of her. He hardened painfully at the thought then broke away to look at her. She was so unbelievably beautiful that his heart swelled.

"We have had this connection since the moment we met. There is something between us, something I believe will grow if we cherish it, feed it, and water it like the rarest rose. I feel as if we have been given this chance, and I for one am willing to risk everything to take it. Marry me Cassandra. Be my wife, the mother of my children. Let me take you home to Rosehill Manor."

She stared at him as if she could not believe her ears. "Do you not want to know what happened before you make this offer?" Although it killed him to think this Parker fellow may have taken her virginity from her before they were wed, he did not care. He refused to consider it. She would be his. He would seer his image into her mind and on her body, so she never forgot who she belonged to.

"No. What happened *happened*. You are free to be mine and that is all that matters."

"This offer is rather generous of you. I am a disgraced woman after all. What about your family? If I marry you will it not bring shame to your parents and siblings?"

He laughed and thought of his siblings, all of his sisters in a line, standing over him, waiting for him to charge out on his white horse and rescue the damsel in distress, and even his brother Stephen participated in the girl's romantic plot. At least Elizabeth would consider it a plot. No, he did not worry about his family or the possibility of a scandal.

"Except for their nosy interference in all of our affairs you do not need to worry about my family." William reached up and kissed the end of her pert nose. "They will stand behind us with unwavering support, and Cassie, this too shall pass."

"Why do you want to marry me?"

He smiled and he took her face in his hands and kissed her again. He kissed her until she opened to him and her arms moved around his neck, and her hands thrust into his hair. He moved his lips from her mouth to her ear and whispered, "I need you Cassie. I have thought of nothing or no one else except you. I want you in my home, in my life, in my bed." Then his mouth crashed down over hers and showed her the strength of his determination. A little mewling sound like a kitten escaped her throat. She kissed him back with matching need and fire, and the determination to possess. He opened his eyes long enough to get a foggy glance at his surroundings and remembered where they were.

"Marry me, Cassandra Chambers."

"Yes, I will marry you. I will be your wife!" She threw her arms around him and pressed herself against him. He held her for several long moments before he pulled away then brought out a small box from his pocket.

He opened the gift and presented it to her. She gasped. "It is beautiful."

The gold ring was set with a large emerald surrounded by diamonds. It reminded him of her eyes, sparkling, and full of life. He removed it from the box and placed it on her finger.

* * *

The moment the word "yes" left Cassie's mouth, the Prescott women swooped down and pulled her into a whirlwind of planning, shopping, and fittings. Her transformation took place in twenty-four hours time, which turned out to be a good thing, since it gave her less time to think, and less time to consider what she had done.

As she walked down the stairs to the drawing room to meet Lord William, she knew she would say yes. If she turned down his offer she would be well on her way to the far side of England, to the

Yorkshire moors; the land of nowhere. Her family, but most especially Jocelyn, would struggle with the consequences of her actions.

Marriage to a powerful Prescott, and an alliance with such a family, not only saved her from ruin, but saved her family from disgrace. This was for the best; she was sure of it.

Over the next two nights before her wedding, she laid awake thinking about Lord William, his sweet words spoken to her as he proposed, and his fiery kisses. She felt swept away each time he came near, flushed with warmth, and the strongest desire to wrap herself into him and stay there forever. He would make her a good husband: kind and gentle, and *passionate*.

A small part of her worried how her betrayal would make Mr. Parker feel when he heard of her marriage. She knew in her heart she did the right thing. If she would have married Mr. Parker, the marriage would have been a disaster. He would have come to resent her, possibly hate her. No, she did not regret coming back home. She simply regretted leaving home in the first place. She should have taken the time to think Mr. Parker's proposal through, to ask more questions, to form an intelligent, instead of emotional, opinion. Then perhaps she would have cried off, and that would have been that.

She could not turn back the hands of time. A piece of her heart broke and whisked away in the winter winds on that day, but now she had another chance, a chance to start over, to mend her heart, and set things to right. Lord William was her savior, her rescuer, and she was determined to be a good wife to him.

Now there was to be a wedding, and Lady Prescott's personal seamstress, whom she kept in full time employment at Nightingale Hall, created a silver confection to dazzle the eyes. The silk gown flowed down Cassie's body like a waterfall. The cut of the gown held a burgundy ribbon in place just below her breasts. She thought the gown too low cut, and she wondered what her father might think, but all of the Prescott ladies, as well as her mother and Jocelyn, reassured her the gown was the perfect cut and fit, and completely acceptable.

The Chambers family gathered with the Prescott family, the local gentry, and a few close friends in the drawing room of Nightingale Hall for the wedding. Her father did the honor of marrying them then pronouncing them man and wife, and during the ceremony, she noticed how he choked up once, and worked to regain his composure. At that moment, she never felt more loved and forgiven.

Lord William took her breath away in his black suit and white shirt with an elegantly tied starched white cravat. He beamed at her as she entered the room, and his smile melted her heart, and made her feel warm all over. Her breasts strained against the material of her gown, and swelled into tight, little buds. She flushed and prayed no one noticed.

At the end of the ceremony, the groom kissed his bride with the briefest of touches. She was a bit disappointed, but decided he probably preferred to spare her from public display. The kiss may have been fleeting, but she knew there would be many others, and they would be a far cry from short and chaste.

A small part of her forced herself to close off her thoughts of Mr. Parker, and the guilt she felt for marrying someone else so soon after she cried off. She prayed he would understand, forgive her, and find someone else to love. She did not understand why Lord William became her fate and destiny, but deep in her bones she knew this day was right, preordained, and meant to be.

The wedding breakfast was a merry occasion with an abundance of food, champagne, and laughter. She wondered if she would ever get used to the Prescotts. The noise roared in her ears, and she found it difficult to keep up with the flowing conversation, their private jokes, and constant movement. They were a bundle of energy, a force to be reckoned with, and they were a family full of love and affection. She could not recall ever receiving so many smiles and hugs during one day in her life. By the time she was settled into Lord William's carriage to go to Rosehill Manor, she was ready to collapse from exhaustion.

* * *

William sat next to his bride, wrapped his arm around her, and pulled her head to rest on his chest. Cassie did not hesitate or pull away, but instead, closed her eyes and fell into a deep sleep.

She seemed happy today, perhaps a bit overwhelmed, but happy, except for the haunted shadows that occasionally flicked around her eyes. He ran his hand along her arm and breathed in her fresh, clean lemony scent, then wondered how she really felt about their wedding. Was she disappointed her groom was not Mr. Parker? He clamped down on his jaw, and suppressed the envy that rose its' ugly head. She was his now, and after tonight, he was certain she would know it as well.

He hoped his new bride would stay awake for the consummation of their vows. A few hours rest before dinner would do her some good, especially since he had a long night planned for her. He would take his time, savor every moment, show her the ways of physical love and passion, and make her his forever.

William was grateful to his family for their support, and how quickly they pulled together an elegant wedding, complete with flowers and music, an assortment of foods and desserts, and continuously flowing champagne. The day was perfect, and tonight all would be complete.

He smiled as he thought of the surprise he had for his wife. *His wife*. He whispered the words and was thrilled with the sound. Just a few days ago he wondered if he would ever marry, or if he was destined to stay a bachelor. He knew he was a rare one, wanting something most men tried to avoid, or at least put off until they had no other choice. He was not the heir. He did not have to marry. He *wanted* to marry. He wanted children, a house full, and a large family like his own parents.

His father was a living, breathing, example; a nobleman who shocked the *ton* by actually participating in his children's upbringing. He spent time with his children in the nursery, taught each of them to swim and to fish, helped them with their reading and numbers, and made a point of spending private time with each child.

He knew how fortunate he was to have a loving father and mother. He had friends in Society who could not say as much. Most children of the aristocracy were raised by servants and only saw their parents a few times a year when they wanted to parade their heir and offsprings in front of members of the *ton*. He would be a good father to his children, and he had no doubt Cassie would make a wonderful and loving mother.

As they approached Rosehill Manor, William gently shook his bride to awaken her. "Cassie. Cassie, wake up sweetings. We are home." She lifted her head, yawned and wiped the sleep away from her eyes. At that moment his heart flipped over. He thought of all of the mornings he would be able to watch her awaken, and suddenly his future beamed bright as daylight.

"Home?" She stretched and sat up and looked out the window before letting out a tiny gasp. She put her hand to her lovely lips. "Oh my."

"I hope you find it as breathtaking as I do." Her eyes widened as they entered through the iron gate opened by two footmen. The carriage climbed to the top of the hill.

"I never imagined. I did not realize how impressive your home would be."

"*Our* home, *my lady*." He gave her mouth a little kiss and watched as her eyes grew round, and change from light green to a smoky emerald.

Desire welled up then spiraled downward into a place from which he might never return. He drug his finger along Cassie's cheek then stroked her lips with his thumb, before trailing down her long white neck, then dipping to touch between her breasts. She caught her breath and lowered her eyes to where his finger lazily traced a line across her swelling bosom. He swept his hand around the nape of her neck and gently pulled her toward him.

Cassie's mouth opened and yielded to his kisses. He flicked his tongue across her lips and into her mouth and drank deeply as if she were the finest and most costly wine imaginable. He tasted her depths and her warmth, both perfect company for a cold winter night. Groaning, he pulled away and rolled his neck from side to side before he become carried away with his innocent wife in a carriage when their marriage bed awaited them.

"We have arrived," William whispered. The carriage rolled to a stop and the footman opened the door. He stepped down and held out his hand. First came his bride's milky white hand, then her slippered foot, and last her lovely face emerged from the carriage. She looked up in appreciation at her new home.

"Rosehill Manor is magnificent, my lord."

"Call me William."

Cassie gave him a quizzical look before responding. "Very well, *William*."

He took her arm and led her towards the steps leading to the front doors. When they came to the bottom step he swept her into his arms and carried her the rest of the way. She let out a tiny gasp, then wrapped her arms around his neck. At the perfect moment, Scott opened the door to allow his master to carry the new mistress of Rosehill Manor over the threshold.

"Welcome home my lord, my lady."

William set Cassie down and allowed her body to slide down his, ending chest to chest. He held her to him while he spoke, "I imagine you will want to rest before dinner. I will show you to your bedchamber."

"I am rather tired." She agreed and looked up at him while biting her trembling lower lip, questioning him with her eyes.

He took his new wife's hand and led her up the stairs and down the long hallway to the west wing of the house. They came to a private parlor with two doors; one leading to her bedchamber, and one leading to his. A connecting door joined the two rooms. It was an opening he planned to cross this night, but for now he would give her time to adjust to her surroundings, and get some rest.

William opened the door to Cassie's room, and startled the maid out of her slumber. She popped out of the chair positioned next to the warm fire and dropped to a curtsy. "My lord, my lady."

"Katie, this is my wife, Lady William Prescott. She will be your new mistress. You are to attend to her every need. Cassie, this is Katie, your lady's maid. My mother selected her for you."

"A lady's maid?" She seemed a bit confused at first and looked at him as if he must have recently bumped his head. The realization that she was now the wife of a nobleman, and not just a vicar's daughter, must have dawned on her. She screwed up her face a bit, then relaxed and nodded towards Katie. "I am pleased to meet you."

William kissed his wife's cheek and left her in Katie's care. "I will see you at dinner. Try to get some rest." He turned and left while aching for the night to come.

* * *

Cassie sat and stared at the emerald and diamond wedding ring for so long her eyes began to glaze over from the sparkling blur. The day was a surreal dream and she was on the edge of awakening. She spent her wedding going through the motions, moving from one action to another with little conscious thought. Did she really speak vows promising to love, honor, and obey this man as her husband before God and her family?

She remembered eating, drinking, laughing, and dancing. Why did it feel as if the events of the day came from a fictional book? It was all so real, and she had a difficult time coming to terms with it. Over the last two days, she had not had time to think, to digest her new lot in life, or to consider her future. The days were filled by the imposing Prescott women, and her nights were filled by one imposing Prescott man.

Now this man was her husband. This man would come to her room tonight and demand his husbandly rights. The man who kissed her senseless in the carriage and made her body ache for more.

Her future plans went topsy-turvy in such a short time. She had her life figured out for weeks now, ever since Mr. Parker proposed. By now, she was supposed to be Mrs. Parker, the future Lady Winnington, not Lady William. She tried to decide how she felt about that and struggled between what she thought should be while being honest with herself. None of it mattered now, not while sitting in her new room, in her new home, with her new name.

She wiped away the escaping moisture from her eyes and looked at her new surroundings. The room was to her liking, decorated in striped peaches and cream walls, billowing ivory curtains framed in velvet peach, and centered with an elegant four-poster mahogany bed.

Cassie sat on a small sofa grouped with chairs and tables in the corner of the room. Who would have thought of such a thing? A writing desk faced away from the window, and a dressing table complete with mirror sat on the opposite side of the room. Despite the large interior the room was comfortable.

Her lady's maid—something else she would have to become accustomed to, Katie helped her out of her traveling gown and into a day gown, then brought her a pot of tea and a plate of biscuits before she left her to her own devices. The quiet suited her perfectly. She refilled her tea cup, and noticed that the china was Sevres. The quality of expensive furnishing, plush carpet, and fine linens in the sumptuous room spoke of elegance and plenty of blunt.

Cassie's father had negotiated the marriage agreement. She trusted him in this way, knew he would see she was cared for. However, she was surprised to learn her pin money in a quarter year would amount to more than her father's salary in a decade. Her new husband not only provided for her, but settled a large amount on her parents to ensure their comfortable retirement. In addition, he added a significant amount of money to Jocelyn's small dowry. Her father told her about these generous arrangements only yesterday evening. Lord William offered more to her family than Mr. Parker even considered.

Cassie knew the Prescotts were one of the wealthiest, most powerful families in all of England, but until now, she had no idea the extent of their wealth. She still did not know exactly, but for the second son to possess such wealth certainly said something about the family. This was an unusual fate for a simple vicar's daughter, and one she willingly accepted when she said yes to Lord William.

The plush bed coverings beckoned her. She stifled a yawn and decided a nap was in order. She removed her dress and crawled onto the deep mattress then let her tired body sink into its' softness. Her muscles relaxed and she sighed as she pulled the blankets up to her chin and sank into a blissful sleep.

* * *

Sometime later a hand shook Cassie awake. She blinked a few times before it registered whose face stood before her. It was Katie.

"My lady, it is time to dress for dinner. I picked out the lovely green silk gown for your first dinner at Rosehill Manor."

"No! I mean, I am sorry, but I cannot wear that gown. Please get rid of it." If Jocelyn were here she would throttle her for packing that gown. She did not need reminders of her broken betrothal with Mr. Parker.

"But it is so beautiful...I don't understand." Katie looked at Cassie as if she were mad.

"Yes, it is beautiful, but I do not want it. Please, take it away."

"If you wish, my lady, but which one of the few gowns do you want to wear?" Katie appeared dismayed. As the daughter of a vicar, Cassie had little need for an extensive wardrobe, but now that she was a married woman with more pin money than she knew what to do with, she would need to purchase a few more gowns.

"The blue one will do." Cassie got up and washed her face, cleaned her teeth with tooth powder, then dressed in the cerulean blue gown. Katie arranged her hair in a lovely coiffure. Her new maid did wonders with her unruly curls, which now framed her face like a work of art.

Rested and refreshed, Cassie almost felt as if she could face her new husband. *William.* She could see his handsome face in her mind, feel his lips on hers, his hands touching her and making her feel the strangest of things. She trembled knowing what lay ahead. Desperate, she pushed her wayward thoughts away and refused to examine her feelings about her wifely duties, or her fears.

Cassie had some idea about what went on between a man and a woman. The expected pain; the possible pleasure. Considering her experiences with William up to this point, she thought perhaps there would be more pleasure than pain, but that thought did not stop her from trembling.

She took several deep breaths in an attempt to calm her nerves, then followed Katie into the dining room. Katie explained there were two dining rooms: one smaller and more intimate for family, and another for entertaining. Lord William preferred to dine in the smaller of the two. An ornate mahogany dining table centered in the room seated six. A matching buffet table set against the far wall below a tapestry depicting a scene of the King's court during medieval times. A fireplace burned at the end of the room which added a warm glow to the already lit wall sconces and chandelier.

Lord William stood when she entered the room. She noticed her place was set next to her husband rather than at the end of the table. The warmth from the room and the thoughts of intimacy made her dizzy. She hid her shaking hands behind her back and pasted a smile across her face.

"My lord."

William held out a chair for her. She was careful to ease herself down rather than flop. Her mother would be quite proud of her ladylike posture.

"Did you rest well? Did you find your bedchamber comfortable?" he asked.

"Yes, my room is lovelier than I could ever imagine."

The footman set the first course before them, a bowl of soup, and an arrangement of meats, served on blue and white patterned Sevres china. The elegantly dressed table was unlike her usual meals at the vicarage, where simple and plain were preferred. Her mother's finest china and crystal were reserved for holidays and special occasions. The luxury overwhelmed her. "Do you always dine in this fashion?"

"What do you mean?" He raised his brows in question before focusing his attention on a spoonful of soup.

"Everything is so elegant, so rich. I suppose I am not used to such finery."

He chuckled before setting his spoon down and giving her an assessing look. She clenched her fist to keep from reaching out and touching his baby soft hair, thick and rich as a cup of chocolate. He beguiled her with his smile which revealed a small dimple in his cheek she had not noticed before. His large dark eyes peered into her soul, as if he knew all of her secrets. She looked into her soup to avoid the intensity of his gaze.

"You are a Prescott now. You will become used to the luxuries of your new station soon enough." William picked up his spoon.

"I suppose, but it seems wrong to have so much when so many have so little." Cassie pressed her lips together, thinking about the homeless children, and her father's poorest parishioners.

"It is only wrong if we keep it all to ourselves. I contribute to the less fortunate, and I can only imagine that with your great heart, you will want to be involved in charity work. You have already made a fine start by helping Anne with her quest to create a home for the orphans."

She studied her husband for a moment, and decided she was fortunate that she married a good and kind man. She knew young ladies who were married off to men of their station who did not see the injustices in the world, but instead, contributed to them. She wondered if Mr. Parker made charitable contributions, but somehow, in her heart, she knew he did not. On the day they broke off, Mr. Parker seemed more upset at not having what he wanted and of not getting his way. His mother and sisters would have suffered in the end, as well as any children they might have had. His behavior was spoiled and childish. Mr. Parker's reaction startled her at the time, but now that she had more time to think about it, she realized he never showed any charitable characteristics.

William and Cassie talked about Anne's orphan project, ideas for decorating the unfinished rooms, and plans for going to London when the Season began. Cassie had never been to London, never had a season, and never made a come out. This would be her introduction to Society, and her first whirl in London with balls, routes, and parties. She could hardly contain her excitement, and questioned William about everything from Almacks to Vauxhall Gardens. She wanted to visit the museums and Hyde Park, and to see the famed Thames River.

William told her stories of his sister's come outs, the latest *on dits*, and the expectations of a nobleman's wife. Their conversation over the meal was relaxed and comfortable, and it flowed freely throughout the evening. She almost forgot about the night ahead—the moment he would enter her bedchamber and make her his wife. The footman kept refilling her wine glass to the point where she lost count of how much she drank. Her head clouded in a strange fogginess. The room spun, making her woozy when William pulled out her chair so she could stand.

He grasped her elbow to keep her from falling. "I believe, my dear wife, you have imbibed in too much wine."

"Oh, I never drink too much, my lord. I mean, *William.*"

His arm circled around her waist and pulled her close to lean into him. His warm, masculine body was softer than silk. She suppressed a giggle with her hand and wondered when he would take her to bed. The room shifted as her flesh heated, creating a warm pool of wetness in her most secret place. She thought he said something about going to the drawing room, but suddenly she was lifted into the air like a bird with wings, but instead of flying, he cradled her against his chest. She melted against him, wrapped her arms around his neck, then dug her fingers into his thick mane.

They entered their shared suite, then he carried her to his bedchamber door. Her aching peaks quivered in anticipation. She sighed in exhilaration. The room blurred from the light of dozens of candles, and the scent of roses overpowered her senses. He laid her down on his massive bed. The softness surrounded her and eased her into a quiet bliss.

Cassie closed her eyes and dreamed that William kissed her, touched her, made her his, before she fell into a deep and drunken slumber.

Chapter Seven

*W*ILLIAM SAT ON THE BED next to his sleeping bride, and struggled to repress his laughter. He spent the last two days looking forward to tonight, to seeing her in his bed, and now she lay fast asleep. He shook his head in dismay. He would have to speak to the footmen about limiting his wife's wine consumption.

The effect of the wine caused Cassie to become more and more animated. She was such a delightful little package when she lost her inhibitions and rattled on with so much excitement. He loved watching her, listening to her voice, seeing her smile, and hearing her giddy laughter. He watched her hands move as she talked. He was smitten, mesmerized, drawn into her.

He touched her shoulder. "Cassie?" She was out. He removed her slippers from her lovely and delicate little feet. He pushed her skirts up past her knees and swallowed hard. Long, well shaped legs. He slowly untied her garters and rolled her stockings down her legs. Sighs escaped her slumbering throat. He folded her stockings and placed them on a chair along with her garters and slippers.

Now for her dress. He rolled her to her side and undid each button, one by excruciating one, until the milky white skin of her shoulders and back were revealed. He took his time sliding the silk dress from her arms and down her body. He left her in her see through chemise, then laid her dress over the back of the chair and sat beside her to remove his own boots.

He could see her dusky peaks form into tight little buds of desire through the thin material. His eyes roamed her body past her small waist and womanly curves, to the golden thatch of hair at her woman's core. His cock hardened. He wanted to wake her, to remove the rest of her clothing, to touch and taste her, to make her squirm beneath him and beg for more. He wanted to drive into her and make his rightful claim to possess her and make her his. Instead, he stripped off his clothes and eased his body beneath the covers. He wrapped his arms around her waist and cradled her into him. Her back was against his chest, and her bottom against his erection with her legs entwined in his.

"Sleep tight, sweetings." He kissed her hair, drawing her lemony scent deep into his lungs, as he waited well into the night for sleep to claim him.

* * *

Light invaded Cassie's eyelids. She squeezed her eyes tight, and willed the light and her headache to go away. She reached up and rubbed her throbbing head and groaned. Who opened the curtains? She turned onto her back and opened her eyes, blinking the sleepiness away. Since when did her bed curtains turn navy? She rubbed her eyes with her hands and looked again.

Realization dawned. She snapped upward and took in the masculine room. His room; his bed. The well appointed bedchamber was dark and manly. The solid navy blue covers and curtains matched the navy and gold stripes on the walls. His bed dwarfed the oversized one in her chamber. The four posters rose to the ceiling like towers rising to the sky. His bedchamber was majestic; a room fit for a lord with its' fine English furniture and masterpieces of art gracing the walls.

She pulled the covers around her to ward off the chill of the morning after the fire slowed to embers during the night. She looked down and gasped. She could not remember removing her clothes, but here she sat, in her chemise. Had Katie helped her into bed? Surely William would not have removed her clothes. She spied her dress lying across the back of a chair.

Cassie rubbed her temples and tried to remember. They had a lovely dinner and a great conversation. At some point, she began to feel flush with wooziness. *The wine.* The footman kept refilling her glass. How much did she drink last night? *Think, think.* The last thing she remembered was being lifted into William's arms before they headed up the stairs. Did they consummate their marriage? Her clothes were removed, barring her chemise. But could they do *that* with her chemise on?

She did not feel any different. Her head throbbed and she was somewhat nauseated. Her mother told her she would be sore down there after the first time. Yet, there was nothing. She must have fallen asleep, and either Katie undressed her, or *William* did. Perhaps she removed her own dress. At least, she hoped.

A light knock at the door startled her. The door opened and Katie came in with a tray. "Good morning, my lady. Lord William told me to bring you up some breakfast."

Katie sat the tray down on a nearby table and gave her a quick, but assessing look. Cassie squeezed her lips into a tight line. How utterly embarrassing! Surely the maid believed she did *that* last night with *him*. The contents of her stomach threatened to come up her throat. The smell of coddled eggs did not help.

"I believe toast and tea is all I can handle this morning. Could you take the rest away?"

"Of course, my lady." Katie handed her the plate of toast and set a cup of tea on the table beside her bed. She removed the tray and quit the room. Cassie set the plate down on the bed then collapsed back on the pillows.

She never drank so much in her life. Her nerves were on edge last night, and the wine tasted so good. It warmed her throat and loosened her tongue. There was a sense of freedom, an openness she never before experienced. She ate and drank and laughed and talked. It all seemed so perfectly innocent.

Well, there was nothing for it now. She would simply have to pay attention to how much she consumed from now on. She finished her toast and tea then slipped out from under the warm covers, gathered her clothes and entered her own bedchamber. Katie sat and embroidered a piece of cloth while she waited for her mistress.

"Are you ready to get dressed, my lady?"

"Yes. I would like to wear my blue muslin, please." As Katie went to the wardrobe to pull out her dress, Cassie scrubbed her face and cleaned her teeth, then set about brushing her unruly hair.

Her head still hurt, but the pain started to ease, so she decided a brisk walk would do her some good. She wanted to explore the gardens and the house. She needed to meet the staff as well, and consult with the housekeeper. She must keep busy. Her father always said idle hands belonged to the devil. She had no desire to sit around idle.

She wondered if William might join her to show her the grounds and give her a tour of the house. They got along well enough, and she could not deny her attraction to him. In time she hoped they would settle into a comfortable routine, a pattern acceptable for a marriage of convenience.

In her most intimate dreams, she wanted more, but she knew she could not expect more. He was a lord, a member of Society, and everything she knew about his class suggested they did not marry for love.

Of course, she planned to marry Mr. Parker for love. He told her he loved her when he sought her hand in marriage. He was the first man for which she felt a tender, the first man she loved, but, now, everything had changed, including her feelings. She thought herself in love with Mr. Parker for months. She dreamed of him, their wedding day, and the life they would have together. She pictured little blonde haired children with blue eyes, or possibly green eyes like hers. They made a handsome couple. Everyone said so.

William's presence in her life baffled her. She did not understand how she could love one man, yet feel such a wild attraction for another. Was it lust she experienced? She almost made a horrid mistake with Mr. Parker, and nearly came to ruin until William swept in and made her his wife. It all happened so fast she could not process it, or figure out how she felt about it.

Cassie knew only one thing—once the decision was made she was committed, and there was no turning back. She was William's wife now, and she vowed to be a good wife to him. They may not love each other, but they could respect each other. They could get along, and learn to be friends. What was a marriage if not one of companionship? She had accepted her fate when she spoke her vows.

Cassie headed downstairs, taking in her new home. The mahogany paneled walls throughout the house were bare of decor and paintings. She stumbled upon the drawing room with its' cream walls, plush floral carpet, deep green curtains, and sparse furnishing. The room was light and airy, yet unfinished. She moved to the library, partially filled with books, a desk, and two leather brown chairs. Obviously, William only began to furnish and decorate his home. Maybe he would allow her to take over, or at least help. It would give her a purpose and keep her mind occupied.

The doors to the study were closed, so she knocked lightly and hoped William was in the room working. His voice called for her to enter. Her husband stood behind a large, imposing desk. The paneled walls held paintings of landscapes, ranging from the wild sea to flowers in a meadow. Shelves overflowed with books. Large, overstuffed chairs sat in front of the desk, and a couch and tables graced one corner of the room. The study was complete...finished. Masculine—like the man.

A shiver of awareness slithered down Cassie's spine. Their eyes met and held for an eternal breath. He came around the desk and stepped in front of her, then stood only a few inches away. He did not greet her with words, but instead, pulled her into his arms and stole a kiss. As his lips, soft and probing, descended upon hers, she melted against him. He pinned her arms, but she wanted to fling them around him, and dive her fingers into his hair. She loved the feel of his hair, soft and thick.

He broke away. "Good morning, Lady William."

"Good morning, Lord William." William took Cassie's hand and guided her to the couch. He sat beside her and looked into her eyes, which caused her to feel stripped raw and unnerved.

"Last night..."

"You fell asleep. I will have to make sure your wine is limited," William chuckled. Cassie's shoulders sagged with relief. She hated to think she could not remember her own wedding night.

William reached up and touched her face with the back of his hand. "I thought we could spend our first day together getting to know each other. I can show you the house and gardens, then we can take a ride around the estate. I already asked Cook to make us a picnic lunch. What do you say?"

"That would be lovely." She smiled tentatively. She still did not know what to think of this man who was now her husband. He was so good to her, yet she barely knew him. She bit her bottom lip, considered him, and thought of the days, and the nights ahead. They had yet to become man and wife in the truest sense, and her blood boiled with fear and anticipation.

They began their day with a tour of the house. Most of the rooms were still unfurnished. William gave her carte blanche to decorate her new home as she wished. His trust in her caused her heart to tumble in her chest. She could not wait to tackle her new project, to let her imaginings become realities.

The room leading to the gardens delighted her senses. Sunlight streamed through tall, gleaming glass windows. She imagined a perfect sitting room, surrounded by bright colors: green plants and vibrant flowers, light colored furniture, and a breakfast table for two. A perfect room to begin their day.

They walked through French doors that lead to the gardens which stretched as far as the eye could see. Although she had seen many lovely gardens, she had never seen such a sight as this. Winding walkways weaved throughout displays of flowers, plants, and trees. Babbling brooks and ponds with fish were interwoven with bridges, gazebos, statues, and benches.

"The gardens are one of the major reasons I purchased this property. The Duke of Wentworth is known for his gardens on each of his estates. There was a time when an invitation to visit Rosehill Manor was quite the coup. I have retained most of the gardeners who originally worked on the estate for the duke."

"I can certainly see why. A person could easily become lost in the vastness of these gardens. This place is magical. I suspect I will spend a lot of time out here."

They walked, arm in arm, along various paths, discussing the flora and the fauna, as well as plans for the house. William mentioned putting her in the care of his mother and sisters when they went to Town for the Season. She needed a wardrobe worthy of her station in order to attend all of the routes, teas, parties, dinners, and balls. He promised her a trip to the opera, something she dreamed about, but never had the opportunity to attend.

Suddenly, Cassie realized her lot in life might have been similar if she would have married Mr. Parker, who was the heir to a title after all. Somehow the thought did not give her the same sense of comfort as she walked through these lush gardens with her new husband, Lord William.

Cassie discovered a peace within herself, a rising sense of belonging and joy. She found it easy to talk with William, and he listened as if she were the only person in the world. There was a comfort in their blossoming relationship, along with an ease in their ability to get along. Although her nerves were still frayed in anticipation of his touch, and her gooseflesh rose simply because he was near, she believed she were a butterfly wrapped in a cocoon, preparing to spread her wings. The wondrous and delightful feeling made her pray for its continuance.

William stopped in the path where an ivy covered wall brought the gardens to an end, or so she thought. He smiled, took her hand, and led her under an arbor, and past tall bushes. There was part of the wall not laced with plants. He removed a key from his pocket. She realized there was a gate that only a discerning eye would notice.

"I have a surprise for you. He inserted the key and pushed a hidden lever, and opened the gate into a paradise. She gasped at the secret garden; it was wild, untamed, a bit of God's nature manipulated by man, and seemingly untouched. The space was small, but perfect in every way. She imagined the colors that would bloom when spring came.

"This is amazing! It is so unlike anything I have ever seen. Why is it locked away?"

"I am not sure, except to think the duke and duchess wanted to keep this little bit of heaven to themselves. Would you like to swing?" His eyes twinkled.

"Oh," Cassie giggled. She lifted her skirts and ran over to the swing attached to the branch of a tree. He followed behind her. When she sat, he touched her back to push her off. His hand burned her back with a touch that turned liquid and pooled in her belly. The cool air snapped against her skin as she swung higher and higher. Their laughter carried in the wind, and she delighted in the sense of freedom. It was a moment that brought back childhood memories. Joy overtook her and made tears sting her eyes.

Cassie swung and they laughed until William caught her by the waist and brought her back down, wrapped his arms around her, and rested his hands on her stomach. The warmth against her back stilled her breathing. He reached down and kissed her along the side of her neck, which caused her skin to tingle. Her breasts heaved, uncommonly heavy and sensitive.

William's lips trailed along her neck and across her temple. His hands moved up and cupped the underside of her breasts. His touch burned through her redingote and clothes and scorched her bare skin. She caught her breath then leaned back against him.

He took her hand and pulled her to her feet. He twirled her around and hauled her against him. His warm hand grasped the nape of her neck and brought her mouth closer and closer, until their lips were only a breath away. She noticed the clean and woodsy scent of soap and man. Cassie closed her eyes in invitation.

William's lips captured her mouth in a slow, tantalizing kiss that singed her nerves from her head to her toes. She opened her mouth and he took the opportunity to dive in with his tongue. She met him in a battle of desire and need, Every inch of her throbbed, and cried out for something she thought might be within her grasp, yet could not quite reach it.

She wrapped her arms beneath his coat and around his waist. She touched the small of his back, and was amazed at his strength. She wondered what it would feel like to touch his skin, to feel his skin against hers. The tender tips of her breasts tightened in response to his machinations. She desperately wanted to rub her hardened nipples against his chest. It seemed like such an odd, wanton thing to do, but she could not help herself. She wanted, *no*, she *needed*, to feel her naked breasts against his chest.

Eventually he tore away from her, breathless and ragged. Cassie bit her lip. Disappointment gathered in her bosom. She did not want him to stop. She wanted to know what it would be like to be loved him. She wanted tonight.

He led her out of the secret garden, locked the gate behind them, and headed through the winding pathways back to the house. He stopped at one point and observed the low, gray clouds that waited to burst. "Perhaps we should hold our picnic indoors today. It looks like rain on the horizon."

She stopped and shielded her eyes from the sun with her hand. The wind began to whip her coat and skirts, as the sun hid behind darker clouds. A roll of thunder shook the earth in the distance. A keen sense of regret settled within her bosom. She had looked forward to their ride to see the rest of the estate, and their planned picnic, but nothing could be done about it. She nodded in agreement and they made their way to the house as the first drop of rain touched the tip of her nose.

* * *

Before the rain came down at a steady pace, William grabbed Cassie's hand and led her to the house. The rain fell before they made it through the door. He laughed and tugged her damp body into his arms, then crashed his lips down on hers.

Since the moment he first laid eyes on her he wanted her. He could not have her then, but he could have her now. Should he wait until after dinner? Would she feel offended or shy if he took her to his bed now? In the light of the day? He wanted to show her the ways of love, to spend the night exploring every inch of her.

William's heartbeat accelerated as he took the kiss deeper into the depths of her mouth, until she groaned and wrapped her arms around his shoulders. How fortunate his luck had turned around, giving him this chance to build a life with the woman of his heart. *Did he love her?* He considered his feelings as he ran his hands up and down his wife's back. *Love.* Such an elusive thing, but not impossible. He knew it could happen. It was rare among the *ton*, but he had grown up watching two people in love make a happy life with each other and their children.

When does one know if he loves another? He knew for certain he loved his family, his parents, his brothers, and his sisters. He would lay his life down for any of them without a second's hesitation. Would he do the same for his wife?

Yes.

He would give his life for Cassie. Did that mean he loved her? Did he know her well enough to declare his love? Perhaps he was just falling in love, on the edge of a cliff, waiting for the perfect moment to tumble. If he told her he loved her now, he was certain he would scare her away. No. It was too soon. This was not the time.

First he would make love to her and teach her the physical side of love. And he would woo her. He would spend time getting to know her heart and her mind. He only hoped he would recognize when the time was right, when his heart was sure. He pulled his mouth away from her lips and watched the confusion and disappointment pass over her face. The rain changed his plans. He took her hand and led her out of the room and up the stairs.

Scott awaited them at the top of the stairs with a concerned expression on his face. William might have laughed at the man's stiffness, if the hairs on the back of his neck did not suddenly rise in alarm.

"My lord, you have a visitor." Scott's voice sounded troubled.

"Who is it, man?" asked William.

"Mr. Miles Parker."

Chapter Eight

WILLIAM STIFFENED.
Cassie paled.

What could Parker be thinking? They were married less than two days, and he decided to pay a visit. The man must be mad. Cassie started, but William held her in her place. He wanted to grab the interloper by his cravat and throw him out, but he was raised to show a certain amount of decorum while in polite company. He would not act rashly. What would it prove anyway?

"We will go together." In a possessive gesture, William laid his hand on Cassie's lower back and led his wife into the drawing room to meet her former betrothed.

Parker stood next to the fireplace with his hands behind his back. His face was a tight mask of controlled anger. He pasted on a fake smile when they entered the room. "My lord, my lady." He bowed, but his eyes never left Cassie's face. William kept his hand at her waist and tugged her close.

"Mr. Parker. Whatever are you doing here?" asked Cassie.

William noticed Cassie's voice trembled, and the tension in her shoulders and defiant stand. Her face lost its' softness and turned hard as she flashed a brittle smile. He clenched and unclenched his fist, aching for a fight. His wife's Mr. Parker was more handsome than he had originally imagined.

"I had to see for myself." He directed a hand towards Cassie. "I came to wish you my felicitations," Parker nodded.

"Thank you, Mr. Parker." Cassie replied with her hands in front of her. William noticed the white of her knuckles as she fought to keep control.

"Is that all?" asked William.

"Well, no. Not exactly. I mean...I...hoped to have a word with Cassie. Alone."

"She is Lady William Prescott now. And the answer is no."

"William, please. I owe him that much," Cassie pleaded. Everything in him wanted to deny her, to say no, to knock the man flat on his bum. He had ruined her, disgraced her, and now he had the audacity to come here and request a private audience?

"You owe him nothing," said William between clenched teeth.

"We have left things unsaid. Please, my lord." Cassie looked at him with such beguiling eyes he turned away. Although this went against his better judgment, perhaps she was right that the affair needed closure.

"Five minutes." William gave Parker a warning look, then turned and walked out of the room, but he did not go far. He lingered outside of the door in case his wife needed him.

* * *

"Cassandra." Mr. Parker came to her and held her shaking hands. She bit down on her lip and tried to keep from spilling tears. "Are you alright? Are you happy?"

"I am fine, Mr. Parker. Why did you come?" she asked. Why, indeed? It would be simpler not to see him again, to put him firmly in the past where he belonged.

"I was shocked when I read about your marriage in the paper, so sudden, and only a few days after...after we broke off."

Cassie pulled her hands away and walked over to the window. She watched raindrops splatter against the glass and fall into long rivulets like tiny streams in search of their final destination. How could she explain? She could tell him how the disgrace hurt her family, how it ruined Jocelyn's chances for a good match, but in truth, how she wanted to marry William. The moment she learned of her husband's offer she experienced a sense of relief, of elation, of wonder.

"My parents were sending me away to live my great-aunt in Yorkshire. I could abide my punishment, my disgrace, but dear Jocelyn did not deserve the backlash of my actions. Lord William offered me the chance to right my wrongs...to end the scandal, and to keep my family and I from ruin. And suffering anymore embarrassment." She turned to face Mr. Parker. His look was hard, unforgiving.

"We could have married. You did not have to return home in disgrace, Cassandra." He stepped towards her, but she stepped back, forcing distance between them.

"We have already been over this, Mr. Parker. I could not allow you to sacrifice your inheritance, your only means of support. You should have considered your mother and sisters. You would have come to resent me, and that is something I could not bear."

"Is he good to you Cassie?"

"He has been nothing but kindness. I could not have asked for more." She said nothing but the truth. Cassie looked at Mr. Parker in his yellow canary coat and green pants. Something shifted inside of her. His wardrobe always amused her so, but now he appeared silly and brass. Oh, he owned a piece of her heart, but something had changed; in him, and in her, as well as in everything else.

"He will never love you like I do, and I am certain you will never love him. We were destined, Cassandra. You and I should be husband and wife right now."

Cassie's breath caught on his words. Would William love her? And what about her feelings towards her husband? She enjoyed his company, and craved his touch. But could she love William? She looked at Mr. Parker and felt her heart wrench in two. His familiar face had kept her company in her dreams for so long, but now, even as he stood before her, he began to fade away.

She realized she wanted him to leave; needed him to go. She was amidst a fog, where two men swirled around her, pulling on her from each side like a child's game of tug-of-war. Tears pricked her eyes. Could she love two men at once?

"What is done is done. I am Lord William's wife now. It is over. Please, Mr. Parker, please go." Cassie met his eyes. She saw a hardness there, a coldness she never noticed before. He bowed and quit the room, quit the house, quit her.

She sank down on the couch and choked on a sob. William rushed into the room to her side, but when she looked up at him, his face was distorted in compassion and fury.

Cassie stood. "I am fine except for a headache. I think I shall rest awhile." She walked past him, shoulders stiff and erect, back straight, chin up. She felt like a little soldier called into battle, except in her case, it was the battle of her heart and mind.

Cassie made it up the stairs. Her knees threatened to give out before she could fling herself on the bed. She allowed the sobs to crest and flow. She cried for a life that might have been. She cried for her near ruin and momentary disgrace. She cried for relief, for what she had now, and for what she hoped to hang onto. Finally spent, she fell into a deep, dreamless sleep.

* * *

William stormed into his study and slammed the door behind him. His fist itched to rearrange the dandy's face. First, Parker charms Cassie into leaving with him in the night, then brought her home unmarried and ruined, and now he dares to show his face at Rosehill Manor. What Cassie could have seen in the man he could not understand, but her eyes spoke volumes. His wife loved another man.

Damn! He was a fool who allowed his cock to lead his head. He wanted her with every fiber of his being, and he thought, over time they might grow to love each other, and build the kind of lasting relationship his parents had. He strangled himself with his own mistake.

The moment he heard of Cassie's dilemma, he charged off like a knight in shining armor to rescue his damsel in distress. He poured himself a glass of brandy, downed its contents, and smashed the crystal against the stone fireplace. Sinking into a chair, he rubbed his face with his hands, embarrassed at his own foolishness.

Her face flooded his mind and he envisioned her green eyes, pert nose, and lush lips. He imagined her golden hair, and thought about how much he looked forward to removing her pins and running her hair through his fingers. Her sweet laughter rose up and rang in his ears. He wanted to embrace her, hold onto her, and never let her go.

"She is mine." The words fell from his lips in a desperate whisper. By the laws of England, he owned Cassie, possessed her as one owned land or a house or a trinket, but her heart, her mind, her soul, belonged to someone else.

He leaned back in the chair, his head cushioned against the leather, and closed his eyes to his torment. Things were going so well between them. Granted their marriage had yet to be consummated, but he had plans for tonight, to take her loveliness and make her his own. They shared similar values, ideals, and comfortable conversation. There was a contented ease in their budding relationship. His heart twisted and plummeted to his stomach.

He wanted her and needed her like a starving man needed food and water, like someone desperate for a breath of fresh air. He could choose to fight for her heart, or turn his back on all he ever wanted, and live in a loveless marriage of convenience.

William sat in his chair for what seemed like hours as he contemplated his future with his bride. He would not let that little weasel of a man stand between him and his wife. He would not share Cassie's body, heart, or mind with another. He would continue his original plan. Tonight, his wife would be his in every sense of the word.

* * *

Cassie turned and stretched before opening her eyes and remembering the day's events. William and Mr. Parker flooded her mind like a carriage trapped in a raging river. She started to sit up, but fell back onto the bed. Her were eyes dry, and her body was weak from the turbulent emotions. She stared up at the peach canopy. How could she face her husband?

She ran through their pleasant morning: their tour of the house, their walk in the gardens, and the wildness of the secret patch of earth behind the hidden gate. She loved how the wind whipped across her face as he swung her in the air, and she recalled how their laughter merged into one sound. The happiness they shared in those moments could not be compared to any other moments of her life. She had never known such abandoned joy. And his kisses. *Oh heavens!*

Cassie's body melted in a storm of fiery sensations at the very thought of William kissing and touching her. Although she was somewhat nervous, a bit unsure of the unknown, she looked forward to becoming his wife in every way. Her skin tingled with anticipated pleasure. She only prayed he would come to her tonight.

He seemed so angry earlier. *Furious.* Mr. Parker's timing could not have been worse. Another man who was angry at her. Well, it could not be helped. She sighed. The guilt she amassed for rushing into marriage with William after her run to Gretna Green resulted in such dismal failure. She had no choice really. She could not allow her family to suffer for her indiscretions. William gave her another chance, an opportunity to rectify the situation, and in truth, after sharing sinful kisses with the man, she could not help but want more.

She heard a small knock at the door before it opened. "Beg pardon, my lady, but it is nearly dinner time."

Cassie sat up and threw her legs over the edge of the bed. It was time to face her husband. She washed up and changed into a pink muslin gown. Katie worked miracles with her tangled hair, and after a quick survey of herself in the mirror, she deemed herself presentable. She gathered her wits about her, put starch in her back, and made her way to the dining room.

William, his face reserved and his eyes shuttered, stood when she entered. She tried to smile, but managed only a slight lift of her trembling lips.

"Good evening, my lady."

"Good evening to you, my lord." They both paused as the footman placed their soup in front of them. William did not waste time on pleasantries, instead, he picked up his spoon and focused on his meal. She did the same.

The silent air in the room crackled like the fire in the hearth. The tiniest sounds of silver clanged against the china and echoed in her ears. Tension mounted in her shoulders with each spoonful of soup.

The lack of even the most basic conversation put her nerves on edge. She started more than once to engage in polite conversation, but he only managed a nod, grunt, or syllable.

She could not stand to spend a lifetime of meals in unbearable silence. He knew of her circumstances when he proposed to her. Surely he could not blame her for Mr. Parker's unexpected visit. The entire matter left her distraught. If only Mr. Parker had let her be.

"The rain has finally lifted," she said.

"Yes."

Cassie pursed her lips. She wanted to shake him, to force him to show emotion, to talk to her, to yell at her if need be. "I enjoyed our walk through the gardens today, especially our time in the secret garden."

William paused, his spoon full of pudding halfway to his mouth, a flicker of raw emotion ran across his features. He nodded, but did not say a word. Cassie gripped her own spoon in frustration. She finished her pudding, leaned back, and watched the man she married. His brows lifted in question.

"I will leave you to your port, my lord." Cassie rose to leave, but William's hand caught her arm.

He stood along with her, and looked so long into her eyes her skin began to tingle. "Await me in your bedchamber."

A sweet sensation swept through her and pooled deep in her belly. He looked intent. She could only guess of his plans. Her breasts stretched to a lush peak against the silk of her chemise and dress. She tried to speak, but only managed a nod before turning and leaving the room.

Cassie took her time walking up the stairs. Each step seemed heavier than the last. A storm brewed inside of her, a mix of anxiety and fear, along with desire and anticipation. She knew what he meant, what he wanted, but she did not know if this was how she wanted to experience her first time. If only he would have carried on some semblance of a conversation at dinner. He left her feeling unsure and now her nerves stretched like a wet rope pulled from two ends.

She entered her bedchamber and paced the length of the carpet. It was too soon to retire. Katie was probably having her supper now. She thought about the revealing piece of white silk her mother gave her for her wedding night. You could see right through the material. Thin straps barely held it up, and then there was the V that dipped baring the shadow between her breasts.

No, she could not put *that* on. Perhaps she should wear her ordinary gown that covered every bit of her skin when buttoned to her throat, save her hands and feet and face. She could slip beneath the covers and pull them to her chin. Her mother explained that her husband would most likely pull the covers down and pull her gown up. She shivered at the thought of her nightgown rising above her waist to reveal her most private parts.

The air left the room which left her heated from head to toe, and throbbing in a particularly sensitive spot. How could she do this when her husband was so angry with her? It was not her fault that Mr. Parker came to the house today.

She wanted to throw herself on the bed and scream into her pillow. It would be her luck her husband would choose that moment to enter her bedchamber. How long would he make her wait?

Cassie wished William would come up and get on with it. She walked over to the window and pushed it open. The cold air slapped her face and cooled her heated body. She reached to undo her buttons, but could only manage the first few. She needed Katie to help her out of her clothes, or perhaps her husband would help her.

Flushed with heat, she moved to the table beside her bed and poured a glass of water from the pitcher. The tepid liquid did nothing to cool her insides. Cassie sat on the side of the bed and wrenched her hands together for what seemed like ages before she jumped back up and retreated to the open window. She embraced the cool night air as soaked through her clothes into her heated skin.

The sound of the nightingale's song, the lover's call, mingled with the sound of his footsteps as they approached her room. The creaking of the door, the click of the lock, the deep breaths she expelled as he came to her caused her to shiver with anticipation.

William wrapped his arms around her, drew her to him, and kissed the nape of her neck. She turned her head to give him better access, and to allow him the freedom to trace his tongue on the outside edge of her ear. Moans escaped her throat. Fire burned low in her belly as his hands found the buttons she could not reach.

One by one they released, baring her skin to his eyes and his touch. The brief contact of his fingers brushed the skin on her back and made her tremble, but his when lips followed the same path, she groaned.

Cassie's stormy emotions were stripped from her as he stripped her of her clothes. She wanted him, wanted his mouth on her lips, on her body. She craved it all, needed it all, and she prepared herself to beg him to give her everything.

She never knew such sweet torture existed. She never understood what a man could do to a woman's body, to her heart, and to her soul. Oh, she had enjoyed Mr. Parker's tingling kiss once, but *this*...this made her want to scream with need and desire.

The material of her gown brushed across her shoulders, over her breasts, then slid to the floor. The cool outside should have chilled her skin, but she was warm; hot. William swept her into his arms and carried her to the bed. She fell into the deep, soft mattress, and looked into his eyes to something dark and burning with desire.

She licked her dry lips and noticed the tense rise of his shoulders. She laid there before him, in her unmentionables, a material so thin he could surely see the duskiness of her nipples and the golden thatch of hair at her private entrance. Her nipples peaked, reached out, stretched against the silk fabric, and ached for his touch.

Cassie watched her husband remove his coat and tear off his cravat. He unbuttoned his shirt, slowly revealing a mass of dark curls

that narrowed to a path beneath his breeches. She swallowed the
lump in her throat, and rose from the bed to pour another glass of
water. He tugged his shirt from his pants and removed it.

His well muscled body appeared to be sculpted by a master artist.
A wide chest, strong arms, and tight stomach made her insides melt
from a raging fire. She squirmed, desperate for his touch. She
reached her arms out to him in invitation. He kneeled down and
kissed her, as she wrapped her arms around his neck and pulled him
closer. She wanted to feel his body connect with her own.

"Patience, love." He sat on the bed and pulled off his boots,
which gave her time to study his strong back and broad shoulders.
She reached up and touched his skin, but pulled her hand back as if
burned. He turned and smiled at her. "You are free to touch me. Do
not be afraid, my ladywife."

Did he see the wanton fear in her eyes? He might think her too
forward, but he said she could touch him. He gave his permission,
and she wanted to touch him so very much. She licked her dry
mouth, then reached out and drew a line down his back with her
finger.

He groaned.

Cassie smiled.

Chapter Nine

NO OTHER WOMAN ever made his cock feel so hard, so near to bursting. He could not take her like a widow or a wanton. She was his *ladywife*, the woman he would spend the rest of his life adoring, the mother of his future children. He must make this night special, make it last, and erase Parker from her heart forever.

Cassie's eagerness pleased him, as well as confounded him. Just today she met with her first love, her former betrothed. He was certain she argued with Parker. He imagined his fist smashing the man's face in for upsetting her.

William stretched out next to Cassie's incredible body. He vowed to take her slow and easy. Her smile took his breath away, encouraged him to continue, and gave him reason to hope. He cupped her face with his hand and bent to taste her lips. Could anything have ever been so sweet?

He touched her shoulder, then used his finger to swirl a path of circles across her chest, and to the tops of her breasts, before swooping his hand across her stomach, over her hip, and down her leg.

She reached up and tentatively pressed her hands on his chest, which burnt an impression on his skin. Her cool slim hands were exquisite as they touched him. She slid her hands across his shoulders before she plunged her fingers into his hair. He deepened the kiss, and swept her mouth with his tongue, then brought his hand back up to rest on the side of her breast.

He pulled away and whispered, "Do you know what is going to happen between us?"

"I have some idea, but I am not afraid."

Gently his lips met hers again for a few lingering kisses before he raised his head. "The first time might hurt. I will be gentle, and I promise it will only get better, no pain, only pleasure."

She nodded and reached up of her own accord to meet his lips, to match his fever with her own and draw him into a heart stopping kiss. After several moments, he broke and began to show her other ways to kiss. He moved his lips across her jaw, down the side of her neck, and across her chest until he reached her soft mounds of enticing flesh. He scattered kisses across the tops of her breasts. She twisted in his arms, moaning in pleasure.

He scraped his teeth over her nipple. The cloth created a friction that sent her spiraling and caused her to cry out. He smiled and took her breast into his mouth, through the fabric. He suckled and nipped at her until she squirmed against him. He left one breast and reached for the other. He pleasured her with his mouth, while he reached up to her other already sensitive breast, and squeezed it, then flicked his fingers across the tight bud.

Cassie dug her fingers into his hair and held him to her. Her lemony scent tickled his nose, bittersweet, yet perfect. He raised his head and gave her a brief, but lingering kiss. "I am going to remove your chemise. I want to see you, all of you."

A tiny gasp escaped her lips, but her wide eyes were pools of dark green passion. He sat up and took his time as he slipped her chemise over her shoulders, and peeled it away from her breasts. As she started to cover her breasts, he grasped her hands and said, "No."

He continued pulling the silk from her body, down her stomach, past the golden triangle, and along her legs until he swept it from her feet onto the floor beside the bed. He took his time and breathed in her scent of lemons and sunshine. He admired her plump breasts and dusky tight-buds that led to her flat stomach, and the place between her legs where he wanted to drink of her nectar. He ran his finger from her throat down between her breasts, circled each nipple and continued down her stomach, then briefly fluttered his hand across her womanly mound.

William lay atop her letting her breasts rub against his chest. He captured her mewling sounds with his mouth before moving on to her breasts. He took one into his mouth and laved the soft flesh with his tongue. He encircled and suckled the tip while attending to her other breast with his hand. She writhed beneath him. Her hips naturally swayed upward and met the hardness of his body.

He ached to remove his breeches and free himself to plunge into her sweet, tight depths, but he refused to give in to his own desires. Not yet, not until he loved all of her, showed her how it could be, how it would be between them. Switching his attentions to her other breast, he continued his sweet torture. She reached for him and wrapped her arms around him. She dug her nails into his back, and cried out in pleasure, and he rejoiced in it.

William trailed kisses across her stomach, licked and kissed the path he created, then reached past her golden curls, and moved his way down her legs, along her thighs, all the way to her toes. He retraced his path, and nudged her legs apart in order to kiss and lick her inner thighs. She wiggled beneath him, and cried out and moaned, as he came closer to her secret depths.

He wedged his shoulders between her legs, and opened her to his gaze, to his touch. She tried to sit up, to see him at the apex of her thighs, and cover herself, but he shook his head. She fell back against the pillows. He used his fingers to pull her folds apart, to find her bud, and gently massage it. Her hips lifted from the bed to meet his caress with all of the pent up passion she stored inside. He swirled his finger around her bud with the gentlest of motions, and wanted so much to suckle her there. Yet, he did not want to frighten his innocent wife. He continued to move his finger along her wet depths as he slipped his body up against hers, and once again he met her breasts with his chest.

William kissed Cassie deeply, mimicking the circular motions of his finger with his tongue in her mouth. To think he only dreamed of this a few days ago. He never believed she could be his, or that he would be able to touch her in this intimate way. He never dreamed he would see her nude body damp with passion across his bed. Her hands explored his body, and gently caressed his shoulders. She swirled her fingers through the dark curls on his chest, across his tight nipples, and down his lower abdomen. He sucked in a breath as she came close, but not quite reaching the hard length of him. Her shy touches sent him spiraling and pumped his blood so hot he was sure it would boil over before he could remove his breeches and sink into her.

He slipped a finger into her wet, hot depths. Her feminine core tightened with tension, and she gasped from the invasive shock. Then she melted against him. "This is where I am going to enter you." He recreated the in and out motion with his finger of what would come, then stretched her with two fingers to prepare her entrance to take him in. In slow motions, he pumped his fingers into her and pulled them almost out while he circled her tiny bud with his thumb and battled her tongue with his own.

Cassie scraped her nails across his back as she reached the pinnacle and soared into that heavenly place where her body shivered and shattered with delight. He broke their kiss to watch the passion sweep across her face, to watch her rise and fall, and shutter back down to earth. He removed his fingers and opened his breeches. Then he slid them down and off his legs. He climbed over her, and pushed her legs apart. He touched her core with his length, and pushed against her opening.

"We are going to join now. Relax and let me enter you."

Cassie closed her eyes and moaned as he inched his way into her hot, tight sheath. The pleasure was unbearable. He had to strain himself to keep from losing control, and to keep from thrusting inside of her and tearing her maidenhead. He pushed further into her then paused before breaking through her innocent layers. She cried out, but he felt her body relax as he remained still within her until she adjusted to him.

"Please...," she begged.

He moved within her, and created a rhythm she soon learned and followed. They moved slowly and sensually to an ancient tune that increased in tempo until they climaxed together. The world exploded into a million shards of brilliant light, as they merged into one. Then he spilled his seed deep into her womb. Together, they cried in unison before he collapsed on top of her. Their breathing and heartbeats mingled into the last notes of a symphony known only to them.

William and Cassie stayed bound together with their limbs intertwined, and his cock buried deep inside of her. He heard her sigh and noticed her wiggle beneath him. "Forgive me, sweetings. My weight must be too much to bear." He slipped out of her, and rolled off, then pulled her to him. He cradled her like a babe in a mother's arms. "Are you alright?"

"I am perfect...wonderful...absolutely delicious." Cassie beamed, and it made his heart flip inside his chest. "I had no idea, not even a clue. Can we do that again?"

William laughed and pulled her tighter against him. "Again and again, as often as you would like."

"I think I would like to do it again now, please." She did not wait for his answer, but pulled his head down for a kiss.

They spent the night getting to know one another, and learning each other's bodies. They laughed and talked between bouts of lovemaking. William could not ask for a more perfect wedding night, even if it were the night after. He wrapped her in his arms after a long night of loving, and she laid her head on his chest then fell into a blissful sleep.

Peaceful and content, William drifted in and out of an erotic sleep where he relived the night over and over again. Tomorrow...his dreams told him...tomorrow he would buy her new dresses and jewelry. He turned to his side with his back against her. *His bride, his lovely bride.* Her face appeared before him, and smiled like sunshine on a gloomy day. Then it faded away. *Cassie!* He called out to her, but she was gone. He turned again and felt her body against him.

William wrapped his arms around her, and took her plump breast in his hand. He kneaded it, and listened to her whimpers. He stiffened against her backside, and readied to wake her. Moans escaped her throat as she arched against him. He came awake, fully aroused, and increased the pressure on her breast. He rubbed her nipple between his thumb and forefinger. She wriggled her bottom against his hardness. William continued his exploration as he rained kisses on her shoulder.

She cried out, *"Mr. Parker!"*

William froze.

His world crashed down around his ears like metal clanging against a stone floor. His face tightened as sudden tension rolled through his shoulders.

Dear God in Heaven, he thought he would win her heart when he took her body. Obviously he was wrong.

He wanted to pull away, and leave her delectable body, while he washed away the bullets shooting through his soul with a strong bottle of whiskey. He eased away from her. His heart wrenched at each small movement. The pain of his foolishness cut through him, sliced him like the sharp edge of a knife, drew his blood, and cut out his heart.

He should have known, and expected her feelings for her first love to stand, rather than wither away like dying flowers on a vine. Exhausted from the lovemaking, Cassie turned into her pillow and mumbled incoherent sounds, bitter to his ears as he imagined she dreamed of her Mr. Parker.

The fire in the hearth died out to nothing but embers, but the coldness that gripped him came not from the sharp penetrating air of the room, but from deep inside him, where self-preservation fought to close him off to her forever.

William donned his clothes and looked back at his sleeping angel, who was fully loved and sated, with her peaceful innocence in his bed. *His wife.*

He closed the shutters of his heart, and quietly left the room.

* * *

Cassie stretched like a kitten waking from a long nap. Never before had she felt so relaxed, and so completely and thoroughly loved.

She almost purred.

Deeply satisfied, she reached over and felt the empty space in the bed. She frowned, turned on her side, and pulled the covers over her naked body.

Slivers of a red-orange dawn peeped through the window and illuminated his space in colorful shadows. Where was William?

Cassie ran her hand along the bed sheets and over his pillow, and sought his warmth. Perhaps he was an early riser. Surely he did not return to his own chamber after what they did last night.

She sighed, contented by his loving, but frustrated by his leaving. Why was he not here, in her bed, soothing her throbbing body? Now she knew why she throbbed down there, and she wanted to feel him again, deep inside of her, thrusting in her until the ache eased and she felt that wonderful splendor all over again. Warmth tinged her face at her naughty thoughts. William would most likely be shocked if he knew that she was thinking such sinful, wanton thoughts. Couples did not make love in the daytime, or *did they*?

Cassie snuggled deeper under the covers. She reached up and touched her full breasts, and the tight buds of her desire. She recalled his mouth on her, and the exquisite pleasure he gave her *there*. Her hand moved to the secret place he touched last night, now sensitive, but still wanting. Every part of her craved his touch again, but she was alone, so all she could do was turn into her pillow and groan.

* * *

Rosehill Manor left little room for escape. William could only go so far before he ran into his wife. He knew he could not avoid her forever, and if he were honest with himself, he did not *want to* avoid her, especially her bed. Annoyed by his own self-imposed life long prison sentence, he knew he needed some space and time to sort out his muddled thoughts and feelings. He could not do that with his wife in his constant presence.

During the night William debated leaving Cassie in the country while he went to London alone, but he decided it was best to avoid unnecessary gossip. After all, there was no one else but himself to blame. William knew about Cassie's feelings towards another man *before* he offered for her. She could not switch her feelings overnight, despite his attempts to make her forget. Time and attention were his only weapons, but right now his own wounds were too raw.

Cassie's cry in the night for Mr. Parker cut deep. He needed a certain amount of distance before he made a besotted ass of himself. Somewhere between twilight and the rising sun, he realized his dilemma as a fallen man. All of his life he admired his parent's unconditional love, but their love was two sided, unlike his sham of a marriage, where only one heart was engaged.

In London, he could keep her busy with fittings for new dresses and social engagements. He would need to escort her on occasion, but for the most part they could follow separate social agendas. He could escape her by spending time at his club and Gentleman Jackson's.

As William sat down for breakfast, Cassie breezed in with a smile so brilliant he nearly lost his resolve. The woman took his breath away, and this morning she looked particularly pleasing in a lavender gown with a deep cut revealing her delectable breasts. He schooled his expressions, stood and greeted his wife, but could not take his eyes off of her. His wife's golden locks, let loose, reached her waist and formed an angelic vision that never looked so lovely.

Cassie's eyes fluttered downward, and a blush sweetened her milky skin. Her shyness after last night's passion touched a deep cord inside of him, a place he desperately tried to close up and lock away. The temptation to sweep her into his arms and carry her back upstairs almost won out, but he fought off the thoughts in the same way a man being choked would fight off his attacker.

"Good morning, William." Cassie's face glowed and her heat radiated around him, and tightened the already protruding bulge in his breeches even further. Her eyes were dreamy as if last night meant something, but he remembered her cry and tightened the reins on his heart.

He fought for control and normalcy. He forced a smile to curve his lips, and he reached to kiss her cheek. The softness of her skin tormented him, so he turned to the buffet to fill a plate with coddled eggs and kippers. She followed and did the same, blushed and turned from him more than once before they made their way to the table.

Yes, London would be a good thing. Lots of diversions. His family being the first on his list of ways to keep his little wife occupied. "I have instructed Katie to pack your things. We will leave for London this morning."

Cassie's fork stopped halfway between her plate and her mouth, her full pink lips gaped open. The idea of yanking her onto his lap and kissing her mouth took hold of him. Instead, he took a deep breath and gathered his composure. Is there a name for a madness of the heart?

"Today? So soon?" She lifted the fork to her mouth and took a bite of her egg, then had the audacity to dart her tongue out and lick her lips.

William held back a groan that threatened to escape his own lips. His attraction towards his wife vexed him. "The Season is about to begin. You will need time for shopping and fittings and such."

"What about our plans for Rosehill Manor?"

He stumbled. The renovations were almost finished, but the house still required decor and furnishings. He thought of another way around this new obstacle. "You can consult with London's premiere designers and order everything Rosehill Manor requires from our London townhouse. By the end of the Season, the house will be complete, and when we return our home will be in order."

"I feel as if I have yet to become used to one place, and now you want to go to another. Not that I am arguing. I have long looked forward to seeing London, but it is just that I feel as if my life is a sudden rush in so many unexpected directions." Cassie held her teacup and looked at him with her startling green eyes.

"Are you complaining of too many changes in scenery in such a short time span?"

She set the cup down. "Yes, I suppose I am. In one week's time I have been halfway to Scotland and back, married, moved into Rosehill Manor, and now you want me to leave for London. Could we not wait a fortnight more?"

Halfway to Scotland and back. William tossed his napkin down and stood. "No madam, we will not wait. We will leave for London in an hour." William marched out of the room, and left Cassie in shock.

Cassie moved from the first blush of love to the first moment of reality in her marriage in a single heartbeat. What, pray tell, brought that on? What angered him so? What did she do to displease him?

Last night, William seemed more than pleased. Good grief! All she did was express her feelings about so much change at once. Perhaps she should not have mentioned Scotland. It reminded him of her disgrace.

Cassie's blood simmered. William knew of her ruin when he proposed marriage. The incident with Mr. Parker yesterday was uncomfortable at best, but she thought him over his anger when he came to her last night, and took her to his bed. Everything felt so right with the world, but now, she was unsure.

Well, there was nothing for it. This week was one adventure after another, and now it appeared she would be adventuring again. She finished her breakfast and made her way to her room.

"Everything is packed, my lady. I left out a traveling dress for you." Katie curtsied and waited for her instructions.

Cassie did not know if she would ever get used to having a lady's maid. "Thank you, Katie. Lord William wanted to leave soon, so I had best hurry." She changed into her serviceable gown and went to the front hall to meet her husband.

Her husband's efficient staff brought the carriage round and stowed their trunks away in record time. William handed her up and they were off to London Town. *London.* She might have been thrilled if William was not so out of sorts, and if the trip had not been announced just this morning.

Cassie looked out the window, and avoided her husband's sour disposition. This was a side of the man she could live without. She much preferred him smiling and cheerful. Right now he reminded her too much of her father, who almost always wore a puckered look on his face as if he swallowed a canary. She chuckled at the thought.

"What is so funny?"

"Nothing, my lord. I am simply lost in my amusing memories."

"Would you care to share these amusing memories?" he asked.

"I was thinking how you remind me of my father, a dour expression indeed, as if you just swallowed a canary. The vision I created amused me."

He twisted his lips as if he debated between a scowl and laughter. "I am glad my mood entertains you, my lady."

"Why are you out of sorts, William?"

He hesitated, then sighed. "I am sorry, my dear. I do not know why I feel so agitated this morning. I suppose I have not been good company."

"No, you have not, but perhaps, you can make it up to me." Cassie had his attention now. She thought about how she awoke this morning and wanted him near her. Last night's magic lingered, and now, more than ever before, she wanted his kiss. He turned to her, and his expression softened a bit. She pleaded with him with her eyes. Perhaps it was wanton of her, but she could not help herself.

"And how might I make it up to you?" William's voice changed to a husky, intimate tone.

"You can start by kissing me, *husband*."

Cassie must have said the right thing because William's lips crashed upon hers. There was something different in his kiss, something possessive, and punishing. She relished it, and kissed him back with everything she had. She threw her arms around him, opened her mouth and met his tongue in a passion filled battle. He yanked her onto his lap, and before she knew what happened, he had her dress was halfway down her waist.

He burned a trail of kisses down her neck until he found her breasts and drew one into his mouth. She cried out, and squirmed on his lap, desperate for release. His mouth tortured one breast before he turned to the other. William's hand found the hem of her gown and slipped up the inside of her skirt to the slit in her drawers. Wetness pooled there and she opened her legs to give him better access. She panted and gasped as his fingers thrust into her core and he tantalized her with the movement.

Her climax burst through a foggy cloud and split into waves of pleasure. She screamed before she descended from heaven and he pulled her against him. She sat in his lap, half dressed with her breasts pressed against his coat. His arms were wrapped around her with his hands running over the smooth skin of her back when the carriage came to a sudden stop.

"London." William pulled her dress back up and helped her with her buttons. She moved to her seat beside him and straightened her skirts. What an amazing ride she just experienced. Who would have thought one could seek such pleasures on the road?

She looked back up at her husband, the man who changed moods like a woman changed her clothes. William's smile faded, and was replaced by a hard mask of indifference. Where did he go when he shut himself off like that? But most importantly, why did he go there?

Chapter Ten

WILLIAM SENT A NOTE to his family's London home before he went to his club and left Cassie to her own devices. The fully furnished and decorated townhouse was large enough for entertaining, yet still warm and inviting. After she looked around, she wanted to add a few feminine touches to the masculine environment, especially in the drawing room.

Her own room was a feminine creation of rose and silk. The housekeeper, Mrs. Maudley told her that William's sister Elizabeth took charge of decorating this room for him. Cassie wandered the house, talked to the staff, and finally found her way to the drawing room where she sat by herself. She watched the city pass by from behind the window, as she searched for her husband's form, and hoped for his return.

A familiar coach and four made its way up the street and stopped in front of the house. The Camberley crest marked it, and a footman opened the door to four young women—Anne, Elizabeth, Mary, and Jane. She scolded herself for her impulse to run out to greet her new sisters, instead, she stood and waited patiently for the butler to announce their arrival.

Like little mother birds the sisters flocked into the room, and surrounded her with hugs and warm wishes.

"How is married life with our brother, dear? Is he treating you well?" Mary pasted a mischievous grin on her face, as if she expected an answer that would give her a reason to scold him.

"Very well. William is the kindest of souls." Cassie rang for tea as the ladies found their seats.

"I must admit I am rather surprised that you are in London already. I thought William would keep you to himself for at least a fortnight," said Anne as she stirred cream into her tea.

Cassie did not miss the assessing glance her friend and new sister gave her. "William thought I would need time to shop and deal with fittings before the Season got into full swing." She lifted her teacup to her mouth to hide her expression. Something told her this was not the full reason for their abrupt departure from Rosehill Manor.

"Where is that brother of ours? Why is he not here laving attention on his new bride and greeting his dear sisters?" Mary sat down her cup and straightened her back. Suspicion clouded her eyes.

"He said he had some business matters to attend to." Cassie bit into a scone. One could not answer questions if one's mouth was full.

"It is a bit odd, but no matter. We are excited you are with us now. All of us need to acquire a new wardrobe for the Season. That is why we came to Town early on. Tomorrow, Madame Colista will bring her staff to Camberley House for fittings. You must come." Elizabeth patted Cassie's hand.

The conversation turned to the latest *on dits*. Cassie listened to the chatter, but she did not hear it. She could not help but wonder about William. When would he return? Where had he gone? She was acting silly. A man of consequence did not sit around his home holding his wife's hand. She made a sincere effort to enter the discussion at hand.

"I had it on good authority from my friend Miss Blakely, who heard it from her mother's friend, Lady Chancery, who got it from her friend, Lady Dorchester, who is acquainted with the duchess of Rochester, that Prinny threw a terrible temper tantrum just last week. They say he rolled onto the floor in a fit of temper, pulled at his hair, and cried like a babe. Do you think he is as mad as his father?"

"Dear Jane, I do declare you could write the gossip column for the paper with all of the *on dits* you manage to find yourself privy to," Elizabeth chuckled.

"I will leave the writing up to you, dear sister. Did you hear about the recent wild house party at Lord Rutherford's?" Jane waited for her audience to give her their full attention, but at that moment, William entered the room.

"William." Cassie stood, then quickly realized how anxious she appeared. She faltered a moment, then strode toward her husband and lifted her cheek for a kiss.

"Cassie. Sisters. I see you did not waste any time once you received my note. I hope you will embrace my wife and help her plan her wardrobe for the season."

"Do we have carte blanche to spend your money then?" Mary smiled and raised her eyebrows at her twin.

"Within reason, Mary. It is a shame mother is not here. I thought to ask her to sponsor a ball to introduce Cassie to Society. What do you think ladies?"

"Oh, I think mother would be thrilled, William," said Jane.

Cassie could not imagine such a thing. A ball in her honor! The prospect frightened her, but excited her at the same time. If only William's smile reached his eyes. Something was amiss.

The tide of the chatter turned to the ball, as William took his leave. Cassie wanted to follow him and demand he tell her what was wrong, but she did not dare. She feared acting the part of a nagging wife.

"Cassie, you must come to dinner at Camberley House tonight," said Anne.

"Oh, yes, do come, Cassie." The Prescott sisters spoke and nodded their heads in unison.

"I must ask William, of course." Cassie hesitated, unsure how her husband would want her to answer. She could not imagine he would turn down an invitation to dine with his family. They were close, that much was obvious.

"Oh bosh! Mother would have William's head if he even thought to turn us down. We dine at seven." Mary was adamant, and the look her sisters set upon her told her they brooked no argument.

"Of course, I am sure it will be alright. Tonight then."

* * *

William sat in the carriage and scowled. He did not want socialize with his perceptive family. He could not blame Cassie for accepting the invitation. She had no idea what he was thinking, and she could only assume he would want to go. Besides, his sisters never accepted no as an answer. He knew they would badger Cassie if she hesitated in the slightest before agreeing.

There was nothing to do except carry on. His acting skills would be tested tonight. He still chafed over his unexpected encounter at Whites with Miles Parker. *Damn the man!* He insinuated his way into William's card game this afternoon. He should have folded and left, but too many curious eyes were focused on him, all of the gossiping dandies who loved the next *on dit* as well as any woman.

Cassie's betrothal to Mr. Parker was common knowledge, and her sudden change of grooms stirred a few yakking feathers. He hoped her escape to Gretna Green had not reached the ears in London, but he knew how fast scandals flew across England. William held his own, did not fold, but ended up losing twenty pounds to that blackguard.

He suppressed a growl at the memory. He found it difficult to concentrate on cards when he wanted to reach across the table and smack the smirk off the man's face. Parker used the opportunity to drop hints of his intimacy with Cassie—*the bastard*. She was a virgin when he took her, but that did not mean she did not succumb to passion's play with her betrothed. He did not want to question his wife's morals, but he could not seem to help himself. Had she played loose and fast? Had he married a wanton?

Clenching his fists, he shoved such thoughts from his head. Just because she allowed *him* liberties while engaged to Parker, did not mean his wife was a fast woman. After all, he was on the other side of those passionate moments.

Cassie stayed close to the window and looked out at the London sites as the carriage made its way to Camberley House. William, however, avoided her glances. They spoke barely two words to each other over the evening. The tension crackled through the carriage. Was Cassie thinking about their carriage ride just this morning? He almost smiled. Almost, but not quite. Their shared lust meant nothing. She may have given him her body, but, after all, it was her duty. Her heart? That she could keep to herself. It pained him more than anything that he could not make her share her heart.

Dinner with the Prescotts never failed to amuse him, but tonight was a rare exception. How could he act jolly when he was so damned melancholy? He pretended to be at a boring soiree, and pasted a Society smile on his face. Years of practice should count for something.

"Cassie dear, what do you think of Rosehill Manor?" asked his mother.

"It is quite delightful. I am looking forward to making it a home." Cassie's smile failed to reach her eyes.

Did his wife regret marrying him? Bothered by the sadness in her green eyes, he turned towards his brother Stephen."Are you taking Prince to the Epsom Derby next week?"

"Yes. Would you like to come along? I believe Prince has a very good chance of winning the purse. I bet Cassie has never been to a horse race. It would be quite the treat for her." Stephen raised his wine glass to his lips, as his dark eyes assessed his new sister-in-law.

William was like a bug under a looking glass. Did his brother suspect the marriage was not what it should be?

"I will ask Cassie if she is interested in such a thing." He bit into his beef and chewed until the taste turned to dust in his mouth.

"Cassie, William and I were just discussing going to Epsom Derby next week. My horse, Prince, is a prime candidate for taking the purse. Would you like to come along?" asked Stephen

William glared at Stephen for his impertinence, but the rest of the family chimed in, and made the decision for both of them.

He watched as Cassie's eyes widened. His family caught her in their web. Once she accepted the situation, her smile turned genuine. It appeared they would be going to a horse race. If only he could race out of here and return home. He rubbed his aching temples.

The ladies parted company with the gentlemen and left them to their port. *Thank God*. He took a deep drink and looked up to see his father's and brother's eyes focused on him. "What?"

James smirked. Stephen looked away. His father gave him a direct look that never ceased to make his stomach turn. At seven and twenty, he could not imagine what he had done to get himself in trouble. The last time this happened he was still in leading strings.

"You are not happy. What is going on?" The Marquis of Camberley managed the most direct route in any conversation.

"I am perfectly happy. Why do you ask?" William studied his port.

"Humph." His father answered. William did not want to continue this discussion.

"It is the curse." James could not have portrayed himself more serious than at that moment.

William wished he had something to throw at his younger sibling. "I am married, am I not? That knowledge alone should put that ridiculous curse where it belongs—in a storybook."

"Married, yes, but happy?" asked his father.

Could his father pull any harder punches? "It takes time for two people to adjust to living with one another. We are just beginning to learn each other."

"Your mother and I did not have an easy time of it at first either."

William sat his glass down and looked at his father. He noted his father had caught Stephen and James' attentions as well. Their parents never fought, disagreed, or appeared out of accord with one another, at least not in front of their children. He could not imagine his parents having difficulty adjusting to their marriage. *They* were perfect.

"Despite what you might think, we are not perfect. In fact, we fought passionately when we first married. Your mother bonked me on the head once with a crystal glass. Drew blood. She thought she killed me." His father laughed and wiped away tears with the back of his hand.

His sons stared at him. *His mother?* Granted, she certainly wielded a powerful look when needed, but he could not imagine her as violent. The years must have caught up with the old man.

"I will never forget it. The crystal cracked my head open. She had to call for a surgeon to stitch me up. The pain of that glass hitting my head did not compare to the pain I felt in her despair. I loved her. I still do, of course, but in the beginning, I did not realize just how much I loved her until she almost put me in the grave. It was my own fault though."

"Whatever did you do?" William watched Stephen and James who were just as rapt with attention in his father's story. Stephen's eyes grew round while James chuckled in amusement.

"I took too long to realize the gift I had been given." His father finished off his port and stood. "Let's join the ladies, shall we?"

The men entered the drawing room, and the first face William saw was that of his wife. She wore the rose colored dress as when he first met. Somehow her glow seemed deeper, more womanly tonight. Her soft mounds peeked over the top of her bodice, and made his mouth water for her delicious taste. He wanted her. Despite her feelings towards him, he still wanted to bury himself deep within her sheath. How could any man not want such a delectable beauty?

He thought of Parker, his cutting remarks and the smirk on his face. The man was an idiot to let her go. And he was damn glad of it regardless of the circumstances. He may not have her heart, but he had her. She was his wife. *His.*

He approached Cassie's side and took her hand in his. She startled at the gesture, but quickly relaxed and continued conversing with Anne. He did not miss Anne's eyes flick over their hands before she looked between them.

The family made plans for their upcoming trip to the derby, as well as the ball in Cassie's honor. The Prescott ladies would plan a grand event to titillate the *ton*. He expected nothing less, even though his wife were a mere vicar's daughter, she would take Society's breath with her beauty and charm. And he would secretly revel in his fortune at finding a wife, *despite the damnable curse.*

* * *

Cassie breathed a sigh of relief as the carriage pulled up to their townhouse. The night had been difficult. Her husband constantly changed from hot to cold from the moment he entered the drawing room. When he took her hand she was surprised by his affectionate gesture, and she warmed with the pleasure of it. Did he have something on his mind that had nothing to do with her? It was a possibility. Perhaps she only imagined his displeasure with her. Would come to her tonight? Once they alighted from the carriage, there was no time to consider his plans.

William swept her into his arms and carried her up the stairs. "I believe, my dear, it is time for bed."

Her face burned from embarrassment as they passed the butler, footman, and a maid. She wanted to tell William to put her down, but she could not bring herself to say it. Instead, she buried her face against his shoulder.

Once they entered his bedchamber, he let her down, but held onto her so that her body glided down against his before her feet touched the floor. He tightened his hold against her and touched her cheek with the back of his hand. "So beautiful. So very beautiful."

His voice whispered across her skin and she shivered with the expectation of what he would do to her body. He turned her around and unbuttoned her dress. "I will be your lady's maid tonight." His fingers burned her back, and sent heat throughout her body. The rose silk fluttered to the floor and sent a sweet breeze across her heated skin. He pressed a kiss to her shoulder, and more down her back as he wrapped his arms around her front and tugged at her corset strings. She breathed deeply when he released the corset from her body, and left her in her thin chemise.

William quickly divested her of the rest of her clothes. He pressed against her back with his rigid erection making itself known against her bottom. His arms swept around her and his hands moved across her breasts then down her stomach. His fingers reached her mons and brushed her curls. He whispered in her ear, "I want to taste you there tonight, to put my mouth on you, to kiss and lick you there until you come apart."

Cassie shivered as he swept her into his arms once again and carried her to his bed. He gently laid her naked form across his bed while never taking his eyes off of her, as he stripped his clothes from his body. She met his dark and stormy eyes and followed them to her core, where she lay open and exposed, ready to take him into her body. The heat and wetness of her mound flowed and throbbed.

She scanned his wide shoulders, muscled chest, and followed the line of dark curls until they reached the bulge which would soon fill her. Art did not do a man justice, at least not this man. He was everything beautiful and her hips rose instinctively off the bed to meet his offer of gratification.

"Patience, love." William knelt before her, grasped her legs, and opened them to him before he pulled her forward. Her bottom met the edge of the bed as he wrapped her legs around his shoulders.

He could not be serious? Surely this was a sin. William smiled at her before delving between her legs and kissing her there. His tongue swept across her most intimate places, then twirled and suckled until nothing else mattered except his mouth against her. She wiggled on the bed, but he held her tight, and continued his torture until something swelled so deep inside of her she thought she would burst into flames.

Cassie grasped his hair and tugged downward to keep him in place until she lost all sense, then wept with the pleasure of it. Her dam burst and sensation swept across her body. Her hips lifted with eagerness off the bed. Tears escaped and flowed down her cheeks. William left her burning core, then moved over her and slipped inside to begin another round of exquisite torture.

This time his movements were not as slow and gentle. He pumped into her, and slammed against her thighs, then took her to new depths of bliss. She met his rhythm thrust by thrust until they reached beyond the stars, and he spilled his seed deep into her body. Their perspiration mingled as he lay over her with his chest pressed against her aching breasts. They breathed the same rhythm as their lovemaking, slowly descending to reality. William pulled out of her and gently cradled her in his arms.

Cassie snuggled against her husband. A few days ago she nearly missed out on this moment. A different decision and she would be in another man's bed. She was glad things turned out they way they did.

Chapter Eleven

"THIS EMERALD GREEN would be splendid on you." Lady Camberley held the silk against Cassie. *Such lovely fabric, and so costly.* She nibbled on her bottom lip. She spent more today on one dress than she normally spent on her entire wardrobe for a year.

Lady Camberley looked at her oddly before she handed the fabric to Madame Colista. "Make something stunning from this."

"Of course, my lady. You will be the diamond of the ball when I am done with this dress."

Cassie watched Madame Colista flitter away. Outfitting six women for a season must be an overwhelming task.

"Shall we sit down and enjoy a cup of tea? I would like to speak to you while my daughters are occupied." Seamstresses surrounded the four sisters and measured, pinned, and tucked. Cassie was fortunate they insisted she submit first, so now the ordeal was over.

She sat down on a settee at the far end of the drawing room. She looked over the rim of her cup, and watched her mother-in-law. She hoped whatever bothered Lady Camberley had nothing to do with her. So far, Lady Prescott showed her kindness and open arms.

"How are you and William getting along dear?"

"Fine, thank you."

"Humph."

Did Lady Camberley detect that things were not quite right? How utterly embarrassing! How could she explain something she did not understand herself? Should she ask Lady Camberley about William's mood swings? She feared his constant change in temperature had to do with her. She was stumped as to why he offered for her in the first place.

Granted, they shared two sinful, lustful, intimate moments while she was still betrothed to Mr. Parker. Once near the river and once at Mulberry House. Her cheeks flushed from the memory. "It is rather warm in here."

She could not think of any other reason why a man from such a noble and powerful family would offer for a mere vicar's daughter. William must have felt some sense of honor towards after their scandalous indiscretions.

None of her fairytale made sense. He treated her well during the day. If you counted polite conversation at breakfast and a hurried retreat as *doing well*. The nights, however, were something else. He changed into a different man when he visited her room. She knew not what to make of it.

"Adjusting to marriage takes time. Lord Camberley and I did not get along very well at first. It took awhile for us to come around to each other, but in the end, I could not have been more blessed." Lady Camberley's eyes turned dreamy, and her features softened in such a way she suddenly looked much younger than her actual years.

"William and I get along fine, my lady," said Cassie.

"In bed, perhaps, but what about outside of the bedchamber?"

Cassie nearly dropped her cup. "It really is quite warm in here." Surely she just turned three shades of red. *Good word!* She did not want to discuss bed play with her mother-in-law.

"I have distressed you, my dear. I am sorry, but, I sense things are not as they should be. Call it mother's intuition if you will. I know my William. He is not happy."

Cassie closed her eyes and wished she could do the same to her ears. *Not happy.* Guilt enveloped her and squeezed the air from her lungs. She should not have married William. She brought her shame on his family, and now he regretted their marriage. When William proposed, he seemed to truly want her, want this marriage, but now, she was unsure.

She was so confused. Although she once believed herself in love with Mr. Parker, she could not imagine doing with him what she had done with William. Her world had shifted in such a short time, and her feelings were shifting as well. Pain seared her heart as she thought of William as unhappy. She wanted to be a good wife to her husband. But how could she if he kept his distance except at night?

"Cassie. Do you still love Mr. Parker?"

The air left her lungs. How was she supposed to answer such a question? She looked around the room, and searched for an escape. There was nowhere to go. She was well and truly trapped.

"Perhaps it is for the best if you did not answer."

"I...uh...I..."

Mary grabbed a biscuit and plopped down in a nearby chair. "I am done with my fittings, thank goodness. I do not understand why women have to have so many changes of clothes. Morning dresses, walking dresses, dinner gowns, ball gowns. It is ridiculous if you ask me." She looked curiously from one to the other. "Did I interrupt something serious? You both look like startled deer."

"We were just talking, Mary," said Lady Camberley.

"Talking about how William is so unhappy, I suppose," said Mary.

Dear heavens! William's family must despise her for the sham of their marriage.

"Oh, do not get your feathers in a ruffle, Cassie. It is William's own fault. It is not as if he could expect you to fall madly in love with him only a day after returning from a spoiled trip to Gretna Green with your betrothed. He may be mad about you, but he cannot think you can turn your feelings on and off so easily." Mary bit into her biscuit as if they were discussing the weather.

"Mary! Must you be so brass? I am sorry, Cassie. I did not mean for our conversation to turn so sour. I do not blame you, truly, I do not," said Lady Camberley.

What exactly did they expect her to say? Could William be mad about her? She warmed at the thought. But no, he was too cold to her. At least he was cold during the day. But the nights...

"It is the curse." Elizabeth poured herself a cup of tea and sat down.

"What curse?"

"Oh, William did not tell you? Hmm...probably not. He doesn't believe in it. You see, a long time ago, the third Marquis of Camberley, and his brother, the second son, fell in love with the same woman." Mary's eyes twinkled.

Elizabeth picked up the story from there, "Lady Monica, of course, married the marquis."

Anne walked up to join them. "But the second son, Lord John, had a jealous fit of temper."

"And when the marchioness refused to be his lover, he stabbed her with a knife," added Elizabeth.

She looked back and forth as the sisters told their tale. What could this tragic triangle have to do with William?

Jane wandered over, obviously entranced with the story, and not wanting to be left out. "As she lay dying, she set a curse on Lord John."

"And every second son of the Marquis thereafter," said Anne.

"Which is odd when you consider it, since she in fact, cursed her own son," said Elizabeth as she nibbled on a biscuit.

"I never thought about that." Anne screwed up her face in consideration.

"Nevertheless, she did curse her own son, and every second son thereafter," said Mary.

Jane continued, "According to legend, the second son of the Marquis of Camberley was cursed to rejection."

"He is never to find his true love, or to marry. He is destined to remain a lonely bachelor," said Elizabeth.

"But William married Cassie," said Jane.

"So the curse came to an end," added Anne.

"Except that William is unhappy," added Mary.

"Mary!" The entire lot of them turned on Mary. She simply shrugged her shoulders.

Cassie paled. She could not believe in some silly curse, but she did believe William was unhappy. She was quite sure of it now. What could she do? They were bound to each other for life. She did not know how to make her husband happy.

"Oh posh. He is only unhappy because he believes his wife loves another." Mary lifted her brows towards Cassie.

Mr. Parker. Mary meant Mr. Parker. What could she say? She was once betrothed to Mr. Parker. She could not change the past.

"How can you say such a thing? How would you even know such a thing?" Anne screeched.

"We are twins," Mary stated as if that said it all.

"He was quite desperate to marry," said Jane.

She swallowed hard before responding, "Desperate?"

"Perhaps not desperate." Jane grinned.

"No, not desperate, but he did want to marry. I cannot imagine why," said Mary.

"He is the only one of us who actually wanted to marry," said Elizabeth.

"To the bane of my existence." Lady Camberley's face puckered as she rolled her eyes at her daughters.

"Unfortunately, his suit was rejected," said Anne.

"Twelve times," laughed Mary.

"I guess thirteen is his lucky number," said Jane.

Thirteen. She was number thirteen. She could not imagine why twelve eligible women turned down his suit. William was incredibly handsome with his dark, thick, wavy hair and chocolate colored eyes. He was wealthy beyond compare, and from a powerful family. He must have had his pick of young misses thrust at him by matchmaking mamas.

Did he marry her because everyone else rejected him? Did he think her so desperate she would not turn him down? Well, she *was* quite desperate. Ruined. Disgraced. But that is not why she said yes.

Why had she said yes?

His smile. His kiss. His touch.

Where was a fan when one needed to fan one's self? The room was overly warm. Hot, in fact. Burning. Could they not douse the fire?

"Cassie, dear. Are you quite alright? I believe my daughters overstepped themselves." Lady Camberley screwed up her face like the sternest schoolmarm. Everyone had the decency to blush, except Mary who grinned as if she were having a great deal of fun. At Cassie's expense. Could this conversation get any worse?

She nearly burst into tears. The last place she wanted to have a good cry was in front of his sisters and mother. It was bad enough they thought she made William unhappy. How much worse will they think of her if she turned into a watering pot?

She fought to get her emotions under control, and considered her words carefully before she spoke. "Thirteen is *my* lucky number. If the other ladies had not rejected him, then where would I be?"

"In Yorkshire with your great aunt, I suppose," Mary sneered.

"Enough Mary. You are being quite rude." Anne came to Cassie's defense. "Mary is closest to William, so naturally, she is somewhat protective, but she does not mean to offend. I am sure of it. We are all worried about the two of you. Are *you* happy, Cassie?"

Yes.

No.

Maybe.

Cassie bit her bottom lip. Life would be much simpler if

everything would go according to her plans. She was supposed to be Mrs. Parker right now. Instead, she was Lady William Prescott. A rather urgent and dramatic change in her life plans. One that still rendered her speechless. Everything happened so fast. How could she reconcile herself to it all? On one hand, she could not imagine living without William in her life, but on the other hand, if she were honest with herself, she did miss Mr. Parker.

Happy? More like confused. *Very confused.*

The hairs on the back of her neck lifted as if her husband's warm breath blew across her skin. She sensed him before she saw him. How odd. She looked up and met his gaze. The room closed in and washed away the insane conversation with his mother and sisters. They were the only two people in the world. Cassie smiled.

He did not smile back. His face was impassive with no expression or emotion. *William was unhappy.*

Cassie watched as her husband walked over and greeted each of his sisters and his mother. He came to her last and placed a kiss on her cheek.

"Are you ladies done? I thought I would escort my wife back home."

"Yes. We are quite done." Lady Camberley gave warning glances to her daughters.

"Good. Then shall we?" William offered her his hand. She said her goodbyes and climbed into the carriage.

* * *

While on the drive to their townhome, William thought about the distressed expression on his wife's face when he entered the drawing room. She looked as if she were about to burst into tears. What had his family said to her? He clenched his fist. If they said something to upset her, to make her unhappy...

Cassie sat across from him in the the carriage and stared into her hands. Did she miss Parker? He hardened his jaw at the thought. His extreme dislike of the rogue was only natural, except, there was something else. He could not quite put his finger on it, but there was something that disturbed him about the man.

As soon as they arrived, Cassie went straight to her room, claiming a headache. He noticed the drawn lines on her face and her pale complexion. He wanted to comfort her and wrap his arms around her and hold her forever. Instead, for the sake of his own heart and sanity, he retreated to his study with a glass of brandy.

There was a knock at the door, but before he had a chance to respond it opened. Stephen waltzed into the room.

"Brother," William said. "Pour yourself a glass."

Stephen nodded and poured his brandy then took the seat opposite of William. They sat quietly for a few moments before Stephen spoke, "I just came from Whites."

"And?" He braced himself. He could tell by the set of Stephen's jaw and the anger in his eyes something was wrong.

"Talk of Miles Parker wagged on every tongue. Apparently, I just missed the lout when I arrived."

Every muscle in William's body tensed. He had the terrible feeling the rest of the story would prove not to his liking."Go on."

"The man came in raging drunk, hollering about challenging the bastard who stole his woman. He put a bet on the books that you would be dead by sunrise tomorrow."

William sat his glass on a side table and stood, ready to tear the idiot limb from limb. He growled, "He gave up his claim to Cassie when he returned her home disgraced. She is *my* wife."

"Of course. I thought you should be forewarned. According to Banks the man was well into his cups. He would not be fool enough to carry out such a threat, especially after announcing it to every gentleman in Whites." Stephen finished his brandy and rose. "If you need me, send a note around."

"Yes, thank you, Stephen."

His brother turned and clasped him on the shoulder. "Keep your wife nearby. I suspect the besotted fool might try something that would force you to defend her honor."

Stephen's words echoed in his head long after he left. He could keep Parker from his wife, but could he keep his wife from Parker? A dark scowl crossed his face. He was tempted to go upstairs and remind his pretty little wife who she belonged to. Then he remembered the sadness on Cassie's face when he found her with his family.

Was his wife unhappy? Should he have left her to her disgrace? She might not be happy if she were in Yorkshire, but at least he would not have to endure watching her. And despite everything, he found he could not resist going to her room at night. Last night proved that. He wanted her like no other woman, and when they were together, he thought she wanted him too.

Although his wife may think herself in love with Miles Parker, he was certain of the connection between *them*. The passion was clearly etched on her face when he entered her sweet body. Cassie wanted *him*, needed him.

Why did this have to be so damned complicated?

He started to quit the room and head upstairs when the door opened. "William?"

His lovely wife entered the room. She had changed into a simpler gown of dove gray muslin. Her hair fell down past her shoulders to her waist. *Air.* He needed air.

"Are you feeling better?" he choked out.

"Yes. *No.* I would like to talk to you." She squared her shoulders with the determination of a soldier preparing for battle. He wondered what they were about to battle over.

He motioned for her to sit. "Would you like a glass of sherry?"

She hesitated, "Yes, please."

He poured her a glass and handed it to her, then sat in the chair across from her. *Distance.* If he sat too close, he might be tempted to do something before she could say what was on her mind.

"Are you unhappy?" blurted Cassie.

Stunned, he did not say anything, but he sat up straighter, leaned forward, and creased his brow. Such an odd question.

"Are you unhappy?" he asked.

"I asked first," she said.

"What brought this on, Cassie?"

"Just answer the question." She held her hands together until her knuckles turned white.

He moved from his chair to the settee where she sat. Then he took her glass from her, sat it on the table, and turned to face her. The sadness in her eyes was more than he could stand. He lifted her chin and kissed her sweet mouth. "Does this feel unhappy?"

She pushed against his chest which startled him. Her eyes were closed tight for a moment, and then she opened them. "I am not talking about...this..." She waved her hand at him.

"What? This?" He kissed her again. This time he captured her head with his hands and took her mouth with more pressure, and willed her to open to him. She bit down on his lip.

"Ow! What the hell did you do that for?"

She stood abruptly and paced the room. "It is what you deserve. I am trying to talk to you. *Talk.*"

"Talk, then. Do go on."

She stopped and turned to face him. "Do not scowl at me. I simply want to have a conversation. Is that too much to ask? A conversation without your hands all over me."

He threw up his hands in exasperation. *Damnation!* What did the woman want from him?

"I am sorry. Please, sit back down. I promise to keep my hands to myself."

"I will stand." She crossed her arms over her chest. Her bosom rose and fell like the crest of waves.

How could he listen to her *talk* when he could not take his eyes off of her breasts?

"I do not want you in my bed at night if you are going to ignore me during the day."

He became as still as stone. She did not want him in her bed? A man is better off a bachelor for life than to live his life in a cold marriage bed. And what about children? Surely she wanted children. How long had he known her? A few weeks. Not long at all. He never asked her if she wanted children. He just assumed.

Cassie reacted to him, so warm and passionate and giving. She could not have faked it. Did she close her eyes and pretend he was Parker? *Damn her. Damn Parker.*

He grasped her by her shoulders. "You are my wife. You will do your duty."

"Of course. I just wanted..."

Did he see fear on her face? He had never done anything to cause her to fear him. Her eyes welled with tears. God, she was going to cry. If she cried, he would be lost.

"What? You want Parker? Is that what you want? Then you should have married the bastard!" He let go of her shoulders, perhaps a bit too hard. A sob tore from her chest, but he ignored it. If she wanted to cry over Miles Parker, then let her. He was not going to stand around and listen to it. He left the room, left the house, left her.

* * *

Cassie fought to control her emotions. Sobs threatened to take over. Her interview with her husband did not go well. Why did William think she wanted Mr. Parker? *I do not want you in my bed at night if you are going to ignore me during the day.*

"Poor choice of words," she said aloud. William latched onto the first half of what she said, and never heard what she meant. She wanted him to talk to her, to spend time with her, to be as they were on that first day of their marriage—one precious day before Mr. Parker showed up and spoiled everything.

What was she to do? She wanted to have a civilized conversation with her husband to discuss how they might get along. If they aired their feelings, then surely she could figure out how to make him happy. Instead, she only managed to anger him. She should have practiced her speech first. What a mess she made of things!

She picked up her glass of sherry and downed the contents. She tucked her legs beneath her, leaned back against the pillows on the settee and closed her eyes. She wished she could go away to sort out her feelings of all of the insane change of events over the past couple of weeks. It was too much, too fast. She needed time to think.

Scott tapped on the open door and entered the room. "You have a visitor, my lady."

Who could possibly want to see her? She knew no one in London except for William's family, and she just came from Camberley House a couple of hours ago. She did not want to see or talk to anyone. Perhaps Scott could tell this person she was in bed with a headache.

"Who is it?"

"Mr. Parker, my lady."

Could this day get any worse? She did not want to see Mr. Parker. She could not *handle* seeing Mr. Parker. Her emotions were too raw, too close to coming undone.

"Tell him..."

"Good day, Cassandra." Mr. Parker did not wait to be announced. He pushed his way around Scott. "If we could be left alone?"

Mr. Parker was dressed in black breeches and a black coat. Odd. She had never seen him in anything but bright colors. He looked so dashing and handsome it squeezed something inside her heart. She tried to push away the feeling, but realized she could not shut off her emotions. She pressed her lips together in a hard line. Her feelings for Mr. Parker were no longer relevant while her feelings for William were *confused.*

Scott looked at her for confirmation. Resigned to this interview, she nodded to the butler who left the door open when he quit the room.

She stood. "Mr. Parker."

"I have news," he said.

"Oh."

"My uncle cocked up his toes this morning." He screwed his lips as if he were trying to force away an inappropriate smile.

"Oh, I am sorry, Mr. Parker."

"No need to be sorry. He was a crabby old man who made everyone around him miserable. I am Viscount Winnington now." He came over to her and took her hands. "If only fate would have been more kind. Just a few more days and we would have married, Cassandra."

She pulled her hands from his and turned her back. "It is too late for us. I am married now, Mr. Parker, *Lord Winnington.* I am sorry to hear about your uncle, but it does not change things for us. I think it would be best if you go now."

He placed his hands on her shoulders. She tensed. His hands no longer held the warmth they once did. Coldness flowed through the fabric of her dress to her skin. "Divorce him Cassandra. We can be together now. My name will protect us."

She whipped around to face him. "Are you mad? We would be cast out of Society. Beyond ruined. Beyond disgraced. Our trip to Gretna Green would be nothing compared to a divorce."

"I do not care about Society. I care about you. I love you, Cassandra. We were meant to be together."

He attempted to pull her into an embrace, but she resisted. She wiped away an escaped tear. "No. We are not."

She stiffened her spine and raised her chin, then met his eyes directly. She refused to allow him to make things worse for either of them. What was done was done. She wanted him gone. "Please leave."

"I see. I am sorry for bothering you." He bowed, turned, and left.

Tears fell like a rushing river after a storm. She escaped to her room and locked herself in for the rest of the day.

Chapter Twelve

A WEEK LATER, Cassie entered the dining room dressed in a maroon riding outfit. She thought the color darkened her green eyes, which gave them a smoky, exotic look. She pinched her cheeks for color, but her face still looked pale, so she indulged in a touch of rouge to give her complexion a glow.

Since their argument, William kept away during the day and at night. Not once had he come to her bed. He left the house early and came home late. She filled her own days with correspondence, shopping with Anne, and attending a few of the smaller engagements with the Prescott girls.

So far, nothing had turned out as it should. Her husband avoided her, and with the exception of Anne, the Prescotts behaved chilly towards her. They were polite, yet standoffish. She wanted to ask Anne what she did wrong, but she did not dare bring up the subject. She did not want to drive a wedge between her only friend and the Prescott family. She found herself missing her quiet home, even her stoic father. Boring as it all seemed, it was much better than the clawing loneliness she experienced now.

Today the entire family would be attending the derby. She hoped William would not forget her, or leave her behind. She had seen so little of him in the past few days, and then only in passing. He barely spoke to her. She did not have any idea what to expect.

The dining room was empty.

Just like the hollowed out shell of her heart.

Disappointment pricked her skin like a thousand needles, and she pressed her lips to keep from crying. How could a marriage work if two people never saw each other? She fixed herself a plate, sat down, and stabbed her eggs with her fork. He was such a spoiled child. A few moments of his precious time was all she asked for. First, he does not listen to her, then he bellows at her and stomps out of the room, and now he spends his days ignoring her.

She wanted to throw something. Hit something. Scream. William should be ready and waiting to go to the derby. He told his family they would be there. But alas, he had not come to breakfast all week. Or luncheon. Or dinner. Her fork clashed against the china.

"Are you trying to break the dishes?"

Her head snapped upward as her dropped fork clattered against the plate. *William.* The air escaped from her lungs. He was handsome in his riding attire, so much so, she felt her heart squeeze, and her skin tingle in anticipation of his touch. If only he would touch her.

"I see you have decided to come out of hiding and grace me with your presence," she snarled.

His face hardened. Their stares battled before he finally broke and walked over to the buffet. "I am sorry if I have neglected you. I have had a great deal of business to attend to."

"I see." Except that she did not see. What business could keep him both day and night?

"I understand your Mr. Parker called on you the other day," he said.

Did she detect a sneer in his voice? Could he be jealous? No, she doubted that. "Why did you marry me?"

"Because I wanted you."

"In your bed."

"In my life."

For a man who wanted her in his life, he certainly did not act like it. Nor did he take advantage of it. He took a bite of toast and snapped open the morning paper. So that was how it was going to be. Ignored. *Again.*

She wanted to snatch the paper out of his hand. "Mr. Parker came to tell me that Lord Winnington passed away."

He glanced over the top of the pages. "Yes. I heard. I am sure he is thrilled to own the title and the fortune now."

"I am sure he is saddened by his uncle's passing."

He grunted. She picked up her fork and stabbed a kipper. Why was he so angry? She did not know what to do. She sat her fork down and observed her husband. He held the *London Times* in one hand while drinking his cup of tea with the other. He was absorbed in the news of the day. In a rush of madness, she jumped up and grabbed the paper out of his hand.

Startled, he looked up. "See here!"

"Why are you ignoring me?"

"I assumed you did not want to be bothered."

"Do I look like I do not want to be bothered? Do I look as if I am pleased to be ignored by my husband? I am lonely and miserable and I want to go home!" She clenched her fists and stamped her foot. She felt stupid. Like a spoiled child. Worse than a child.

A long moment passed before William stood up and wrapped his arms around her. "God, I am sorry, Cassie. I am so sorry." He kissed her ear. And her temples. And all of her face until he found her lips.

She wanted him to hold her. She realized at that moment how much she missed his warmth, missed his arms around her, and his mouth on hers.

A cleared throat broke the moment. *The footman.* Good grief! William nodded towards the footman in dismissal. He took her face in his hands. "Let us start over. Shall we?"

"I would like that."

"Shall we go to the races?"

She nodded. Maybe all would be well after all.

* * *

William believed himself the worse kind of cad. He allowed his insane jealousy to rule his head. He neglected his bride. They may not have the love he hoped for, but they were married, and bound to each other for life. He must make an effort to have a successful marriage. One day, his wife might come to love him, or at least care for him. Besides, he missed her. He missed her smile and her laugh, her intelligence, and her wit. And there was no denying he wanted her in his bed.

The last few days gave William a chance to think. Cassie told him she did not want him in her bed, but if he remembered correctly, the statement was conditional. She wanted him paying attention to her during the daytime. There was reasoning in her request; unfortunately, he could not bring himself to spend his days with her. He longed for days like the first where they talked, laughed, and enjoyed each other's company.

Spending time with her made him vulnerable to his feelings, and it exposed his feelings to her. He could not do that because he could not sacrifice his heart. She already had a firm hold on his emotions, and since her heart could never be his, he would be left with nothing but pain.

Avoiding Cassie forever was not an option either. He could not blame anyone but himself. He trapped himself when he offered for her. He did not take the time to consider her feelings for her former betrothed. He had rushed into the situation blind, and now he must pay the piper.

The ride to the derby took longer than expected. They were stuck behind a trail of carriages going in the same direction. He attempted polite conversation about the weather, Stephen's horse, the competing horses and the odds, and a few of the most outrageous *on dits*. They became reacquainted and seemed relaxed in each other's company by the time they arrived.

William escorted Cassie to the Prescott box where they found his family waiting. Stephen and James were tending to King, and his father was about assessing the competing horses. The ladies dressed in their finery made William wonder why Cassie dressed in her riding habit.

He turned and saw her strained, pale face. He leaned down and whispered in her ear, "Whatever is the matter, dear?"

"Apparently, I am not properly dressed for this event. Why did not you tell me?" she hissed in embarrassment.

"I suppose I do not give much attention to lady's fashions. I did not realize." Another mark against him. He probably should have noticed her attire, but truly, he did not think of it. Who could possibly keep up with which garment a lady wore to which event?

"William. Cassie." Anne hugged them both and then whisked his wife away to the corner, where they fell deep into conversation. His curiosity almost got the better of him, but Mary took hold of his arm and led him in the opposite direction.

"Walk with me William. I would like to take a look at the horses." Mary took his arm and as usual, he allowed her to lead the way. He spied his spunky sister's determined expression and smiled because she most certainly had something on her mind.

They walked over to the stables where the grooms kept a suspicious eye on anyone coming near their charges. Mary ignored their stares as she stopped and admired each horse, then stroked their necks and noses and whispered sweet nothings. She had a way with horses that at times appeared magical.

"What is on your mind Mary?"

"What makes you think anything is on my mind, beyond which horse will win today?" Mary turned and flashed a brilliant, yet impish smile at him. "Place your bets on Prince."

"Of course, now out with it." He took her by the elbow and pulled her away from the horses and waited for her response.

Mary placed her hands on her hips. "Men. You all believe you can command us mere ladies who should bow down and serve you. I do not know why you are determined to believe something is on my mind." She started toward the barn's exit.

"Fine then, do not talk. It does not matter to me. I am sure I do not want to hear whatever you have to say." He walked past her as she grabbed his arm.

"Cassie's former betrothed visited your home this past week." She let it out on an exasperated sigh.

"And how would you know this little piece of information?"

"I have my connections, but that is not the issue," Mary huffed.

"What is the issue then?" he asked.

"Your wife's former betrothed called on her while you were out. Does that not concern you?" Her hands were on her hips. Anger flashed in her eyes and color rose on her cheeks.

"If I did not trust my wife, I suppose it would be an issue. As it happens, Miles Parker visited my wife to inform her that his uncle cocked up his toes. He is now Lord Winnington." Just the fact that he knew of the visit and the reason should put this silly business to rest, except for the fact that he was dealing with Mary.

"Whatever possessed the rogue to visit another man's wife to tell her of his good fortune? Are you sure that is the only reason for his visit?"

William clenched his teeth and hardened his jaw to keep from firing back a nasty retort. No one doubted that Parker, or, Lord Winnington was a besotted idiot. Yet, the last thing he needed to do was to ruin the bit of progress he made with Cassie by allowing his jealousy to rear its' ugly head.

"Mary, I will not have you spreading malicious gossip, even if it is only for my ears. Cassie is *my* wife. Winnington may be a thorn in her memory, but he is not her lover, nor will he become her lover, if that is what you are saying."

"No, no. I am not saying anything of the kind. I just do not care for the man sniffing around your wife. I only meant to warn you, dear brother."

"Then I am warned. Let us return to the box."

And then he saw Cassie with Winnington.

His insides turned cold as Mary clutched his arm to keep him from tearing the purple peacock in half.

Cassie threw back her head and laughed. Usually, he loved her smile and her laughter, but now he wanted nothing more than to turn away. The leech at her side ate away at his flesh, and boiled his blood, until he tensed his muscles into solid rocks. He clenched his fists, his jaw, and his heart before moving towards his enemy.

He would maintain his control, behave as a gentleman, keep his wits about him, and not bring embarrassment on his family. At least that is what he told himself as he strode toward the sniffing dog.

"Winnington," he ground out between his teeth.

"Lord William." The man's face turned to stone, and his eyes darkened like those of a lecher. The bumbling blackguard had the audacity to paste a faked smile on his face.

"I did not realize you enjoyed the races," William returned in his own pasty smile.

"My uncle had a disdain for the races. I did not want to do anything to give the old codger a reason to cut me off." He dared step closer to Cassie, who stiffly watched the two men exchange icy retorts.

"Are you saying that sending a young woman to her disgrace is less disdainful and risky than attending a horse race?"

Cassie stifled a gasp and paled. Two marks against him this day. He should mind his tongue, but something about Winnington made him want to challenge the man to his death. Swords or pistols came to mind.

"*I* did not break my engagement. In fact, I traveled immediately to London to have it out with my uncle, to force his hand in giving me his blessing, but by the time I returned, it was too late. You stole my betrothed right out from under me."

Cassie's milky white skin looked as pale and translucent as a haunted angel. Her green eyes turned to dark muddy pools, and reflected hurt and shame. His worst nightmare cut through the fog and pulled him into something so stark, so real, he could not face the daylight.

He watched and waited with bated breath, as he half expected his wife to throw her arms around another man. Instead, she turned on her heel and marched away. A breath he did not know he held blew out, and shuddered throughout his body. He turned towards Winnington and grasped the man by the cravat and squeezed the bloody air out of his lungs.

"Stay away from my wife, Winnington."

Winnington sputtered and gasped for breath before he turned the same color as his purple coat. Since it would be beyond the pale to commit murder on a racetrack with half the *ton* as witnesses, he let the bastard drop to the ground. Winnington held his throat, and sneered with the venom of a viper, but William turned away from the nodcock and followed after his wife.

* * *

Cassie sat in their carriage. Her hands trembled and tears streamed down her cheeks. She could not go back and face William's family now. She needed a place to be alone and think about everything. Her thoughts tumbled through thunderous clouds. The look on William's face frightened her. For a moment, she thought her husband and former betrothed might kill one another right in front of her eyes. Mr. Parker, no, *Lord Winnington now*, purposely egged William on. Why? And what did he mean when he said he went to London to confront his uncle? Had he truly planned to return to marry her?

Her heart ached from the tugs in so many different directions. When she spoke to Lord Winnington he made her laugh. She almost forgot how much she enjoyed his company. And, it had been awhile since she laughed with such freedom.

The last time she laughed was with William on the day after her wedding. *Walking, talking, swinging.* The memory wrapped around her shoulders like a warm hug. She wanted everyday to be like that day, and every night to be like the one engraved on her body and soul.

But what about Lord Winnington? She tried to define the difference between her feelings for the two men. At first the lines blurred, but now she understood her first love was not her true love. Yet, was she in love William?

She loved her nights William, but as of late, he spent precious little time at home. Hurt swelled in her heart when William left her alone. He reminded her of a leopard who constantly changed his spots. If only he would act consistently in her presence.

As they traveled to the derby today, she thought perhaps they had a chance at happiness. He attempted to converse with her, and even though she did not sense the same level of comfort in their conversation as they once experienced, she believed they were on the right path.

The door to the carriage opened, and a body, a presence, larger than life itself, entered and sat down next to her. He said nothing, but put his arms around her and pulled her into his warm embrace. A tear slipped down her cheek as she rested her head against his chest. Warm. So deliciously warm.

They sat like that for several minutes before she felt his lips touch her head. She wanted to stay like this forever. Her heart shifted a little, as if she went from girlhood to womanhood in a single moment. Her old dreams of wedded bliss with Mr. Parker gathered on the wind and flittered away, only to be replaced by something more fulfilling.

A serene sense of forever held her to him. The world drifted away, and left them alone, and, at that moment, she knew she loved him.

In a moment of daring, she lifted her face to him, and touched her finger to his strong mouth. She offered him a silent invitation to kiss her, to love her, to give her his heart.

William answered her invitation by giving his mouth to her. She opened her lips and accepted his tongue into the depths of her mouth. He tasted like warm honey, and a sweet sensation overtook her, flushed her skin, and gathered in her secret place that ached for him.

She melted into his kiss, long and lingering. His tongue thrust in and out of her mouth, and she met him and matched him kiss for kiss, thrust for thrust. His kisses were the only ones she wanted. Mr. Parker's tingling kisses left her like an insignificant childhood memory in the foggy distance of her past. She craved her *husband's* kisses, *his* hands on her, *his* body merged with hers. She wanted his company, his conversation, his thoughts and opinions, and in this brief second in time, she was determined to have all of him.

Cassie acknowledged she would fight for her husband. She did not know or understand what brought him to her, fate perhaps, but she would not let him abandon her to lonely days and unfulfilled nights. Her fingers tangled in his thick, soft hair, and she held him to her, set his mouth to hers, and gave him all the love in her heart.

In the back of her mind she heard a tap on the carriage door, and a groan in William's throat. She ignored it, but it came again, and this time louder.

"Cassie. Cassie! Are you in there? Are you alright?" Anne's voice echoed through her foggy brain.

"Go away," muttered William.

She pulled away. "I am fine."

The door opened and Anne stammered, "Oh, oh, I am sorry. I thought you were alone. I will just leave now."

"No. It is alright. We were just talking," she said as William chuckled. "Let us go and enjoy the races, William."

"Of course, my dear." William stepped down, then helped Cassie out. He squeezed her hand, and gave her a warm, knowing smile.

When they returned to the Prescott family box, she noted the odd stares from William's family. Mary eyed her with disdain. Elizabeth and Jane's eyes twinkled with curiosity. And William's mother appeared deeply concerned. At least the men were attending to Stephen's horse. William escaped almost as soon as they entered the box. *Traitor.*

She pasted a smile on her face and tried to appear cheerful. She wondered if her face appeared tear stricken, *or well kissed.* Could the women guess her improper behavior in the carriage? At least the gentleman in question was her husband. They cannot fault her for a few moments of privacy with her own husband. Could they?

Oh drat! They probably thought she was the worst kind of wife, a country bumpkin, totally unsophisticated to the ways of London life. She could not change her background, or turn herself into a lady of the *ton.* She *was* a vicar's daughter, a simple country miss, an innocent in their world of privilege. Whatever the consequences, she accepted this life when she married William, and she would make the best of it.

Cassie would try to win over William's sisters one at a time. Mary stood at the window eyeing the track with what could only be envy. Mary's mouth watered as if she stared at a plate of sweets. Not one for sitting in the background, waiting for life to happen to her, she decided to start with the one sister who seemed to dislike her the most.

"When does the race begin?" she asked.

"Soon."

"Anne tells me you are an expert horse woman. She says that you have a special way with horses."

Mary shrugged her shoulders, but never moved her eyes away from the activity outside.

Anything in life worth gaining came with struggle, at least that is what her father always said. She turned toward the window and watched as grooms walked the horses along the track, brushed them down, and whispered words of encouragement in their ears. She caught sight of her husband with his brothers and father. They leaned against the fence and talked, laughed, and smoked smelly cigars.

"Do you think Prince will win the race?"

Mary turned towards her with a look of dismay on her face. "Of course." She turned back towards the window.

Cassie wondered if the conversation was an effort in futility. "Do you not wish you could ride on the back of Prince during the race? It must be an exhilarating experience."

"Society and their dratted rules. The only thing women are allowed to do is bat our eyes at eligible gentlemen and discuss the weather. We are nothing more than ornaments to hang on a man's arm. We must ride side saddle in confining skirts, while we simper, whimper, and faint at the hint of scandal. It makes my stomach turn." Mary harrumphed. She was like a little bird trapped in a cage and Cassie pitied her.

"I always thought Society's rules were meant to protect ladies from the sins of the world," said Cassie.

"Protect us? No. They are meant to keep us ignorant of men's debauchery so that they may continue acting the fools they are."

Cassie pressed her lips together to hold back laughter. She could not think of anytime in her life she heard anyone speak with such vehemence and passion. Her parents brought her up to believe it was her duty to act like a lady, to marry and produce children, and to turn a blind eye to a gentleman's indiscretions. Gently bred young ladies should stay innocent of the world's sins. Should they not?

Hearing Mary made her question what she knew about the world.

Of course, marriage taught her much already. The few nights she spent with her husband went far beyond her imagination. She felt ridiculously wicked for wanting to do it again.

She did not have time to question Mary further or even consider their odd conversation. The men came indoors and William whisked her away to go and make their bets. She placed an extravagantly foolish bet of ten pounds on Prince. Although the entire Prescott family felt certain Prince would win by a landside, it occurred to her they might be a bit prejudice. William's bet of one hundred pounds astounded her. Their servants made an eighth of that amount in a year, and yet they had bet one hundred and ten pounds on a horserace. The guilt squeezed her consciousness.

As they headed back to their box to watch the race, a palpable energy charged the air that left her breathless and excited. She crossed her fingers and hoped for success. Despite everyone's excitement, and even her own, she had to squash a lump that continuously threatened to rise in her throat. William held her hand as the race began. She held on for dear life and promised herself she would donate her winnings to charity if Prince won. Perhaps she could convince her husband to do the same.

The charge in the air made her feel insanely giddy. She joined the chorus of voices, "Go Prince, yes, go, yes!" as Prince crossed the finish line a victor. William picked her up and swung her around, and then shocked her by kissing her fully on the mouth in front of his entire family. Lost in his kiss, she heard the thunderous cheering and celebration over their win as if it were coming to her through a tunnel. She forgot herself and wrapped her own arms around William and thrust her hands into his hair, dearly wanting to feel close to him, to have him hold her, make love to her, but somewhere in the midst, reality waved its' flag in front of their eyes, as they joined the rest of humanity.

"How much did I win?" she asked while trying desperately to catch her breath.

"One hundred pounds my dear. What will you spend it on?" William's smile made her knees weak. The moment reminded her of their moment in the secret garden where the world seemed perfect.

"Are you quite serious? One hundred pounds? Oh my!"

"You can go on a shopping spree on Bond Street tomorrow," laughed William.

"Oh no, I would not dare," Cassie's voice and her convictions rang clear, "I shall donate my winnings to Anne's home for orphans."

The collective air went out of the room at her statement. Everyone turned and stared at her as if she had two heads. Then Anne rushed over and took her hands. "Oh, my dear, dear Cassie, that is a most generous offer. I shall do the same with my winnings!"

"Count in my winnings as well," said William. Cassie wanted to fling her arms around her wonderful husband. Her heart burst with pride, and another thing—*love*.

"I will give my winnings as well," piped in Jane. "I did not need a new bonnet anyway."

"It is not much, but I will contribute mine too," said Elizabeth.

"Oh, count mine in too," Mary muttered.

"This is so wonderful. We have raised such generous children, Lord Camberley." Lady Camberley smiled up at her husband.

"And they follow by example. We will give our winnings to your home as well Anne. It is a worthy cause," said Lord Camberley.

Anne beamed and Cassie nearly cried from happiness. The collective winnings would make a substantial start for preparing Mulberry House. Stephen and James, beaming from their victory, walked in at that moment.

"Ten thousand pounds! Prince is a sure fire winner," cried Stephen.

"We are all ecstatic with Prince's win, and each one of us has agreed to contribute our winnings to Anne's home for orphans," said Lady Camberley.

Stephen looked around the room. No one dared speak, as they all focused their eyes on the two brothers. The room snapped with quiet energy as everyone waited for Stephen to answer.

"Oh hell, I will contribute mine as well," said Stephen. A cheer erupted from the room, and except for a disapproving glance from Lady Camberley at her son's inappropriate language in front of ladies, everyone crowded around Stephen to express their thanks.

"I guess I am not getting out of here without adding my winnings to the pot," said James.

"Do not even consider an escape, James Prescott," said Anne as she hugged each of her brothers.

Cassie stood back and watched the large and loving family's

interactions. It warmed her to her very toes. They may not have shown a high regard for her as of late, but she felt as if she started something of value today.

William rested his hand on her waist and looked at her with his dark eyes. She believed she saw something like love shine in his eyes. She would give all she had to see this look on his face every day, and to see his eyes express such emotion. Her heart swelled.

"You did a good thing today, my dear. Let's go home so I can show you my appreciation." The mischievous twinkle in William's eyes caused her to warm all over. She could not wait to see what he had in mind.

Chapter Thirteen

CASSIE FINGERED THE ROSE SILK GOWN as she gazed in the mirror. Katie swept her hair into a coiffure of golden ringlets, leaving one long curl to sweep down and lie across her bosom. Her dress was positively sinful, and for once, she thought she looked beautiful. The tiny diamonds weaved through her curls made her hair shine even more. Despite her self-lecture to not act upon her vanity, she smiled at the angel in the glass reflecting back her smile.

She wanted to please William. She sighed and turned away from the mirror. Since the horse race, he made a point to spend time with her each day. He conversed with her at breakfast and luncheon, escorted her to teas and on picnics, took her on rides through Hyde Park, and to visit various museums throughout London. *And the nights...* Oh, the glorious nights when he entered her room and showed her all the ways two people could love. Sweet shivers ran down her body as she remembered his touch, and looked forward to being alone with him again.

A knock interrupted her dreamy thoughts. "Come."

William entered, but when he gazed upon his wife, he froze. She relished the look upon his face. It was the same look he had when ravished her naked body each night; a look of lust, and passion, and desire. His eyes roamed her body displayed by the fashionably low cut of her gown, then his gaze rested on the tops of her generous breasts boosted by her tight whalebone corset.

"Dear God in heaven," he breathed.

"Do you like it?" she turned for his inspection.

"Do I like it?" he laughed. "I have never seen anyone more lovely, more enticing. In fact, I am quite tempted to forgo the ball and lock myself in here with you for eternity." William pulled a wood carved box out of his pocket and handed it to her. "I have something for you."

"What is it?"

"A gift for my bride."

She opened the box and sucked in a breath, "Oh my." A diamond necklace, bracelet, and earrings glittered inside.

"Here, let me help you put them on."

"I do not know what to say. I never dreamed of owning anything so beautiful or of such value."

"Say nothing, just let me look at you."

William helped her with the bracelet and necklace, and she completed the ensemble by placing the earbobs on her lobes. He came behind her and put his arms around her waist, and rested his hands on her stomach. Their gazes met in the mirror, and she realized how handsome they looked together. She placed her hands on top of his strong lean ones, and settled against his chest. He kissed her ear and her cheek before turning her around.

"You will sweep Society away tonight."

His mouth tenderly took hers in a sweet kiss of adoring reverence. Her bones melted so that she was forced to lay her hands on his chest in order to keep her knees from buckling to the floor.

"Shall we, my lady?"

The crush at a ball thrown in her honor amazed her. Carriages lined the Prescott's drive as ladies in silk gowns and glittering jewels were escorted into the house by finely dressed gentlemen of the *ton*. Liveried footmen dressed in navy and silver, rushed about attending to every need. Camberley House stood tall, awash in the glow of hundreds of candles and the sounds of Mozart.

Cassie stood in the receiving line with the Prescott family, and was introduced to each guest by Lady Camberley. She would never learn all of the names and titles: viscounts, earls, marquis', and dukes, but the most surprising guest was Prinny.

The moment the Prince Regent entered the ballroom, the *ton* stopped and lowered into a bow. The future king made his way down the receiving line and stopped in front of her. She never before imagined she would have the opportunity to mix with such a crowd, much less meet a royal at a ball in her honor. She trembled as she tried to remember the proper protocol.

The prince took her hand and kissed her knuckles—lingering a brief second longer than necessary. She felt William stiffen at her side as the prince gazed at her, raking all of her in, and even letting his eyes rest on her breasts. His blatant perusal of her being shocked her.

"A vision of loveliness. Wherever did you find her?" asked Prinny.

"Tucked away in the English countryside, Your Highness," answered William.

"Perhaps I should plan a trip to the country. I hear breathing good English country air is good for the constitution, and no doubt finding an English rose is even better." The crowd laughed, but she failed to understand the joke. She decided the Prince was rather odd, and wondered about the future of her country in the hands of this man. Of course, she would never say such a thing aloud.

"If you get tired of your new husband, you only have to send a message around and I will be happy to keep your company." Prinny leered at her, as William's muscles appeared to jump from his chest.

William took her hand and kissed it. "You do not need to worry that I will keep my wife entertained, Your Highness."

Prinny threw back his head and laughed. "Of course not. What man would not abandon all else to keep the most beautiful woman in England happy. My felicitations on your marriage." He nodded then moved on. A collective sigh of relief sputtered down the line of Prescotts as the *ton* turned to visit with one another, and the orchestra struck a new chord.

William whispered in her ear, "Do not worry, dear. Prinny is a consummate flirt. His attention on you will elevate your success in Society, especially since he called you the most beautiful woman in England, by which I happen to agree."

"I feel as if I have been raked from head to toe in front of the entire *ton*."

William's hand squeezed hers as the next lord and lady strolled down the receiving line. The end finally came, and not a moment too soon. The first strands of the waltz played, and William whisked her onto the dance floor to open the first set.

Her experience was limited to country dances. Judgmental eyes waited for her to tumble like a country bumpkin, but fortunately, she was blessed with coordination and grace. As her husband swept her into his arms, the strands of music reached her toes, and together they moved about the ballroom as if dancing on clouds.

"You did great, my dear. I expect you will be a smashing success among Society."

The only success she cared about was the success of her

marriage. By the way her husband looked at her, she sensed they were well on their way. She relaxed and enjoyed the dance as the rest of Society fell away, and they glided across the room.

"I was surprised the Prince Regent," said Cassie.

"The Prescotts are powerful and wealthy. Wealthy enough to lend Prinny money without pinching our pockets."

"Why would the Prince Regent need to borrow money?"

"He is a terrible wastrel and gambler. He spends more than his allowance and is forever mounting up his debts."

They spun to the last strands of music before the waltz ended. She was dizzy from the heat and excitement. "I suppose it is naive of me to feel shocked, but I am. I cannot begin to understand it all. There are starving children on the streets of London who could live a year off of the price of one gown, and yet I indulged in several new gowns per day."

William lifted her chin, and forced her to look into his eyes. "Your gown tonight gave work to more than one seamstress. Your contributions to the home for orphans will put food into the bellies of homeless children, give them a warm bed at night, and a chance at survival. Do not forget that."

She pressed her lips together in dismay. Even though his words made sense to her ears, she was still bothered by the extravagance of the *ton*.

"Lord William, do you plan to keep your lovely wife all to yourself, or will you at least allow a mere prince a turn about the dance floor?" Prinny stood with his hand out to her, and of course, she accepted. After all, what could either of them do?

"One dance is not too much to ask." William ground out as he handed her over to the Prince Regent.

"My lady."

She placed her hand on Prinny's arm as he led her out onto the dance floor. She was honored and privileged to dance with the prince, but truthfully, the only prince she wanted to dance with was her husband. Prinny kept a respectable distance, but she wished he would keep his eyes somewhere besides her bosom. They moved about the dance floor with the eyes of Society on them. Their scrutiny made her uncomfortable.

They turned and she caught sight of William partnered with a lovely young lady with auburn hair. Cassie watched the two swirl about the room. She expected her husband to partner with other ladies tonight, just as she would partner with other gentlemen, such as the Prince Regent, so why was there a knot in her stomach?

"Her name is Lady Guinevere, but have no fear, she turned down Lord William's proposal just last Season. Her parents named her after King Arthur's Lady Guinevere, but the *ton* calls her the Ice Princess."

"Why do they call her the Ice Princess?"

"Because her heart is as cold as ice, my dear. Do not worry your pretty little head over the frozen wanton. It is that one there you need to keep an eye on." Prinny nodded towards a lady with raven hair pulled into a coiffure of ringlet curls. She wore an emerald green silk dress adorned with a low cut bodice, and it clung to her body as if she wet it down. Cassie had heard of this fashion, but never imagined a lady would do such a thing in polite society.

"Who is she?" asked Cassie.

"Lady Quartermane. Your husband's mistress."

Cassie struggled for breath. *A mistress? William had a mistress?* Her knees buckled beneath her, but the prince held her tightly and kept her moving across the dance floor. "If you ever find yourself feeling lonely, I will be more than happy to keep you entertained."

How was she to answer such a question? Cassie was certain he saw her discomfiture. "I thank you for your kind offer, but I do believe loneliness is a state of mind."

Prinny laughed. *Loud.* She sensed the sneers of the Society matrons as they turned towards them. Her face burned like a hot flame.

Just when she thought she might perish of utter mortification the music came to an end. The Prince Regent escorted her back into the arms of her husband and went in search of another lady to victimize.

Cassie whispered to William, "Did you not see that your wife was a damsel in distress? Could you not charge in and rescue me?"

He chuckled. "He is harmless, my dear. He would never force himself upon you, but I imagine he made uncomfortable overtures?"

"Oh yes. Prince or not, he is a rake and a rouge, and, and...oh...I am so glad the dance is done!" She grabbed William's arm and held on for dear life, because the night was far from over.

She danced with powerful lords, polished dandies, and elderly gentlemen with fat bodies and smelly breath. Her feet were stepped upon, and her body ran out of steam after dozens of dances with numerous partners.

Sometime in the evening she lost track of time, lost track of her dance card, and lost track of her husband. After an excruciating dance with the Duke of Avalon's third son, she was ready to collapse. As they started to leave the dance floor, a familiar face stepped up and bowed.

Mr. Parker.

No, she must remember now.

Lord Winnington.

His orange coat and purple breeches nearly threw her into a fit of hysterics as she covered her mouth to suppress bubbling giggles. Regardless of his ridiculous, dandified outfit, he looked every inch the noble, and like a golden Adonis. His smile knocked her giggles away and sent shivers down her spine. This time, she did not experience the tingles she associated with his presence. Despite his brilliant white smile, and the sparkle of his blue eyes, she saw something different.

"Lord Winnington."

"Lady William, may I have the honor of the next dance?"

Cassie stumbled. The room and hundreds of guests became smaller. She struggled to get her next breath, then searched the ballroom for William. Where was her husband?

She needed to answer him. Yes. *No.* Maybe. Should she turn him down and risk the appearance of giving him the cut? Should she say yes and risk the squeeze of pain looming within her chest? What would William want her to do? Would he care? Did it matter if she danced with her former betrothed? She could not think. The people, the noise, and the heat whirled around her until she became dizzy.

"Are you quite alright? Here, I think you need some air, Cassandra. Let me escort you onto the veranda." He grasped her hand and placed it on his arm. Her feet moved, but did not recall going across the ballroom and out into the gardens.

"You are not used to such crowds. So many people, so much pressure. Lord William should not have thrust you into Society without a trial run. He should have eased you into all of this."

She heard his familiar, soothing voice echo through the clouds in her mind. Then her husband's name broke through. William. *Where was William?*

"Thank you, Lord Winnington, but I do believe I should return and find my husband now." She started to walk back towards the French doors that lead to the ballroom. They were so far away. How did she get this far? She wanted to go home and lie down.

Lord Winnington grabbed her arm and spun her towards him. He crushed her against his chest. He gripped her tightly as his blue eyes darkened, changed into something far more sinister than she ever imagined.

"Let me go! You are hurting me."

He relaxed his grip, but did not let her go. "Cassie, darling. I have missed you. My heart and soul aches for you, burns for you. Why did you marry another man? Did you not trust in our love? Could you not wait me to find a way out of my predicament? If you had only waited you would be Lady Winnington now."

Tears burned Cassie's eyes at the anguish in his voice. She did not mean to hurt him. At the time, she thought she loved him. Her feelings were those of youthful first love, and a fleeting romance. What they had was not real, or deep, or meant to be forever. How could she tell him her heart changed over the past weeks?

"I am sorry, truly I am, but there is no going back. Please, let me go. I need to return to my husband's side."

"No!" His vehemence startled her. He never raised his voice before. A dark cloud passed over his face. "You are mine. You were promised to me first, and I will be damned if I let another man take you."

His mouth crushed hers, possessive and demanding. She tried to pull away, but he was too strong for her. He pulled her tighter, and held her around the waist with one arm, as he fondled her breast with his other hand. She squealed at the shocking touch. He took full advantage and thrust his tongue into her mouth. She stamped on his foot, but he pinched her breast in cruel response. Why was he doing this to her?

There was a time when she wanted his kisses, but now, she only wanted to get away from him. She tried to push him away in order to run to the safety of her husband's arms. He made her feel dirty and violated. Fear rose in her bosom and the shock of his unwanted attack shook her from the inside out. She managed to slip one arm out of his grasp and punch him on his chest as she fought for air.

He swiftly turned her, backed her up against a tree, and brutally pushed her into the hard, scraping bark. She heard the rip of her bodice and felt his hand on her exposed breast. He squeezed and pinched her nipple as tears came to her eyes. She broke the kiss and screamed when she felt his body yanked from hers.

Cassie sank to the ground, wrapped her arms around her stomach and sobbed. She heard the sounds of fist connecting with face, breaking bones, and bodies crashing to the ground. She looked up in time to see Lord Winnington on the ground clutching his broken nose. William stood over him, breathing hard, with an intensely dark, angry scowl. She cringed from the scene. His eyes met hers, but the desire to fling herself into his arms and sob was met with a sneer of disgust.

"Right yourself now. We will leave out a back gate."

At first, she did not move, still too shocked to register his words until William barked at her. She scrambled to her feet as if threatened by a rabid dog. She raced behind him, followed him to the gate, and waited as he whistled for a boy to tell his coachman to pull around the back. They waited in silence for the coach. A footman jumped down and opened the door. Her husband stood back as the footman handed her up. She collapsed on the seat and fell against the wall of the carriage.

Exhaustion from the nightmare claimed her. She never would have dreamed that Lord Winnington would treat her so abominably. William remained silent and brooded all the way to the townhouse. She longed for him to hold her, to comfort her, but he did not offer, and she did not ask.

When they arrived home, he stepped from the carriage and offered his hand, but his touch was cold, and his eyes were even colder. She understood his anger, but why was it directed at her? She was the victim.

"Go to your room," he ordered. She did not bother to argue with him, or ask questions. Exhausted, she dragged herself up the stairs, as tears streamed down her face.

* * *

William stormed into his study and picked up the first breakable object, and slammed it on the stone surrounding the fireplace. The betrayal cut across his heart, and sliced his pride into ribbons. Maybe he *was* cursed, and was meant to live without the love of one woman. He muttered expletives beneath his breath and paced the room like a caged tiger.

The full force of his idiotic life hit like a blow to his head when he saw his wife in the arms of Winnington. She could not resist her former betrothed. He fumed and admitted he should have left her to rot in Yorkshire.

Damn! They were making progress. *She* was the one who demanded *his* attention. He gave it to her, and look what it cost him. He was the fool of besotted fools. What was wrong with him? The mirror did not show any significant flaws in his physical appearance, in fact, a reasonable person would call him handsome.

He bathed daily, so she could not complain about body odor. He sniffed his underarms and caught a whiff of something unpleasant. Well, hell, it was damned hot in that stuffy ballroom. He poured himself a generous glass of brandy and swallowed the dark liquid. It burned down his throat and warmed him throughout. After he downed the first glass, he poured another.

The bottle of brandy provided the only comfort he would receive this night. He sat down with his glass and bottle, laid his head against the leather chair, and closed his eyes against the waves of pain that pierced his soul.

Her face came to him, like a golden angel coming out of the clouds. So beautiful, so sweet and kind. He mistakenly believed time would bring her to him, teach her to love him, but he now knew her first love was too strong, too real, and the knowledge of it left him without hope.

Chapter Fourteen

CASSIE WRUNG HER HANDS and wondered if she would ever see her husband again. The infuriating man escaped the house by the crack of dawn, and returned late in the night. Where did he go all this time? Her heart broke in two when he sent her to her room and left without so much as a word. Torn between tears of anguish and tears of anger at his betrayal, she decided to continue on with or without him.

She pressed her hand against her belly for the hundredth time since she figured out William's child grew within her. She desperately wanted to tell William her happy news, but drat the man; he did not make himself available for even a moment. Rage shot through her as she thought about how he blamed her for Lord Winnington's assualt. She did not do anything wrong! She wanted to smash something, more than something; she wanted to smash lots of things.

She took several deep breaths to calm herself, after all, what good would it do to break everything in the house? She went down to breakfast and hoped her husband sat at the table enjoying his coddled eggs and toast.

His chair sat empty.

She inquired of the servants who told her William left the house before they rose from their beds.

Over the next several days, Cassie tried to rise early to catch her husband, but the smells of breakfast took her the moment she entered the room. She barely made it back upstairs to the chamber pot before retching her dinner from the night before. The doctor she visited confirmed her pregnancy, then informed her the sickness was normal and it would eventually pass. If only William would come home so she could share her news with him. The news she intended to share the night of the ball.

* * *

William did not want to return to the house and chance seeing his wife. He needed time away to remove Cassie from the place she claimed in his heart, yet he feared the time away made little difference. Realizing his efforts were futile, and his heart hers, he began to accept his life sentence in a loveless marriage. The one thing he would not tolerate was her unfaithfulness. She made a vow before their families and God, and she would keep it if he had to lock her up at Rosehill Manor.

As usual, his thoughts turned sour when she came to his mind, which happened to be all of the time. He wasted his days away from her. There was business to attend to, and papers to sign, and all of this was located in his study. Although the idea appealed to him, he could no longer continue to hide. He needed to stay away from her— *far away*. Otherwise, he might not survive the torment that tore him to pieces.

William entered the house and caught a glance of his wife in a near run up the stairs. What was the hurry? Did her lover come in the night and just now leave? Is he still there? Pure rage filled his soul and before he knew what he was doing, he took the stairs two at a time. He made it to the door connecting their rooms just in time to hear her retch. Good God, she was sick. His stomach turned at the unpleasant sound and smell. He cracked the door and watched as she washed her face and rinsed her mouth, oblivious to his intrusion. She lay down on her bed, like a pale angel framed by golden curls, and his heart twisted.

She was sick after all, and it was his responsibility to care for his wife. He watched as she clutched her stomach and moaned. Quietly, he closed the door and went to the bell pull. Cassie's lady's maid arrived, then he ordered a footman to fetch Dr. Breckman immediately. He paced his room and listened while she retched again. He almost went to her, but in the end, decided against it.

He went downstairs and waited in the foyer for the doctor's arrival. As soon as the man entered the house, William grabbed him by the elbow. "Dr. Breckman, my wife is sick. She is vomiting and holding her stomach. You must see to her immediately."

Dr. Breckman laughed. *Laughed.*

"What is so funny? I just told you my wife is sick!" He bellowed loud enough to wake the dead.

"Expectant fathers are always more jittery than expectant mothers." His eyes twinkled and a smile lit his face.

William pulled him towards the stairs, but the man stood his ground. "What the bloody hell are you talking about? You need to see my wife *now*." William's patience neared the breaking point. Why was the man blabbering?

"Your wife's symptoms are normal, Lord William. Calm yourself. It is too early for a glass of brandy, but perhaps a small amount is just what you need. "Shall we go to your study for a chat?"

The doctor must have lost his mind. Why would he need brandy? How would he know his wife's symptoms were normal? *Expectant fathers and mothers...*

The blood drained from William's face. He shook his head and ran his hands through his hair. He was an idiot. "Have you attended my wife recently?"

"Just last week. I am assuming she has not mentioned her condition to you yet. Perhaps she was waiting to surprise you."

"I am sure she was," he ground out. "I am sorry I wasted your time, doctor. I thought my wife was ill."

"Perhaps it is time to talk to your wife, Lord William."

"Yes, I suppose it is. Send me your bill to compensate for your time. If you will excuse me." He nodded to the doctor and ran up the stairs.

A child. A son. Or maybe a daughter with golden hair and green eyes. The thought warmed the chill within his heart. Why had she not told him?

William took the stairs two at a time. He needed to see Cassie. He admitted he missed his wife. His heart hammered in his chest. The pain of rejection filtered through his brain. He stopped on the top stair and recalled each ridiculous moment when a woman had turned him away. On each occasion, he was disappointed, yet his heart never dealt with the crushing pain he experienced as of late.

Seeing his wife in another man's arms was the ultimate rejection. Bitterness crawled across his skin like livestock from the filth of the London slums. Winnington's mocking smirk slithered across his memory as he recalled how the rogue bested him in a card game at White's. He thought of his wife laughing and talking with her former love at the horse race, and he remembered the lowlife's hands on her in the gardens. He left his wife to her own devices during the day and at night. He left her to the manipulation of her former betrothed. Had he driven her to the Winnington's bed?

William sat down on the top step and rubbed his temples. The thought of his lovely wife gloriously naked in bed with her golden curls tossed about the pillows, and Winnington touching her, making love to her, sent him into a complete tailspin. Had his efforts to protect his own heart resulted in his wife turning to her first love? Did the child she carry belong to Winnington?

The possibility shook his soul, and twisted his insides until he leapt up without conscious thought and stormed into Cassie's room.

* * *

The nausea finally passed. Lately, Cassie was tired to the marrow of her bones. Sleep transported her to a sweet, dreamless place.

The door crashed open. Cassie sat up and clutched her feverishly beating heart. *William. Good heavens!* She fell back against the pillow, closed her eyes, and tried to steady her mind. When she opened them, he scowled down at her. *Now what?*

William's insane moods wore her out when all she wanted was a peaceful marriage. This unnecessary turmoil put a strain on her nerves, and truthfully, she had not forgiven him for his callous abandonment.

"What do you want?" she snapped.

"Do I not have the right to see my own wife?" he sneered.

"You have chosen to stay away for days, and now you come storming into my room as if seeing me is suddenly urgent?" Cassie sat up and pushed her hair from her face. She must look like a fright.

"I think discovering my wife is enceinte is urgent," he boomed.

Cassie sat up and stiffened her spine. "How did you know?" she whispered. She had not told a soul. She had waited and hoped William would come home as she prayed her news would thaw his chilled heart.

"Dr. Breckman told me. Nevertheless, it should have been my wife. You have known, but you did not see fit to inform me of your condition?" William paced about the room like a panther stalking its' prey. Warning bells clanged in her head. There was more to his anger than he let on.

Resentment so deep, so real, rose inside of her, and she needed to gain control of her wits before speaking. "I have not seen you since the ball. I only learned it that day. I intended to tell you that night, but you stormed off without giving a clue as to your whereabouts. You have not bothered to grace me with your presence, *my lord*."

Something like guilt flashed in his eyes before his face turned into a stony mask. *Hate.* She saw it in his eyes. Hate and disgust. *Why?* She wanted to cry out, to grab hold of him and shake him. What had she done to cause such vehemence?

"Whose child is it, or do you even know?" William's clipped, angry tone burned her like boiling oil poured on an open wound.

Her body shuddered from weakness. If she were standing, she would surely collapse. How could he say such a thing? Her hands shook, not from fear, but from an anguish so deep it rose to the surface like the lava of an erupting volcano. Never before had she experienced such hurt; such rage. Not when she returned from Gretna Green. Not when she saw the disappointment in her parent's eyes.

Fury boiled over and she grabbed a pitcher of water beside her bed and flung it at William. The bowl followed. He dodged the crockery, but the water doused him.

She charged at him and beat her fists against his chest. "How dare you! You...you...blackguard. You rotting bloody bastard!" Tears burned her eyes and streamed down her face as her out of control fists pounded the muscles of unmoving wall.

William grabbed her shoulders and shook her until her head snapped back. She could not read the stony expression on his face or in his dark, shuttered eyes. For a brief moment, they stilled and he held her tight until he bruised her arms. She struggled to catch her breath. He pulled her into his arms and rested his chin atop her head. His hands ran down her back and etched an impression on her skin. Torn between leaning against him and pushing him away, she remained rigid, and fought for control of her emotions.

"It is alright, Cassie. I will accept this child as my own."

His words took a moment to sink in. He did not believe the babe within her womb his? What could have possibly possessed him to think she would do such a thing? Cassie took her vows seriously. Did he think she would go to another man's bed? His lack of trust sickened her.

"Go away." She pushed against his chest with the palms of her hand, then turned her back on him, and listened as his footsteps crossed the room, and as the door opened and shut.

She wrapped her arms around her waist and sank to the floor. This time the tears did not come. She sat on her knees with her heart hammering in her ears, for what seemed like hours, before she finally rose, rang the bell pull, and demanded a bath.

Tonight she would attend the Farthington Ball without her husband. She would carry on. And when she began to show, she would return to Rosehill Manor *alone*.

* * *

The Farthington Ball was a ridiculous crush of hothouse flowers and London dandies. Cassie wore a deep blue silk gown cut in the popular Empire style. A gold sash rested below her breasts and drew attention to her fashionably low-cut bodice. Katie piled her golden curls on top of her head, and then weaved in diamonds and sapphires. A small sapphire pendent handed down from her grandmother graced her throat. She positively shimmered, and the attention of the surrounding gentlemen proved this to her.

Her dance card filled up within fifteen minutes of her arrival. She gave herself no time to stop and think about her missing husband, his horrible accusations, or her torn heart. Cassie danced and laughed and soaked in the atmosphere of swirling gowns and flickering candlelight. Living her life to the fullest was the only thing she could do to prevent the shallowness of her marriage from creeping into her thoughts, and taking over her every move. If William did not want her, then she would continue on without him.

Her resolve did not last long.

"Cassie, dear, where is William tonight? We hardly ever see him anymore," asked Anne.

"I would not know. He does not bother to inform me of his whereabouts or agenda."

Anne's brow creased and she pursed her lips. "This is becoming a habit of his. Is something wrong?"

"No, of course not. William stays busy." Cassie attempted to smile, but her lips did not cooperate. She should have kept her mouth shut. She trusted Anne, but, she was water to their blood, and

William came first with his family. Perhaps when her babe was born the Prescotts would see her in a different light. Then again, if William did not accept her babe as his own, what made her think his family would acknowledge her child?

Lord Wortham came to claim the next dance, leaving her no choice but to put her thoughts behind her. Cassie's heart could not stand to dwell on matters.

Despite her attempts to enjoy herself, a facade came over her like a cloak of disguise. Her pasted smile became brittle, and she tried to stop herself from rubbing her dry eyes. She danced and turned with partner after partner, but she could not help but glance around with hope blooming in her heart. She needed to have a frank discussion with her husband, but if he continued to avoid her, how would they ever work through this mess of a marriage?

Her observation skills sharpened as she noticed the difference in the faces of young, innocent girls in their first blush of love, juxtaposed with women who wore fake smiles that never reached their eyes. Recently, she heard tales of ladies who married for convenience, mostly to improve their social and financial statuses. True love was rare among the highest circles of Society.

Stephen partnered her for a waltz. He was tall and handsome like his brother with the same dark, wavy hair and chocolate eyes. His smile was warm and pleasant, but she did not react to him in the same way as William. They moved across the room while she waited for the inevitable.

"Where is William tonight?" The concern in Stephen's eyes caused her to bite on her lip.

"I am sure he is quite busy," she said, even though she knew the excuse sounded weak.

Stephen watched her, his gaze intent. Had William told Stephen about her condition, and his awful suspicions?

Stephen said nothing more. She started to excuse herself to the lady's retiring room when a strange hush came over the crowd. She turned to see what caused the fuss when she spotted her husband on the arm of another woman.

She stilled as Stephen took her arm amid a flurry of whispers that turned into a roar inside her head. Cassie watched her husband escort the woman into the ballroom. The raven-haired beauty wore her hair piled high on her head. Dark, exotic eyes with long lashes fluttered against her face. Her cranberry gown shimmered in the candlelight like that of a fairy princess.

"Why?" whispered Cassie.

"Lady Quartermane," Stephen muttered.

Cassie sucked in a deep breath. *William's mistress. Here. In front of the entire ton.* Heat burned her cheeks as mocking faces turned towards her. She caught William's eyes, which he raised, daring her to say or do something. She wanted to slap his face. Imagining the red mark gave her a small sense of satisfaction, but it was not enough to cool the rising anger.

William turned his back, cutting her in front of everyone. She gathered her composure and pretended she did not feel the humiliation, or the eyes of Society watching her, and the pain that wrapped around her throat and choked her.

Anne came to her side. "Cassie, I ripped the hem of my dress. Could you help me?" Not waiting for an answer, she pulled Cassie forward.

Cassie followed her sister-in-law to the lady's retiring room. The hot sting of tears clouded her vision. The burn of deceit followed her out the door. William slammed her heart against the wall, stomped on it, and threw it back into her face.

What happened to the William she loved?

Oh God, she loved him.

Despite her husband's cruel treatment as of late, *she loved him.* She wanted him to return to her, to hold her, to make love to her, to accept their child. Tears flowed down her cheeks as she reached the retiring room. She swiped at her wet cheeks with the back of her hand.

Anne locked the door and pulled Cassie into a hug. "Oh, Cassie, I am so sorry. I do not understand what caused William to act like an idiot."

Cassie tears turned into sobs. Anne handed her a handkerchief to wipe her eyes and blow her nose. She crumpled it in her hand. "I suppose I should buy you a new one."

"Talk to me, Cassie. What is going on?" Anne took her hand and implored her with her dark eyes—*chocolate eyes like William's.*

Cassie sniffled. She needed to talk to someone. Suddenly, she wished for Jocelyn, who was so young and innocent, and would certainly not understand marital problems. Anne was older, but she was also unmarried. She pondered what to do, then started blabbering. "I am enceinte."

"Oh Cassie, that is wonderful. However, I do not understand. William has always wanted children. Why would he treat you as if you had the plague?"

Cassie took a deep breath. "He believes the babe is not his."

Anne gasped, "No."

"Yes."

"How could he think such a thing?" she asked.

"I do not know or understand it myself. A couple of weeks ago Lord Winnington cornered me in the garden. I did not want him to touch me, but he forced a kiss on me. Then William showed up and bloodied his nose. I think my husband blames me, or believes I wanted Lord Winnington's affections. He leaves early and does not come home until late. He will not talk to me, Anne."

If the handkerchief were paper, it would have been torn to shreds by now. Cassie pulled at it as she tried to stop another round of tears. She was at her wits end with her emotions running high, and she did not remember a time when she felt so rung out.

Anne took a deep breath and whispered, "It is the curse."

"What? That silly ancient curse about women rejecting the second son? *I* did not reject him, so how could it possibly be the curse?"

"William married you within days of breaking off your engagement with Lord Winnington. Jealousy runs hot in my family. Nevertheless, I think it is more than jealousy. He fears you will break his heart."

"That is ridiculous. I wanted to marry him."

"I thought you did too," Anne took her hands, "but does William know that?"

* * *

Revenge tasted bitter. The *ton* looked at him with a combination of disgust and speculation. William witnessed the humiliation flood his wife's cheeks, so he turned his back, and gave his own wife the cut direct in front of all of Society. He handed the harpies more fodder for their gossip. And he felt like the world's biggest cad.

He wanted to punish Cassie for her betrayal, but in the end, his punishment worked both ways. A birch across his bare ass could not feel more painful than the tug at his heart. His lovely angel turned to a sour taste in his mouth.

William danced once with Lady Quartermane then left the ball much to her chagrin. He escorted his former mistress home before he made his way to Whites. The corner table gave him little solace. He spent more time in the corner than in his own home. Perhaps he should have taken the curse seriously and stayed away from marriageable women. If so, he would not be in this position with a wife who loved another man, and a babe on the way that may or may not be his.

William downed his brandy. The chair next to him scraped the floor as Stephen pulled it back and made himself welcome. *Great.*

Stephen drummed his fingers on the table. "Would you like to explain to me why you showed up with Lady Quartermane and cut your wife in front of the entire *ton*?"

"No." William started to rise, but Stephen put a hand on his shoulder.

"What you did tonight is not only an embarrassment to your wife, but to the entire Prescott family. What the hell is going on?"

"She is pregnant."

Stephen looked surprised at first and then baffled. "Isn't that a *good* thing?"

"Not if it is not mine."

"What?"

"I caught her in the garden at our ball with Winnington. The damn blackguard's hands were all over her."

A footman brought Stephen a glass of brandy and refilled William's glass. They sat for a few moments in tense silence.

"Are you sure you saw what you think you saw?" asked Stephen.

He thought about it. Not for the first time. The dark shadows in the garden made it difficult to see, but it did not stop him from realizing Winnington was all over his wife. "I bloodied his nose for it."

"Damn. What did Cassie have to say for herself?" asked Stephen.

"She did not say anything. I dragged her home and sent her to her room. The next time I spoke to her was after Dr. Breckman told me about her condition."

Stephen sat up straighter, and William saw the calculating look in his eyes. When others looked right past the obvious, his brother had the uncanny ability to see the pieces of a puzzle and how they fit together. "And when you did talk to her, what did she say?"

William screwed up his face at the unpleasant memory. "I asked her if the babe was mine and she threw crockery at me."

Stephen howled with laughter. Other gentlemen turned their way, curious about the sudden upheaval. William's face colored. He did not relish the entire *ton* knowing his business, but after tonight's foolishness, he had no one but himself to blame.

"What the hell are you laughing about?" he scowled.

"Are you telling me your wife was not a virgin on your wedding night?"

"No, I am not telling you that. Of course, she was a virgin." He could not imagine his brother's point in this ridiculous conversation.

"Tell me William, why would an innocent, bed another man only weeks into her marriage? Do you truly think her brave enough?"

"She loves him," William snapped.

"How do you know?"

The question sunk into William's mind like a drowning vessel. The evidence piled up against Cassie, did it not? Conflicting memories and feelings assailed him. The blind rage he experienced when he saw Cassie backed up to a tree with Winnington's hands and mouth on her resurfaced. He tried to remember the look in Cassie's eyes. Was it fear or relief?

What if she had not welcomed Winnington's attentions, but instead, the man forced himself upon her? Visions whirled in his mind as he recalled how she fought for his attention the day of the race, and how she responded to him *after* the episode with Winnington. He pictured her angelic face, her dazzling smile and pleasant laughter as he pushed her on the swing. William thought of his wife naked, beneath him, on their marriage bed.

No—he did not know anything for certain.

Chapter Fifteen

CASSIE SLEPT UNTIL NOON after an exhausting night alone. She fretted throughout the night, then woke to an overcast day that matched her mood. The sun hid behind ominous clouds, leaving the house dark and full of shadows. At least, she kept the contents of her stomach *in* her stomach thus far.

She put on her dove gray muslin gown, made her way to the drawing room, and sat by herself, knitting a pair of booties for her babe. She sighed with resignation at the knock on the door. With the partially knitted booties in her lap, she closed her eyes, and tried to prepare herself to smile and act as if all were well.

Lady Camberley and Lady Anne swept into the drawing room. The women hugged her first then assessed her. The small gestures of affection caused her to lose her resolve, and a tear slipped past her defenses.

"Oh dear, I am shocked by my son's behavior. I would not put such a thing past James, *but William*. He is my *good* boy." Lady Camberley dabbed at her own wet eyes with a handkerchief.

"What are you knitting?" asked Anne.

Cassie looked down at the knitting in her lap and burst into tears. The women flanked both her sides, patted her hands and back, handed her fresh handkerchiefs, and gave her words of encouragement. She could not seem to help giving into the weariness that sucked at her in like quicksand.

A few minutes later, her tears spent, the awareness of acting like a watering pot filtered through her foggy mind. She rang for tea, and once they were settled with their cups of tea and crumpets, Lady Camberley asked, "What pray tell, is going on?"

"I am going to have a baby." Cassie pressed her lips together. She caught Anne's eye who decided to act surprised at the news.

Lady Camberley placed her hand over her heart. "Oh, that is wonderful! *A baby.* A grandchild. I cannot tell you how pleased this makes me. But that does not explain William's actions, or your sadness."

She hesitated to talk about such a private matter. Anne knew and had not condemned her, but Anne also proved to be her greatest ally among the Prescott family. Cassie wished for her own mother and sister.

"William is under the impression this babe is not his."

Lady Camberley's face turned stark white. For a moment, Cassie wondered if her mother-in-law would have a case of the vapors, but she managed to pull herself together. "Why would he be under this impression?"

"Lord Winnington made unwanted advances on the night of the ball, but William saw only what he chose to see. I swear to you I have not been unfaithful." Anger swelled in Cassie's breast. There were times when she thought about everything and wanted to thrash her husband for his rash conclusions.

"Did you tell him the truth?" asked Lady Camberley.

"He has yet to give me a chance. He leaves before I wake, and returns after I go to sleep. The last time I saw him, he discovered I was with child, then accused me of foul behavior. I confess I lost my temper and raged at him. I have not seen him since."

Lady Camberley drummed her fingers against her teacup. "I see. You are going to have to convince him."

Cassie watched her mother-in-law's expression, and wondered what plan she was calculating, "It is impossible to convince him when I never see him."

"This behavior is not like William. He is not one to avoid confrontation or problems. He generally charges any situation head on," said Anne.

"Yes, you are right. I suspect he is afraid this time," said Lady Camberley.

"But what could he fear? I do not know how to reach him."

"Anne, I would like to speak to Cassie alone. Go the library and see if William has a new book we could take to Elizabeth." Lady Camberley commanded and her daughter retreated without question.

"Anne is unmarried, an innocent. I am going to give you advice from one married woman to another. You need to convince your husband of your loyalty. Go to his bed tonight and wait for his return. Seduce him."

Cassie nearly spit out her tea. This is not the first time William's mother said something scandalous to her. She did not dare answer.

Lady Camberley laughed. "Do not be embarrassed, dear. How do you think William came to be? Now, you listen to me, and listen well," she took Cassie's teacup and set it down, then took her hands in hers, "You must fight for your marriage. William wants marriage and children, but if he believes this is not what you want, he will retreat rather than risk his heart."

Hours later, after Cassie's guests departed and she contemplated Lady Camberley's words, they finally sunk in. Sitting around waiting for William to make an appearance, waiting for him to come to her, was not working. If she wanted William, she needed to take matters into her own hands.

Cassie ordered the staff to move her things to William's bedchamber. She waited for her husband by readying his room and herself. After a long, hot bath soaking in sliced lemons, she donned her silk wrapper then dried her hair by the fire.

Katie brushed out her golden curls, leaving her hair fallen to her waist. Cassie selected a flimsy silk gown the color of her green eyes. She admired all of her preparations in William's bedchamber. She recreated the surprise William had for her on their wedding night—the night she imbibed in too much wine. Hothouse roses in vases littered the room along with dozens of candles. The navy blues and gold's of the bed linens, carpet, and curtains added warmth to the romantic atmosphere.

Her hands trembled, but she was determined to carry her plans through. She needed to convince William she wanted to be his wife, wanted him in her bed, and in her life. She nibbled on a strawberry from a plate of fruit, cakes, and cream. The wait might very well make her mad. She walked around the room, running a finger along the masculine bedpost. Imagining what she would do in this bed caused her to blush, but she refused to back down.

She found a copy of Shakespeare's *Hamlet* on William's bedside table, poured a glass of wine, and then snuggled under the covers with his book to wait him out.

* * *

Weariness crept beneath William's skin. Tired of hiding out, hiding away from his wife and his life, he decided to go home. Since he ceased coming home before midnight, Scott stopped waiting up for him. He used a key to let himself in the front door. A withering candle burned for him. The glow gave him enough light to find his way to his study. He used the flicker of flame to light another candle before sinking into a chair.

The quiet of the house should comfort him, but his tangled thoughts, mixed with grief, anger, and guilt, enveloped him in a tight wrap. Certain Cassie slept, he decided to wait until morning to talk to her. They needed to come to some sort of understanding.

He rested for awhile before making his way to his empty bed. He wanted his wife beside him, but he could not bring himself to invite her and risk rejection. If she indeed loved Winnington, and carried the blackguard's child, then she would not desire her husband's bed.

William clenched his fist, and attempted to fight away the madness that threatened to eat him alive. Every time he thought of his angel in bed with another man, sharing her body, growing large with his seed, William wanted to smash Winnington to smithereens.

As he approached his bedchamber, he noticed a stream of light at the bottom of the door. Thinking his valet forgot to snuff out the candle, he mentally planned to chastise him the next day.

William opened the door and first noticed the dozens of candles that gave the room a golden glow. The smell of roses assailed his senses, but his eyes were drawn to the bed. *Sweet heaven.* He closed the door with a quiet click.

His angel lay beneath the midnight covers with her crowning curls shimmering in the candlelight. Her closed eyes against her porcelain face made her look like a sleeping beauty. Even in the darkened room, he could see her blushed cheeks and rosebud lips. Struck by her loveliness, he moved to the side of the bed and stared down.

A small whimper escaped her throat as he watched her stir. His gut tightened at the sad sound. Why had she come to his bed? Should he wake her or not?

William shed his clothes and slipped beneath the covers. He pulled her against him, allowing her silken hair to caress his bare chest, as her bottom pressed against his hardness.

He breathed in her lemony scent—fresh, clean, innocent. He dreamed of this every night, of holding her like this, in his bed. Although she may have betrayed him, he could not help but want her. He brushed his lips across her shoulder and closed his eyes against the agony of wanting her. He wanted to wake her and relieve himself, but he knew the release would only extend to his body, not his heart or his mind. Tired of the torment, he forced his mind to concentrate on sleep.

Dawn reached its' red and orange fingers through the slits of the curtains. Hard and frustrated, William woke in a tangle of arms and legs. Cassie's soft skin pressed against his back. He resisted snuggling deeper into the covers and pulling her closer.

William eased his body from hers and left the bed. He stood before her and considered his next move. He planned to talk to her today, to find common ground on which to piece together their crumbling relationship. Now, he wanted sanctuary.

As long as Winnington remained in close proximity, he was unable to reach his beloved's heart. They needed to return to Rosehill Manor, but that meant too much time alone with her in a closed carriage. Perhaps he would ride alongside, or ride ahead. William picked up his clothes and dressed as he watched Cassie sleep.

He stopped to scrawl a note leaving Cassie the choice to follow. He pondered how he might win her over. As he left the bedchamber, he found a footman and ordered his horse brought round.

"Give this note to my wife when she comes down for breakfast." He handed the note over to Scott as he left the house. He prayed his wife would follow.

* * *

Strong arms embraced Cassie in her sleep, but were gone when she awoke. The absence startled her. His presence during the night intruded on her dreams. She turned over and swept her hand over the warm indention in her bed. He came. He slept. He left.

She threw his pillow at the air and cried out a stream of inappropriate words as she struggled into her wrapper. Then, she prayed for forgiveness and plopped down on the edge of the bed as she shook her head in frustration. Bound for bedlam, she went to her room to dress. Katie brought her pressed, pink muslin morning gown, then took her time braiding and wrapping Cassie's errant curls into a respectable coiffure.

A small glimmer of hope teased her mind. William had not insisted she return to her room in the middle of the night, but instead, he lay beside her. She smiled at the vision, but she did not count herself victorious. Perhaps her efforts paid off in a small measure of success. If only she had not fallen asleep. What time had he finally come home, and what had he done while he was gone? Did he come from Lady Quartermane's bed? She shook the image from her mind as she could not bear to think of him with another woman.

Scott bowed to her as she entered the dining room and handed her a note. "From his lordship, my lady."

"Thank you, Scott." She took the folded vellum to the table and sat down in the chair. Her heart was heavy with anticipation and dread. It was the first piece of communication her husband extended to her, and she prayed for positive contents.

My lady wife,

I am returning to Rosehill Manor. You may choose to stay or follow in the carriage.

William

Cassie reread the note several times before she tucked it beneath her plate. She debated whether he issued an invitation or an ultimatum; not that it mattered, she would follow. After she finished her first breakfast she could stomach in days, she informed Scott and Katie of her decision, and then changed into a marsh green traveling gown. Before she left, she sent a note to Anne to let her know of their departure.

One part of Cassie regretted leaving the excitement of London, but after her husband's distasteful behavior, she had no desire to attend another Society event. The only way she could survive the *ton's* harsh judgment and biting gossip was to return to the city with William established at her side.

She entered the carriage with Katie beside her. Scott followed in the traveling coach, and half a dozen footmen rode alongside her for protection. At Rosehill Manor, William could not hide at his club, so she might be able to convince him of her innocence and loyalty. She relished the challenge, and prepared herself for the fight of her life.

* * *

The afternoon sun heated William's skin as he rode Mirabelle across the fields. He took a chance leaving London with his sleeping wife in his bed, even though he left behind a note with an ultimatum.

It seemed the only wise thing to do since he realized he could not force his wife to love him. She needed to search her heart and make a decision. Either she wanted this marriage, or she did not. Either way, they were bound for life. However, he refused to give her his heart if she loved another.

William needed to know if there was hope. The die were cast now. His heart ached to think she might choose Winnington. He clenched his fist. She might love another, but she was married to him. His standards and expectations refused to allow his wife to carry on behind his back with another man. She might choose to stay with him, but he set the ground rules. They might live separate lives, but she would do her wifely duties.

Who the hell was he kidding? He could not imagine breathing the air without her. He prayed she would follow him to Rosehill Manor. What if she did not? What if she stayed behind? What if she declared her love for Winnington? The curse upon his head squeezed his heart and sucked him dry. It made his humiliation complete.

William squinted into the sunlight at the sound of horses and wheels. His heart swelled as he recognized the carriage. An unexpected pleasure rushed through his body. He smiled for the first time in weeks.

William pressed his boot against Mirabelle's side, and trotted towards the front of the house as the carriage pulled to a stop. He leapt down and stood waiting for his wife to emerge. He held his hand out to her, and watched as various emotions, the first of which being surprise, flickered across her face.

"My lady." He gallantly offered his arm and Cassie accepted. A smile spread across her face and reached her eyes. He let out a breath he held since his departure from London.

"William."

Just his name on her lips, softly spoken, punched his heart as he realized how many pointless weeks he wasted avoiding the very sight of her. No matter how hard he tried, he could not escape his need for her.

They walked into the house where she immediately excused herself. Reluctantly, he watched her go, but he knew she needed time to rest and freshen up after her long journey. Luncheon would be served soon, therefore, giving him the opportunity he needed to begin repairing his mess of a marriage.

He decided to freshen up as well, and an hour later, he joined his wife in the dining room. What struck him first was her sad eyes. He stood in the doorway and watched her push food around on her plate. *She missed Winnington!* He forced himself to push the dangerous accusation from his mind.

"Cassie." Surprise flickered across her face. He gestured to the footman to move his place setting next to her, rather than at the end of the lengthy table, then he sat down.

"William," she swallowed, but smiled.

"How are you?"

She sat her fork down, and looked him in the eye. "I have not been unfaithful to you. This babe is yours."

William pressed his lips together to hold back his emotions. He forced himself to think clearly and calmly. She had not minced her words. It was time for honesty between them. "You were in the gardens with Winnington. His hands were on you."

Anger flashed in her eyes. "I did not invite him to touch me. He forced himself upon me, and I was glad of your rescue. I could not break his hold. He was much too strong!"

William allowed her words to sink in. If she told the truth, then he did her a great disservice, but if she lied...

"I swear upon God's *Holy Bible* I am telling you the truth. You must believe me!" Cassie touched his arm and he nearly leapt out of his skin.

He might be the biggest fool in the kingdom, but he wanted to believe her. William grasped her hand and held it to his heart. He searched her eyes to find something hidden, but alas, he did not detect secrets tangled within her words.

If her statements were true, then he punished her unjustly for far too long. If not, well, that did not bear thinking. He wanted to believe his wife. He needed to believe her. "You told me once you loved him."

Cassie pulled her hand away, and placed them in her lap. She looked down a moment before raising her eyes to his, "At the time, I believed I loved him, but now I realize I simply believed myself in love. It was nothing more than youthful fancies. The first blush of a man's attention and girlhood dreams."

"And now it is different?"

"*Yes.*"

This time he heard her, and because he wanted to, he believed her.

They ate in awkward silence then attempted small talk. The clang of silver against china echoed in the room and scratched at his nerves. His cravat tightened like a chokehold around his neck. He stopped in the middle of his meal, took off his jacket and laid it across the back of his chair. The cravat came next.

He watched Cassie's curious eyes as he stripped in the dining room. Perspiration dripped down his back, but he unbuttoned only a few buttons at the top of his shirt and rolled up his sleeves. *Better.* He sat back down to her curious glance, then he smiled in response. Picking up his spoon, he dug into his stew with gusto.

He forced himself to focus on his meal. The bulge in his breeches failed to help matters. To start over with her, he needed some time to contemplate the best route to reestablish their relationship.

"Where have you gone all this time? All the days and late nights?" she asked.

The question caught him off guard. He gave her credit for her bluntness. *The minx.* Something shifted inside of him as he admitted to himself how he could not live without her. Where had he gone? *To hell and back.*

"Mostly to my club. Sometimes to Gentleman Jacksons." He did not mention he went to boxing club to fight out his frustrations.

"And Lady Quartermane's bed?" She looked at him directly.

Tension tightened his shoulders, and thickened his tongue. The heat in the room increased, and caused drops of sweat to roll down his forehead. He flaunted his former mistress in the face of Society, and left his wife humiliated. Guilt snaked around his throat then squeezed in a death grip.

"No," he choked out.

"Why did you cut me in front of *ton* with your mistress?"

He did it to punish her, and to appease his own bitterness. He believed she carried Winnington's child. He never believed in the curse his brothers and sisters found so humorous, at least he did not believe until he received the most striking rejection of all. A rejection from one his own wife, or so he thought.

He tried to make sense of it all. "Why did you agree to marry me?"

A flush of pink added a rosy blush to her to her milky white cheeks. His shaft hardened.

"At the moment it seemed like my only choice," she said.

Her words sliced through him. She married him out of desperation. She returned from her botched trip to Gretna Green ruined and in disgrace. She embarrassed her family and her sister stood to suffer the consequences of her actions. He offered for her knowing she had little choice.

"But in all honesty, I wanted to marry you. At the time, I did not understand my own feelings, but, I was drawn to you. I still am." She bit her bottom lip, its' soft and pink flesh invited him to kiss her.

He controlled his physical urges, so they could work through this tangled mess. "This is not the first time I have acted like a complete ass. I am sorry." He rose from his seat and knelt before her. "Will you forgive me?"

"Oh, yes, yes." She took his face in her hands and kissed him soundly.

Her mouth intoxicated him like a fine brandy on a cold day. Aware of the servants, he took her by the wrists and stood. "Perhaps we should finish this conversation upstairs."

"I think that would be a fine idea." Cassie took his hand and the lead. He followed behind, and watched her bottom swish back in forth in a seductive walk. As they made their way upstairs, it occurred to him that he would follow her to hell if that is what it took to keep her in his life.

William closed the door on the curse, on Winnington, on every blasted negative thought, as he shut the bedchamber door behind them.

Chapter Sixteen

*A*S SOON AS THE DOOR CLOSED BEHIND HER, Cassie turned into her husband's arms, linked her hands around his waist and laid her head on his shoulder. "Hold me."

William's arms encircled her, and his chin rested near the top of her head. The warmth of his body drugged her senses, and the smell of sandalwood mingled with sensual man enthralled her. She pulled him tighter in an embrace, and relished the feel of his hard body against hers. His hands ran up and down the length of her back as they comforted and ignited her at the same time. She savored the moment, letting the essence of him burn into her memory.

"I have missed you," he said.

She closed her eyes and took in a deep breath. "Stay with me like this forever."

He chuckled and kissed her hair. "We might need to eat on occasion."

"You are the only food I need." She lifted her head from his chest and smiled up at him. His eyes turned to the darkest chocolate. She licked her dry lips as he caught her in a kiss.

His warm mouth merged with hers, and she opened to him, invited him in, and he came. His tongue stroked hers, and the pressure of his kiss deepened, causing the smoldering in her most private place to burst into flames. She moaned and collapsed against him.

This is how it should be between them. On the way to Rosehill Manor she imagined various scenarios and conversations, but in the end, she did not hold back her words. She risked and triumphed. *For now.*

William broke the kiss and trailed his lips across her jaw and down her neck. Her skin tingled with pleasure and anticipation. His hands moved further down her back and cupped her bottom. She ached for the touch of his warm skin against hers. Her fingers found his cravat and then the buttons of his shirt.

"Do you want me undressed, sweetings?" He started to remove his shirt, but she grabbed his hands and pushed them away.

"No. Let me." Cassie ran her palms along his chest, and took her time undoing each button, one by one. She brushed his chest hair with the tips of her fingers as she made her way down. When she reached his breeches, she pulled at his shirt until it came out of his waistband, then she ran her hands up his bare chest until she pushed the fabric off his shoulders.

Taking a moment to admire William's well sculpted chest and shoulders, she ran a fingertip across his muscles. She walked around him, and touched his arm and back, then moved to his front. She never imagined a man's body could be so beautiful. She placed a reverent kiss over his heart and let her hands wander further down. She took a deep breath, then looked up into his hazy, passion filled eyes. Confidence and power surged through her as she unfastened his pants and shoved them down over his hips.

Cassie drunk in the sight of his naked form with his male part hard, long, and thick. "Can I touch it?"

"You may do anything you please, my lady."

Her hand shook slightly as she ran a finger along his hard erection. She touched a bead of moisture at the tip then brought her finger to her mouth and sucked. His eyes widened and his shaft twitched and grew even longer.

He chuckled at her wanton act, but she did not care. She wanted this man, her husband. She wanted him inside her, in her bed, and in her life.

She giggled as he shuffled his feet with his breeches riding at the tops of his boots while he made his way to the bed. He had a fine backside with tight buttocks. The urge to explore every part of his body with her hands and mouth overcame her.

Heat flushed her from the inside out at the wild direction of her thoughts. She shocked her own sensibilities, then suddenly became shy and cast her eyes downward.

"Come help me with my boots."

She hesitated for a small moment, but completed the task as he commanded. She yanked off one boot and then the other, then helped William remove his breeches from his muscled legs. Her fingers grazed the dark curls around his calves. She studied the hair on his chest and followed its trail with her eyes as it made its way down his stomach, to his belly button, and to the curly mass where his thickness thrust out.

"Turn around." William said as stood up and unbuttoned her dress. She spent so many days and nights dreaming of this chance, that she worried it would never come. Now, here she stood, accepting his assistance as he removed her dress, stays, and chemise.

Once she was naked, he stayed at her back, and wrapped his arms around her. His warmth pressed into her, and yet, she shivered. He trailed kisses across her shoulders and down her back. He wrapped his hands around hers and brought them to her breasts.

"Touch your breasts. Feel their heaviness." He said this as his own fingers flicked the tight buds of her nipples, and desire burned a flame down to where she throbbed with moisture.

She was somewhat embarrassed to touch herself this way in front of him, to feel her own breasts, to give her own body such attention, but she let him guide her in this passionate journey. His hands left hers and moved across her stomach, hips, and bottom, then retraced the burning trail, setting her skin afire. He pleasured every place except the one for which she needed him to touch the most.

"Please," she begged.

"Patience sweetings. I want to savor every moment." His lips followed the trail he began with his hands. His tongue trailed down her spine, with his hands never leaving her. He kissed the round curves of her bottom, the backs of her legs, even her calves. She reached out to grasp the bedpost before she fell to the floor, weakened in the knees.

She spun and her hands hit the bed. She held on for dear life as his fingers made their way up the front of her legs, and past her tender spot where they grazed her ribs and captured her breasts. She cried out at his touch. She wanted him inside of her, now.

Cassie attempted to stand and turn, but he held her captive, and pushed his leg between her legs, then forced them apart. "What are you doing to me?"

"Showing you the many ways a man and woman can love."

One hand left her breast and ran down her stomach until he reached the apex of her thighs. A finger brushed her feminine curls and slid through her moisture. She gasped and moaned at the intimate touches. He continued to pleasure her there until he created a firestorm inside of her that she could not quench.

She nearly wept at the intensity of the uphill climb. Almost there, but not quite, as he flipped her onto her back and climbed onto the bed beside her. She desired his touch to take her the rest of the way, but instead, he traced circles on her breasts with his fingers. The unbearable ache in her body and heart overwhelmed her. She grabbed his hand and shoved it downward and silently begged him.

"Tell me what you want."

She closed her eyes, mortified to speak her desire for him aloud. She whispered, "I want you to touch me there."

His finger dipped into her. "Here?"

"Yes, please."

He did not give her what she wanted. Instead, he moved his hands to her breasts, then captured them both and squeezed before putting his mouth to one nipple. He laved it with his tongue, and suckled until she squirmed and cried and lifted her hips. He moved to her other breast and gave it the same attention. She thought she might die if he did not enter her soon.

Cassie scraped her nails down his back, dug her claws into his flesh, and punished him for unfairly torturing her body in the same way he toyed with her emotions. A terrifying thought crossed her mind—what if he worked her into a frenzy of want and need, then up and left her before completion. She held him to her, and made unfamiliar noises of passion, as he left her breasts and ran his tongue down her stomach, then stopped to dip into her belly button.

Her legs parted of their own volition. The weeks of frustrated tension mounted inside of her. She wanted him, needed him in the same way she needed food and water and the very air in which she breathed. He teased her mercilessly with his kisses and licked so close to the curls at her womanly core, that she writhed on the bed, as he reduced her to puddle of boneless mass.

William stopped and she nearly screamed and pounded his shoulders. He looked into her eyes, "You are mine. Mine." Then he did what she thought he would never do.

He dipped his head between her legs and used his tongue to lick across her pink bud. Her body exploded like fireworks on a summer night, and rose off the bed as waves of pleasure crashed over her again and again. As soon as the last tremor claimed her, he settled his body over her and entered in one, long thrust.

Cassie's scream must have carried through the entire house. William groaned and smiled into her eyes. He moved within her, and she followed his rhythm as they moved in symphony, hitting one crescendo after another until the final cords played. Together they soared to the heavens then floated back down to earth.

He stayed within her and rested. Afraid to say the words aloud, she mouthed, "I love you," as a tear slipped down her cheek.

* * *

William pulled out of her and rolled over. Never in his life had he felt anything like this. No mistress ever caused such a powerful orgasm. Weeks of pent up frustration powered every moment, yet he managed to control his body while he pleasured her to the breaking point.

He planned to wipe every trace of Winnington from her mind and body. He accepted her story of no affair with her former betrothed which released him from his anguish, but he still doubted her feelings. Despite her insistence at making their marriage work, she once loved Winnington, and love was not something easily erased from the heart.

He was determined to hold back a part of his heart until he was sure she eliminated Winnington from her heart and mind forever. He had originally planned to court her, and seduce her into giving herself to him, completely and irrevocably. Instead, he allowed his temper and jealousy to take over and interfere with his plans. It was a mistake he would not make again.

William's advantage over Winnington lay next to him. She was *his* wife. He had the right to have her in his bed every night, and even in the day if he so desired.

He hauled Cassie into his arms until their bodies fit together like two spoons. She sighed and rested against him. He kissed the top of her head, and ran his hand down her side.

"This is where I want to be, you know." Cassie's words came to his ears in a husky whisper.

"I cannot think of any other place I would rather be," he said.

"About the babe..." she turned towards him and peered into his eyes.

His chest constricted. The concern etched on her face stabbed him with guilt. He accused her of carrying another man's child. The distrust stood between them like a stone wall. He would break down the barriers, even if he had to remove each stone one at a time.

William reached down and laid his hand over her stomach. Amazement washed through him at the life that lay within her. For the first time, he noticed the slight roundness to her stomach. Her breasts were heavier, and he wondered how she would look when she was fully round with his child. The thought hardened him; painfully so.

He almost laughed. Never would he have expected to experience such an arousal by the very thought of a woman large with child. William rolled over, parted her legs and slipped back inside of her. Her shudder ran through his own body, and he thought of coming home.

He kissed his wife to keep from telling her he loved her. He wanted to be certain his feelings were returned before handed his heart over completely. He kissed her like a dying man drinking deeply from a well, and sank his member further into her warm body. His tongue danced with hers as they began a private waltz of thrusting and grinding. She cried out her release and he spilled his seed deep within her womb.

He fell on top of her, then voiced a concern that crept into his mind. "I am not hurting you, am I? The baby, I mean."

She laughed. "No. The baby is fine."

"I hope she has your hair and eyes." He pulled out of her and reached to kiss a tempting nipple.

"I hope *he* has *your* hair and eyes," she said.

"I am such a fool. I know without a doubt this child is mine. I let my envy get the best of me. How will I ever make it up to you?"

"I can think of a few ideas," she said she kissed him sweetly on the cheek.

They laughed and wrapped their arms around each other, embracing and savoring the moment. *This is how it should be.*

"But first, I am hungry," she declared.

"I thought I was the only food you needed." He kissed her again to remind her of the feast he offered.

"Yes, well, I might have spoken too soon. The baby needs to eat too, you know."

William kissed his wife's pert little nose, then her mouth, and breast, and stomach before finally getting up and pulling on his breeches. "I shall endeavor to see what I can forage from the kitchens."

"You are my knight in shining armor," she sighed.

He kissed her again before he wrangled into his shirt and padded on bare feet out the door, and down the corridor to the stairs. He made his way through the dark house until he came to the cook's pantry. There he gathered an assortment of ham and biscuits, and fruit and cakes onto a tray. Suddenly hungry himself, he piled the plates high with more food than either could probably eat.

He grabbed two goblets and a bottle of wine. This was how he imagined his life: a home of his own with his wife upstairs in his bed, and his child on the way.

As he made his way back upstairs to the woman he loved, to his future, he believed he almost had everything. Perhaps one day she would come to love him. She desired him, of that, he was sure, but for her to give herself completely, it would mean giving her heart as well.

He debated as to whether or not he should confess his feelings, but by the time he reached the door to his bedchamber, he decided against it. If she rejected his heart, he could never survive it. Better to keep it locked away, and to accept whatever his wife could give.

* * *

Cassie awoke the next morning and found her husband snoring beside her. She covered her mouth with her hand to keep the laughter at bay. He was so masculine, but in his sleep, he reminded her of an adorable little boy. Cassie touched her stomach with her hand and thought of the child growing inside of her.

She imagined a little boy with thick dark hair and chocolate eyes like his father. Warmed all over from their night of lovemaking, and her imagination, she studied the man beside her. She wanted to reach over and kiss the lean planes of his face and the hard line of his jaw, then move to the smooth full lips of his mouth. The very mouth that spent the night torturing her body with pleasure.

Moisture pooled in her heat, and she had to squeeze her thighs to contain the sensation. *Oh dear.* Just a couple of months ago, she never would have imagined such things. Her naivety struck a chord in her as she wondered what else she did not know or understand. Cassie had the distinct feeling there was more.

William moved and the covers slipped revealing the tops of his legs. His hard cock thrust upward. She jumped back in surprise. The man was sound asleep, yet as hard as a rock, just as he was before coming into her. She now knew what he looked like when he deflated, and fought the giggles that rose at the sight of him in such a shocking state while asleep.

She studied his manhood and wondered if she could get him inside of her by climbing on top of him. The very idea made her wiggle her sensitive spot across the sheets. She contemplated it, and tried to decide if the position would work. On a wild impulse she climbed above him, then sank her warm depths over his shaft.

William's eyes snapped open and a lustful smile greeted her. "Well, good morning."

"Good morning to you, my lord." She moved her body up and down as blissful sensations rolled through her. He groaned and she watched him as he closed his eyes, then gritted his teeth as if he were in pain.

She reveled in her own power as she threw back her head and rode him. Their thrusts met and her bottom slammed against him. She held her breasts and pinched her nipples the way he taught her the night before. Overcome with her own release, she battled upward then broke apart and shuddered until her breasts met his chest. He thrust inside of her once more to release his seed.

Cassie lay across him, with his body still inside of hers. She fought to gain her breath, and she decided she liked the wonders of the marriage bed.

"I do not believe I have ever experienced such a pleasurable morning. You can wake me like that every day of my life and I would never tire of it."

"Truly?" she asked as she climbed off and sank down beside him.

"Truly."

They lay together in the quiet of the morning, as the sun rose and lit the room in the dawning light. He pulled the covers over them and held her, and she fell into a half sleep, content like a kitten rolled into a ball by the hearth.

A knock at the door broke through Cassie's consciousness. Embarrassed at being caught naked in William's bed, she yanked the covers over her head. They were married, but the knowledge of what they had done made her want to hide under the covers.

"Stay here." William got out of the bed and put his breeches on before cracking open the door.

She heard the housekeeper speak. "I am sorry to bother you, my lord, but there is footman from Camberley House downstairs who insists he must see you in person. He says it is a family emergency."

Cassie sat up in bed, and held the covers over her naked body as a sense of dread slithered down her spine.

Chapter Seventeen

A RUMBLE OF THUNDER echoed in the distance. The wind picked up during the morning, and the sky darkened as ominous clouds moved over the estate. The weather change from bright to dark over the past hour, and Cassie tried desperately to shake the bad feeling that twisted inside her stomach.

As soon as William heard the housekeeper's message, he dressed and ran downstairs to hear what the footman had to say. When he returned it was only long enough to hand her a missive. kiss her, and run out the door to get on his horse.

She read the message several times, but something seemed amiss. *Return to Camberley House immediately. Mary is hurt.*

The message came unsigned, and William mentioned the footman must be a new hire, for he never saw him before. She asked him to wait, to allow her to dress so she could go with him, but he did not want to lose any time. The fear in his eyes and panic in his voice unsettled her.

Mary was William's twin, and she knew, and understood, that nothing in the world could keep him from riding as fast as he could to be at his sister's side. She would do the same if the message brought news to her of Jocelyn.

"Excuse me, my lady, but I thought you might like some luncheon. I brought you a tray." Cassie did not hear the housekeeper enter, but was grateful for the consideration. Worry caused her to forget about food, but once she saw the sandwiches and fruit laid out before her, her stomach rumbled.

The crack of thunder startled her. Her hand jolted and splashed the liquid onto the new carpet as she poured a cup of tea. She cursed her clumsiness then went over to the bell pull.

A young maid entered the room. "You rang, my lady?"

"Yes, I am afraid I have made a small mess."

"I will take care of it right away." She curtsied and left the room.

Cassie nibbled on a cucumber sandwich and sipped her tea. She feared for Mary, but also for William, who was riding on horseback in this weather. Her imagination ran wild, too wild, and it left her anxious and worried.

What if William's horse caught his foot in a pothole in the road? What if he caught lung fever after riding in the wet weather? What if Mary was badly injured?

Guilt gripped Cassie. Her relationship with Mary was strained at best. There was a wall between Mary and herself, and no matter how hard she tried, her sister-in-law gave her little wiggle room. Mary did not trust her.

For that matter, Cassie never understood why her husband did not trust her. She never did anything improper since she married William. She thought of the night Winnington attempted to have his way with her. She did not encourage or want his advances. Her former betrothed's behavior shocked and frightened her.

Half an hour later the clouds burst and the rain came down in a glass sheet. It pounded the roof, and turned the silence to a deafening roar. So loud was the rain, she did not hear the knock on the drawing room door, or notice the door creak open until the housekeeper stood before her.

"My lady, you have a visitor." The housekeeper wrung her hands.

A knot in Cassie's stomach tightened. "In this weather? Who is it, Margie?"

"Lord Winnington."

Oh dear God. She instructed Margie to send him away, but manners he pushed past the housekeeper. He had the uncanny ability to show up at the most crucial moments.

Margie curtsied and left. She did not like his sudden appearance. The timeliness of Lord Winnington's arrival was odd. How did he know she was at Rosehill Manor?

Cassie remembered the unsigned missive, but it was brought to William by a footman from Camberley House. Or was it? William had not recognized the man, but the man claimed to be newly hired. Surely, she was allowing her vivid imagination to run away with her.

She took a deep breath and prepared herself for the unwelcome confrontation with Lord Winnington. A small part of her sunk into sadness. She had once dreamed of a life with this man, and now, she must to turn him away forever. She fought off the rising guilt and stiffened her spine. Mr. Parker, now Lord Winnington, was a girlhood dream. She loved William, her husband. She would put Winnington firmly in the past where he belonged.

Cassie did not stand when he entered the room, but instead, sat and gaped at his clothes. At one time she thought his taste in clothing adorable, but now he appeared silly, dressed in bright yellow breeches and an orange jacket. The colors clashed and blinded her senses. Lord Winnington looked positively ridiculous.

"I am glad you are pleased to see me, my darling." Winnington bowed in front her as if she were the Queen of England.

She schooled her features, then stood and lifted her chin. "I cannot imagine why you would think I am glad to see you, Lord Winnington."

"You are angry with me. I understand. I got carried away and took liberties. I apologize, darling."

"Do not call me *darling*." Thunder rumbled and lighting cracked at the end of her command.

"My, my, you are quite snarly today. No matter. All will be well soon." Winnington sat down in the chair across from her and crossed his legs.

Cassie's discomfiture wore on her like itchy fabric. She did not know what to make of him.

"Why are you here?" she asked.

His pearly white teeth set against a handsome face with blue eyes. For a moment, Cassie almost lost her resolve. He captured her attention with his handsome smile. The memory of their first encounter flooded her mind. At one time she thought him the most handsome man in England, but in truth, he compared poorly to William. She supposed she would always carry a small tendre for Lord Winnington since he was her first girlhood love.

Cassie understood the difference between girlish dreams and those first fluttering feelings of romance. There was a powerful, all-consuming love which blossomed in her heart when she thought of her husband. The bold line she crossed caused her to never turn back. It was time to convince her former betrothed things were over between them.

"Do not worry, Cassie. I have worked everything out. It is a great sacrifice on my part, but truly, the end result is all that matters."

He spoke in riddles which vexed her all the more. The conversation was at an end as far as she was concerned, and he should be on his way away from Rosehill Manor. However, the rain did not help matters since he would probably expect to stay until the weather blew over. This would not do at all.

"What are you talking about?" Cassie clung to her cup, and sipped her tea for the lack of anything better to do with her hands.

"I should have insisted we continue our trip to Gretna Green. I only wanted to please you, dear Cassandra." Lord Winnington continued, "I thought I would try to work things out with my uncle one more time, and if he still refused, well then, I would simply have to wait until he cocked up his toes."

"Sir, at the time, the situation was impossible. We cannot continue to hash out history, Lord Winnington. What is done is done. I am quite content now. I suggest you find yourself a young miss and marry her. It is the only thing left to do."

"No, it is not. I have found another way for us to be together." His smile did not reach his eyes.

Cassie trembled. Something was not right. Her skin crawled with a sense of foreboding. "It is not possible, Lord Winnington."

"Anything is possible if you set your mind to it. You were promised to me Cassandra, and I shall have you." He walked over and stood in front of her, which forced her to look up into his face.

She did not care for the turn of this conversation, or his complete lack of regard for her married state. She would never betray her vows before God and family. He must be daft. She wondered how she missed this side of him before, but in all honesty, how well did she really know him?

He courted her for weeks before offering for her, then he traveled between her small village and London for months. His visits lasted a few hours, but grew further apart over the months. Eventually, Lord Winnington stopped coming all together, and their communication was reduced to letters. When her father received a new vicarage, and the family moved, he wrote he would not be able to visit her there. She did not see him again until he came to take her to Gretna Green.

"That is enough! I will not be your mistress, Lord Winnington."

He laughed. "No, I do not want a mistress. I already have one of those. Of course, I had to break it off now that I am leaving the country..." Winnington's voice trailed off and left Cassie cold.

Humid air squeezed at her lungs. Fear sped up her heartbeat. His words drummed in her head like the raindrops upon the roof. A silent storm brewed inside while a raging storm blew outside. Something terrible was about to happen.

* * *

Pelting cold rain pierced William's face, and whipped his body, but he pushed on. The lack of visibility forced him to slow down. He could not risk the life of his horse, or an unforeseen accident, which might prevent him from reaching London on time.

On time for what? The lack of information disturbed William, and scratched at the back of his consciousness. Why would his family send such an elusive missive? The new footman failed to know anything at all. He claimed to have been given the missive and told to ride like the devil to deliver it.

If something happened to Mary, he would have sensed it. Nothing reached him except the odd feeling this mission was all wrong, but his twin sister often behaved recklessly, and put herself in unnecessary danger. He imagined a fall from a horse, or a tree. He envisioned her lying on the ground, broken and pale, with the life drained from her, but he shook the vision away because it did not bear thinking.

He dared race to London, to push Mirabelle as fast as possible, but the mud and muck, along with the senseless pouring of rain, slowed him to a near crawl. He was suddenly glad he had not allowed Cassie time to dress and accompany him. In her condition, she did not need to be out in this weather.

William pushed on, and prayed as he followed the muddy London road.

* * *

Winnington reached down and yanked Cassie up by her arms, then pressed her against him. She screamed as his mouth crashed down on hers, and drowned out the sound. Struggling to free herself, she stomped on his foot. He ignored it.

She tried to pull free of his grasp, but his hands held her like manacles. He broke the kiss and pushed her down on the couch. She wiped her mouth with the back of her hand. Anger and fear twisted her stomach into knots as she yelled, "Why did you do that?"

"It pains me to know you have been in another man's bed," he sneered.

"Lord William is not another man. He is my *husband.*" She clasped her trembling hands until her knuckles turned white.

"Yes, well, we shall rectify that mistake." He paced in front of her, with his hands clasped behind his back. "Once we are in America, we can change our identities. No one will ever know."

"What?" She watched his movements twitch, and noticed the shine in his eyes. *Good heavens, he was mad.* "You cannot be serious?"

"Do not worry your pretty little head over it, my dear. I will take care of everything. If only this incessant rain will stop." He stopped and turned towards her. "We will have to leave now, before Lord William returns. Although I imagine he is still plodding his way to London in this horrid weather."

"How do you know he is on his way to London? And what do you mean we will have to leave? What madness is this?" She started towards the door, but he grabbed her arm and yanked her back to him.

"Stop acting like a ninny, Cassandra. I am rescuing you from your sham of a marriage. I am afraid you will not have time to pack, but no matter, I will buy you everything you need once we reach our destination."

This had gone far enough. Her entire body shook with outrage. "I will not go anywhere with you. I want you to leave *now!*" She tried to free herself from his painful grasp, but he fell to his knees and wrapped his arms around her legs. He held her to him, and placed his head on her stomach.

"I will never let you go." Sobs tore from his throat and she swayed from the uncomfortable position he held her in. She was forced to grab onto to his shoulders to keep from falling to the floor. He cried like a baby and kept his grip.

"You must let me go," she pleaded. *This could not be happening.* He was like an out of control, willful child. To think, if she married him instead of Lord William, how her life might have been with this ridiculous man as her husband.

"Never. You are mine! Mine. You were promised to me and I shall have you."

He kissed her stomach through the fabric of her dress, and she shuddered with disgust. She pushed on his shoulders, and tried to wiggle out of his grasp, but the movement caused her to lose her balance.

Cassie landed on the floor with a thud. Winnington fell on top of her, and before she could react, his mouth found her breast. She pushed at his head. "Get off of me!"

Instead, he yanked her bodice down and released her bare breast. His mouth descended at the same time his hand covered her mouth, and muffled her scream. He sucked her breast as she pounded his shoulders and back. Her legs were trapped by his body, which prevented her from kicking him.

He lifted his head and grinned. "We do not have time for this Cassandra. I will pleasure you to your heart's desire later." He replaced her bodice, but did not remove his hand. "I suspect you might scream, but I am warning you, if you do, I will not wait to take you. I will have you here, on the floor. It is not exactly romantic, but I will do what I must to keep my wife in line."

He removed his hand and she screamed as he crashed his hand back over her mouth. His light blue eyes turned dark and his face became red with anger. He forced apart her legs with his body, and thrust his arousal between them. *Surely he did not intend to rape her?* If only one of the servants would come into the room, or William would return.

"Are you going to scream?"

She shook her head no, so he removed his hand and replaced it with his mouth. Sobs tore from her throat as he forced his tongue into her mouth. She choked on the uninvited invasion. His lower region rubbed against her intimately while his hand squeezed her breast. She fought him, not expecting him to let up, and fearing the worse, when he suddenly jumped up.

He stood over her as she lay on the floor. Shocked, she stared up at him. Cassie started to push herself up when her eye caught a glint of metal.

He pointed a pistol at her. "I hoped it would not come to this, but it appears your time with Lord William has brainwashed your mind. Now slowly get up and do not make any sudden moves."

"Why are you doing this?" she whispered as she returned to her feet. She recalled him bragging once about his ability to hit his target with pistols. She could not risk the baby growing inside of her.

Think. Perhaps she could use reason talk her way out of this madness. Except he was not a reasonable man. He was a madman! How had she misjudged him so?

"I love you. I have loved you since the first moment we met. I planned my life with you, but you lost patience, and married someone else. Why did you do that to me?" His hand shook and she flinched.

Cassie was speechless, but oddly enough, she noticed the lull in the rain, and the incredible silence and stillness. The afternoon sun hid behind dark clouds, but allowed just enough light to escape and encase the drawing room in murky shadows.

She grasped for time to make him see reason. "I did not think of the consequences to my family, to Jocelyn. I brought disgrace upon their heads. You must understand that."

He sighed then pointed the pistol to the floor. She let out a pent up breath.

"Why did I listen to you? If we would have continued on to Gretna Green, you would be Lady Winnington right now. My uncle was right. Women do not know what is good for them. We men have to protect you from yourselves." He raised the pistol at her again. "Go."

"Please, Lord Winnington. You cannot mean to go through with this," she pleaded.

"Enough!" He came closer and placed the gun at her back. "Move."

They walked out the door and down the stairs. Margie entered through a side door into the foyer. "Oh, my lady. Is there something I can get for you?"

"I am taking Lady William on a ride." He pressed the pistol into her back.

"In this weather?" Alarm crossed Margie's face.

"Lord Winnington is going to help with Lady Anne's home for orphans. We are having a committee meeting today, rain or shine." Cassie's voice quivered. She prayed Margie would realize something was wrong and send for the magistrate. "When Lord William returns, remind him about the meeting. I do believe he forgot."

"We should hurry while the rain has stopped." A slight push forced her forward. Cassie silently mouthed the word help.

"Of course, my lady. Do be careful." Margie curtsied and ran from the room. She was Cassie's only hope.

Sprinkles of rain touched Cassie's face as Lord Winnington rushed her out the door to his phaeton. The wind whipped her dress, and she wished she had her cloak. The fashionable phaeton did not provide much protection from the elements. She shivered as Winnington set the horses in motion.

Chapter Eighteen

THE RAIN LULLED AND ALLOWED William a chance to gallop his horse down the London road. For the past quarter hour, he worked on the bothersome puzzle within his mind. The handwriting on the missive troubled him. He did not recognize it, nor did he look at it again to study it. He had not thought to bring it with him, but instead, he gave it to Cassie.

The note was short and to the point. Unsigned. Perhaps it was written by a servant, but he could not imagine any member of his family leaving such a task to a member of their staff. No, one of his family must have written it. What if none of the family members were home?

Nothing about the message made sense. The footman said he was new to the staff. If so, then why would he be entrusted with such an important message? Yet, the man wore the Camberley livery.

He saw a coach and four in the distance heading his way. He slowed down then moved over to the side to allow the travelers to pass. As the coach neared, he noticed the Camberley crest, and his heart dropped to his stomach as a sick sense clawed his insides. He moved into the middle of the road and waved at the coachman to heed.

Why would a family member travel on the road out of London if Mary were in London hurt? At that moment, the rain came down hard enough to give him a thorough second soaking which interfered with his visibility. He cursed the skies as he waited for the coach to come to a stop. William jumped off of his horse, ran to the coach, and yanked the door open.

Stephen sat inside, "William! What the hell are you doing?"

"Mary?"

"What about Mary? Why are you riding out in the rain? Or did you get caught? I was on my way to see you. Mother was quite concerned when you and Cassie left Town with hardly a word or reason."

"Stop blathering, damn it! Is Mary alright?"

"Of course she is alright. Why would not she be?"

The hairs on the back of William's neck prickled. "She is not hurt?"

"What the bloody hell are you talking about? I just came from Camberley House not an hour ago. She was taking tea with Mother."

"I received a note from the new footman. It came unsigned. The missive said Mary was hurt." William's heart raced.

Stephen sat up straighter as alarm registered on his face. "New footman? There is not a new footman. As you know, Father handed the responsibility of hiring new staff over to me. And Mary is not hurt. Who would send you such a note and why?"

"If only I knew the answer to that question."

"Tie your horse to the back. We will go on to Rosehill Manor. I would like to see the missive and this supposed footman."

"I doubt our *new footman* will still be there." William clenched his fists at his sides. Why would someone want to lure him to London? *Cassie.* A sense of dread clutched his heart.

"Ever since Winnington made a threat against you, I arranged to keep an eye on him. He booked a cabin for two passengers to America. The ship leaves tomorrow morning. Considering he just came into his title recently, I thought it odd for him to leave the country now," said Stephen.

Winnington. William wondered if he sent the false missive. But, why? Panic reached up and grabbed him around the throat. Thunder rumbled and the rain came down harder. This damnable rain would slow them down. He could move faster if he rode Mirabelle.

"What are you thinking?" he asked.

"Winnington blabbers when he is drunk, and apparently he was deep in his cups again two nights ago. No one took him seriously, considering his state of mind and all, but now I am wondering if he was not boasting after all. He carried on that he would steal your bride away because she was betrothed to him first. Perhaps he did have a plan in place."

"I will kill the bastard."

* * *

Cassie noticed they were on the road to London. The lull in the rain did not last long, and the skies soon opened up. Her teeth chattered from the cold drenching as Winnington chattered nonstop. She considered jumping out of the moving vehicle, but thought better of it. He could stop and overtake her, and really, she did not want to risk breaking her neck or hurting the baby.

Placing a hand on her stomach in a protective gesture, she searched for a way out of this ridiculous situation. She gripped the seat in response to Lord Winnington's reckless driving, and hoped fate did not deal a cruel hand and throw her out of the phaeton. They moved at a dangerous clip, considering the hard rain and sticky mud.

"Could you slow down please?" she asked.

Winnington ignored her and kept going at an alarming speed. At least he put his pistol away. If she escaped him in London and made her way to Camberley House she would be safe. She did not have any money on her, and would be unable to hire a hackney, but she was strong and could walk. She prayed an opportunity presented itself.

"Once we are in America, we will change our names to Mr. and Mrs. Parker. I hear Boston is a modern community. We will buy a house and settle in. It shall be a grand adventure." Winnington talked in this vain the entire time. Cassie believed his mind slipped and wondered how she could get him back to reality.

"What about your mother and sisters?" she asked.

"Do not worry. I set them up for life. They are fine."

Perhaps she could appeal to his sense of responsibility and honor. "And what of your title, and your responsibilities to your estates?" She pressed her nails into the palms of her hand to keep from reaching over and throttling the man. He might become angry and shoot her right here on the London road. Cassie bit her lip until she tasted blood.

"Lord Winnington, I am cold and wet. Could not we find shelter until the storm passes?"

"Call me Miles."

"What?"

"Call me by my given name, Cassandra. *Miles*. I want to hear it on your lips." He turned and smiled at her as if they did not have a care in the world.

She suppressed the temptation to argue or refuse. Battling with him might tempt him to do something drastic. How far would he go if she pushed him? The edge of a cliff came to mind. It was better to try and appease her kidnapper. He might give her the moment she needed to escape. "Miles," she whispered.

"Much better. I am sorry for your discomfort. Once we are in London, you can have a hot bath and change of clothes. I took the liberty of purchasing a traveling wardrobe for you."

The very idea unnerved her as she wondered how long Lord Winnington had planned this farce. How long would it take William to discover the missive was fake? Would he return home right away? She retraced the events of the day in her mind. William left for London first thing this morning. He should have arrived and discovered the truth at this point. He may be headed down the London road in her direction.

Hope swelled before bursting into bits. If they crossed paths with William, Lord Winnington might shoot him, or her, or both of them. *Oh dear God.* She closed her eyes and prayed for Lord Winnington to come to his senses. *Please let William stay in London.* She prayed for a way out of this tangle that she may return home in to the arms of her husband.

The strong desire to have William's arms around her shook her to tears. She forced down the great gulps of air that threatened to rise into sobs. Salted tears ran down her face in the disguise of raindrops. Her love for William and their child dominated her mind for the next half hour. Winnington kept quiet, leaving her in solitude with her turbulent thoughts, which matched the horrendous storm.

Why did everything have to turn so very wrong when William finally came to her? At last, she had hope they might make something of their marriage, something beyond convenience. Now, she wondered if she would ever see her husband again. Would she be able to escape her captor? Or would she be forced to go to America and live with Winnington as his wife? Bile rose up her throat, and she covered her mouth with her hand then swallowed it back down. *No, no, no.* She would not go to America with Winnington, but instead, she would find a way to escape him.

Cassie shivered from the cold rain. If Winnington did not shoot her, she may very well collapse from lung fever. Regret ate away at her. She loved William, yet, she never told him, and he believed she loved Winnington. What if he thought she left with him because she wanted to go, not because he forced her with the gun? Hopefully,

Margie would figure out her predicament and report the truth of the situation to William. If he thought the worst of her though... well, it did not bear thinking.

Surely, after last night William would know in his heart he could trust her. She may not have told him she loved him, but she was certain she showed him.

* * *

Stephen placed his hand on William's shoulder. "Stay calm. Panic will only serve to keep you from reasonable thought. If Winnington goes to Cassie, do you think she would willingly go with him?"

William's mind churned with memories as his marriage flashed before his eyes, both the good and the bad, but mostly, he envisioned last night. She swore to him she did not want Winnington, and he believed her. "No, she would not."

William believed her and trusted Cassie. He knew in his heart she had not lied. The weight of the burden of his trust in her, lifted from his mind, and changed to a deep, compounded fear. What if Winnington took her against her will?

He rubbed his throbbing temples. "We cannot rely on assumptions. We do not know for sure Winnington is responsible for the false missive. But, if not, then who and why?"

"My instincts tell me Winnington is behind the fake message. I am afraid the man is possessed with his former betrothed. *Your* wife."

William's imaginings took a sinister turn. He remembered the night of the ball when he found Winnington's hands on his wife. Cassie's fear streaked face came to him. At the time, he assumed she was fearful of being caught in a tryst with her lover, but, now, he understood her fear came from something else. His innocent wife was attacked and he accused her of a sinful wrongdoings. He was no better than Winnington, and most certainly a fool. William banged on the coach rooftop and demanded the coachman speed up.

"Stay calm. Cassie is most likely at Rosehill Manor sitting cozily by the fire."

"I love her." He had not meant to say it out loud, but there it was. The words had sat on the edge of his consciousness for some time

now. He tried to hide from them, tried to close them out of his mind, to keep them from invading his heart, but they were there all along. *He loved her.* From the first moment he laid eyes on her, he believed her his angel.

He closed his eyes against the pain. He saw her with her golden curls down to her waist, naked in all of her glory, smiling a brilliant ray of sunshine. The fresh scent of lemons wafted through the carriage. No wonder Winnington was obsessed! He might act just as rash if their positions were reversed. No longer able deny his feelings, he confessed he loved his wife.

Regret swelled inside, and left him empty and numb. Last night, he made love to her, and attempted to show her he loved her, but he never said the words. With four sisters, he understood the importance of words to women. He should have said the words. Three simple words, but no, he held back, afraid of being hurt, or rejected by his wife.

William slammed his fist into his thigh. That ridiculous curse affected him more than he would admit. After a series of rejection, he began to question his judgment. The curse scratched at him, wormed its way into his heart and soul, and gave him an excuse for his actions. When he married, the curse ended. *Cassie* did not reject him. She did marry him after all, and, then, out of his own ridiculous fears, he rejected her. He turned his back on his wife. He opened the door for another man to slip in, and this allowed Winnington to continue his obsession.

Now, the damn blackguard might have her in his clutches, and only heaven knows what he would with her. He could not bear to think about it. Impatience shook him, and he clenched his jaw against it. The rain beat against the roof of the coach, and the scent of humid, earth-washed air permeated deep into his lungs. He attempted to calm himself, as the coach came to a shuddering stop.

*   *   *

The wind whipped the stinging rain into Cassie's face. Lightning lit up the darkened sky, and thundered rumbled overhead. "Misery" was the only word she could think of to describe the wretched experience. How much more could she take of the elements or the insanity?

She took hold of Lord Winnington's arm. "Miles, we must find shelter. It is too dangerous to travel."

He cursed under his breath, "There is an inn a little further up. I suppose we can stop there, but I warn you, you will not say or do anything to bring suspicion on our heads."

"No, of course not. I just want to get out of the rain and warm up. We are both soaked through." She tried to look ahead, to see how far to the inn, but the rain came down in thunderous sheets.

The rain and mud forced Winnington to slow down. She prayed the inn was not too far away. Despite his warnings, Cassie planned to stay alert for an opportunity to escape his clutches.

Lightning crackled in the sky, and charged the air, as it prickled Cassie's cold-numb skin. The horses startled forward so quick that Winnington lost control and fumbled the reins. She held onto the sides of the seat as the horses galloped at a dangerous speed, which caused the phaeton to perilously balance on one side or the other. The wild ride tumbled and tossed her back and forth like a child running with a pull-toy.

"Hold on!" Winnington reached over and grabbed the reins as one of the horses lost its' footing and went down. The vehicle crashed into the rear of the horses and rolled to its' side, sending Cassie and her captor flying through the air.

In slow movement, she watched her life pass before her. She saw herself as a child running through the fields with Jocelyn. Cassie reached out to her parents, but their faces melted in the distance, only to be replaced by the face of her husband. She cried out with joy then horror as she realized she might die.

Cassie braced herself for death and prayed for the life of her child. She cursed Winnington for his stupidity as she hit the muddy ground and shattered. Pain radiated throughout her body, and she wondered how many of her bones snapped. She clutched her stomach and begged God to at least save her baby.

A savage cry echoed through the relentless rain, as Cassie lay on top of Winnington. She lifted her head and met his lackluster eyes set deep into his pale face.

"Miles! Miles!" She grabbed his jacket collar and shook him. "Are you hurt?"

He lifted his hand to her her cheek. "Forgive me, my love." His hand dropped to his side, and his eyelids closed as the life drained from his body.

She shook him harder. "No! Oh, Miles, no. Do not die, do not die!" Cassie reached into her fog clouded mind, and tried to break through the cloudy edges. If only he would have let her be and gone on with his life.

Anger swelled as she pounded at his chest. She sobbed and cried with grief for all that was lost. She feared for the child growing inside of her since she doubted she could survive the fall and the weather.

Cassie pushed Winnington's dead body away from her and rolled to her side. A sharp, searing pain coursed through her shoulder, but she turned anyway and sank her face onto the soaked ground. Every inch of her body hurt. She thought of William one last time before the darkness claimed her.

* * *

"What the hell are we stopping for?" William banged on the roof and waited for a reply from the coachman.

"There is a wrecked carriage ahead, my lord."

The blood drained from his entire body and left him frozen in time. The months of his marriage passed before him: Cassie as she stepped from her father's carriage that fateful first night, her golden curls spread across his pillow, her smile and laughter, and the fear in her tear stained face after Winnington attacked her. He shoved the carriage door open and jumped into the rain.

The mud sucked at his boots, and made it difficult to run, but he used every muscle in his body to propel himself forward, toward the carriage, and his wife.

He pictured her broken body lying in the road, with the life draining from her. A savage wail tore from his throat as his body moved quickly, yet in slow motion. There was a downed horse and two people in the mud. One was a woman.

William picked up his feet and moved faster, and prayed like never before. *Please God let her live.* To find his one true love, and then lose her seemed a cruel fate. And oh, the time he wasted that he could have spent loving her. He cursed his own foolishness and damnable luck. He cursed the curse that hung over his head.

As he came closer to the accident he saw Cassie's limp body in the mud. His heart hammered in his chest, and a cry escaped his throat. William fell on his knees next to his wife.

"Cassie! Cassie, do you hear me?" He took her pulse, then praised God in Heaven when he found a steady, pulsing beat. He moved his hands across her body, and searched for broken bones. Once he assessed her, he lifted her into his arms and turned towards the carriage.

Stephen rushed up to him. "Is she alive?"

"Yes, thank God, yes." He continued past Stephen until he reached the coach. John Coachman opened the door and he gently laid her on the seat. He stripped off her wet clothes and threw them onto the floor, then he wrapped her in blankets and cradled her in his lap.

William tenderly rocked his wife's body, willing her awake. He refused to leave her as Stephen and the coachman removed the broken phaeton out of the road. He hoped Winnington was dead in the mud where he belonged. If not, he would kill him by driving a rapier through his heart and send him to hell.

The coach door opened and Stephen poked his head in. "We've cleared the road enough to pass by. One of Winnington's horses is dead, but the other is alive and able to move on. Winnington his dead, of course. We tied him across his horse. I will take Mirabella, and lead Winnington's horse to Rosehill Manor where we can send for the magistrate." Stephen shut the door as the coach lurched forward.

Chapter Nineteen

*W*ILLIAM CARRIED CASSIE in his arms as he burst through the doors of Rosehill Manor. A footman, standing sentry, lost his composure when he saw his master and lady. William paused to order the man to fetch the doctor.

He carried his wife up the stairs to her bedchamber. Katie sat in a chair by the fire mending a gown when William exploded through the door. Her face turned white when she saw her mistress, but she quickly jumped up to assist.

"What happened?"

"She was in a carriage accident in the rain. Bring me towels and her warmest nightgown."

William removed the damp blankets from his wife's body, and briskly rubbed her body down with towels. Katy worked to dry her mistress' hair and wash the mud from her face. Cassie's skin was pale and new bruises appeared all over her body. They dressed her in her nightgown, and covered her with thick quilts, while the housekeeper stoked the fire to roaring.

William placed his fingers at her pulse and put his ear to her heart. *Alive.* He pulled a chair next to the bed and collapsed into it. *Please, Cassie, wake up.* If Winnington were not already dead, he would kill the bastard with his bare hands.

"My lord, you are just as soaked as my lady. You must dry off and change before you are in the bed as well. I will watch over her and call for you if there is any change. *Please.*" Katie wrung her hands and worry etched across her brow.

He wanted to stay beside Cassie, forever and always, but he heard the truth in Katie's words. If he caught lung fever he would be no good to his ailing wife. Besides, only a door separated their rooms. Reluctantly, he left Cassie in her maid's care while he dried off and changed.

He stripped his wet clothes and thought about the time he wasted. He prayed for Cassie's full recovery, and swore to himself he would give her the loving attention she deserved. Guilt pressed him as he recalled how he ignored his wife, and flaunted Lady Quartermane in her face, in front of the entire *ton*.

William stood by the fire and dried his naked body with towels in the same brisk manner he dried his wife. He rubbed his wet head until his hair was dry, then ran his fingers through it to tame it. He dressed in buff breeches and a white shirt, but did not bother with a cravat or boots.

He padded back into Cassie's bedchamber, but she looked the same as before. Her milky white skin was translucent, and the only colors on her skin were bruises of black, blue, and green.

"At least she is not feverish, my lord."

"True. Please go and wait for the doctor. I will stay with her now."

"Yes, my lord." Katie curtsied and exited the room.

William bent over Cassie and touched her cool skin. He agreed with Katie. Her golden locks fell into one long braid across her shoulder and over the top of the quilt. He picked up the end of her braid and ran his thumb over the silky ends.

He loved running his hands through her golden tresses. He loved her lemony scent. He loved everything about her. Her loved her smile and laughter, her kind heart, as well as the way she carried herself with poise and grace.

A tear escaped William's eye and ran down his cheek. He swiped it away, dropped the braid, and slumped in the chair beside her bed. His lashes lay wet beneath his closed eyes. The only thing he ever wanted in life was a wife and children. Not a conventional marriage of convenience, but one of love and mutual respect.

Damn the curse to hell! Believing in an ancient curse went against the very grain of his soul. How ridiculous to live one's life believing in such nonsense. After he received several rejections to his marriage proposals, doubt crept into the corners of his mind.

The twelfth rejection had grated on him. He might have understood if he was ugly, poor, or from a scandalous family, but he was quite handsome, rich, and from a powerful and respectable family. Regardless, he was determined not to let a little curse keep him from his goal.

And then Cassie came into his life. He fell in love the moment he laid eyes on her. She was an angel from heaven with her golden crown of glorious hair, celestial beauty, and green eyes. She did not reject him. If anything, she gave of herself and begged him to do the same.

He cursed himself for rejecting Cassie. He turned from her before giving her a chance to refuse him. If she awakened, he would spend the rest of his life making up for his foolishness.

A soft knock at the door revealed Katie and Dr. Ainsworth. William greeted the doctor as he entered the room. "Ainsworth."

"Lord William." Ainsworth bowed. "What happened?"

"She was in a carriage accident and was soaked through from the rain. She is unconscious."

"What the devil was she doing out on a day like this?"

William bristled. "She was taken by force by her former betrothed, Viscount Winnington. He is dead. Killed when his phaeton crashed."

"Serves the blackguard right. Now leave and let me conduct my examination." Ainsworth set his bag down beside the bed and removed the covers from Cassie's body.

William did not want to leave, but the look Ainsworth gave him left no room for argument. "I will wait outside the door. Oh, by the way Ainsworth, she is with child."

He followed Katie out the door then paced the hallway floor as he held onto hope. Stephen, thoroughly soaked, stomped down the hall. His brother clasped him on the shoulder and asked, "How is she?"

"The doctor is in with her now. She has not awakened."

"Once the rain clears up and makes it safe to ride, I will send word to Camberley House and to Cassie's parents." Stephen shivered from the cold, damp weather.

"Katie, show Stephen the blue bedchamber so that he may dry off and change. Did you bring clothes along, or should I loan you some?"

"I have a small trunk. Listen, I brought back Winnington and sent for the magistrate. The body has already been fetched and carried off."

"Good. I do not even want his dead body in my house, or else I might kill him again." William clenched his fists to keep from punching the wall. Rage boiled below the surface of his deep concern for his wife.

"I will return in a few minutes." Stephen pressed his lips together and patted William's shoulder before going to change.

William sat down on a mahogany bench against the wall, and held his head in his hands. He rubbed his face and tried to make sense of everything, but in truth, nothing made sense to him.

He waited for half an hour before Stephen returned and sat next to him in silence. Margie brought tea and sandwiches, but William could not stomach anything. Stephen, however, finished off the plate.

Finally, Dr. Ainsworth opened the door, and William bound out of his seat. "How is she?"

"Nothing is broken, and her pulse is weak, but steady. She is still unconscious."

"Will she make it, Dr. Ainsworth?" asked Stephen.

Ainsworth took a deep breath. "The longer she stays unconscious, the riskier things become, and of course, if she gets a fever, that will complicate matters. If she does not awaken within the next few hours, I will become gravely concerned."

"She has to awaken." William stated through gritted teeth. "What about the babe?"

"Everything appears to be intact. There are not any ruptures or bleeding. If Lady William wakes up and receives the proper nourishment, I believe the babe will survive," said Dr. Ainsworth.

"Thank you, doctor. I will have a bedchamber arranged for you, so that you may attend her when she wakes up." He strode into the room and sat in the chair at her bedside. He forgot to arrange for the doctor's room, so he got back up to pull the bell pull. Katie arrived before he crossed the room. "Arrange a room for Dr. Ainsworth, and let Cook know we have two guests."

"Of course, my lord." Katie waited a second before asking, "Is she going to live, my lord?"

"Yes."

Relief washed over the maid's face as she curtsied and left. He crossed the room and sank back into the chair. He suddenly wished he had ordered Katie to bring him a brandy, but as usual, his brother knew what he needed most, and pushed a glass into his hand.

"Thank you," he said.

"The storm has passed. I sent a couple of footmen out to send word to our family and Cassie's. You look tired. I can sit with her awhile so that you may rest."

"No, I will stay with her, but thank you. I am glad you are here."

Stephen rested a hand on his brother's shoulder. "I will say a prayer for her before I retire. I think I will go find a book in your library and go to my room. Send word if she awakens, or if you need me."

"Yes, of course."

William squirmed in the uncomfortable chair, and swore to purchase a new, larger chaise with soft cushions. He reached over and picked up his wife's copy of *Pride and Prejudice* from her bedside table. *It is a truth universally acknowledged, that a single man in possession of a large fortune must be in want of a wife.* No truer words were ever spoken, or so he thought. He wanted a wife, and not because he possessed a huge fortune, but because he had a dream.

And he did not want any wife; he wanted an angel—*Cassie*. He read her book because she read it. He read it aloud and wondered if she heard his voice. Could he call her back to the living and tell her he loved her? He wanted to remind her she carried *his* child. She would fight to live, so her child could live. This much he knew about her.

William spent the night reading and talking to her. He talked about their future, decorating the nursery, taking walks through the gardens, riding across the hills and through the forest, and spending nights together in each other's arms. He talked until the edges of twilight cast golden shadows across the room through the slit of the heavy draperies.

He rubbed the sleep out of his eyes with the palms of his hands, and stretched his aching back. Still, Cassie slept, unmoved. He reached over to place a hand on her chest as he waited for the rise and fall that came with breathing. *She lived.* A dry swallow caught in his throat.

"Cassie. Cassie, do you hear me sweetings? It is time to wake up now, Cassie," he choked out with raw emotion. He thought he heard the faintest of sighs. He sat beside her on the bed and took her hand in his. Her long, slender fingers, with their manicured nails were cool to the touch. He saw the blueness of her veins through her milky skin. He rubbed her hand between his and called to her once more.

She did not sigh or move or even twitch. She lay as still as death. He wanted to shake her, to force her to open her eyes, to make her come back to him. He touched her face, and ran a finger across her soft pink lips. *So beautiful!* He took in a deep breath, then stood and crossed the room to look out the window.

He pushed the heavy peach drapes open, and allowed the early morning light to flood the room. Cassie's bedchamber window overlooked a small rose garden, now blooming with fragrant flowers in every color. He decided to have the roses cut and placed in vases around her room. Her room would be cheery, full of sunshine and life.

Sometime later, William heard a light tap at the door, and Katie entered with a breakfast tray. "You must eat something, my lord. Keep up your strength." She set the tray in front of him, then he sent Katie to speak to the gardener about filling the room with roses. He was hungry, so he ate all of his hearty meal before Dr. Ainsworth and Stephen arrived.

"How is she?" Stephen asked.

"The same, although I thought I heard a sound from her this morning, but perhaps it was wishful thinking."

"At least she is not feverish. She must awaken or risk starving to death. We can try sitting her up and spooning soup into her mouth, but she might not swallow it," said Dr. Ainsworth.

"It is worth a try." William went to the bell pull to ring for a maid. A few minutes later he ordered a bowl of broth and a cup of tea.

They propped Cassie up and surrounded her with pillows. They jostled her around and she moaned, but did not open her eyes. William believed it a good sign. He insisted on feeding her, although Katie came and held her head as he attempted to spoon the broth into her mouth. Most of it dribbled down her chin, but she swallowed some of the liquid. Katie washed Cassie, then they worked together to change her into a clean nightgown.

She moaned again and turned on her side on her own. William sat by his wife's side and ran his fingers through her hair. The servants brought in vases of roses until the room burst with scent and color. He read aloud more of *Pride and Prejudice*, and talked about anything and everything from childhood stories, to ideas for improvements at Rosehill Manor, to the latest *on dits*.

Stephen joined William in Cassie's bedchamber for luncheon. A footman brought up a small table and two chairs so they could dine. Stephen talked in a hushed voice as he tried to help ease William's mind. He appreciated his brother's efforts, but, his eyes never strained too far from his wife.

Mrs. Chambers arrived, and clucked at him like a mother hen, then sent him off for a few hours of sleep. She promised to waken him if there were any change.

William kissed his wife before he left, and waited for her eyes to open, but alas, the tale of *Sleeping Beauty* was just that -*a fairy tale.* His sisters loved the stories, and they often insisted on hearing the tale from Elizabeth, the writer and storyteller in the family. He, too, heard the tale many times while trapped in a room, flanked by a sister on each side, who was determined to make him stay and listen as the prince kissed the girl and awakened her. If only his kisses had the same effect on Cassie.

A few hours later, William awoke from an exhausted sleep to Stephen's shoves. "William, come. Cassie has a fever."

He jumped up and ran into Cassie's bedchamber. His wife tossed and turned from side to side and moaned while her mother pressed wet rags to her forehead. He climbed atop the bed into a sitting position, then pulled her into his arms and held her.

"Where is Dr. Ainsworth?" he asked.

"He went for a walk in the gardens. I sent Katie to fetch him," said Mrs. Chambers.

"How long has she been like this?"

"Only a few minutes. She is burning up. We must get the fever down."

Cassie shivered against his warm body, as Mrs. Chambers wiped down her daughter's face, neck, and chest with cool cloths. Dr. Ainsworth arrived and the three of them worked together for the next several hours.

"You must fight Cassie. Think of our child, please. You cannot die," he pleaded with her, not caring that others witnessed his anguish. The only thing that mattered was that Cassie opened her eyes and her fever broke.

His wife's body finally relaxed and her breathing evened. "Her fever has broken."

Dr. Ainsworth touched her forehead with the back of his hand. "Yes, she is cool now, thank the good Lord. Let her rest for awhile before trying to feed her again. If she does not awaken soon, I cannot be sure she will make it."

"She will wake up, do you hear me?" William cradled Cassie in his arms, and then slid down beside her and held her against him through the night.

The sky broke before dawn, and William woke to the sound of moaning. With the candles extinguished, the smoldering embers in the fireplace gave the room its only light.

"William."

"Cassie? Cassie, are you awake?" He shook her shoulder slightly, but her eyes remained closed.

"William," she moaned.

"I am here, sweetings. I am here. Please wake up. Please come back to me." He embraced her tightly, and brushed her hair from her eyes with his fingers. He kissed her hot forehead.

William laid her head gently on the pillow and eased away from her body. He opened the door to the sitting room and called for Katie who slept on a cot. "Cassie's fever has returned. Fetch fresh cloths and water."

Katie's eyes opened wide, and she jumped up and ran out the door to do as he commanded without so much as a proper curtsy. He made a mental note to raise her pay for knowing her priorities.

A few minutes later Katie returned with cool cloths, and William began the task of washing Cassie down. He folded down the bed coverings and removed her gown. Her gloriously naked form was spread before him. She tossed her head and moaned his name, which consoled him somewhat.

By the time the morning light broke across the sky, Cassie's fever broke once again. They dressed her in a fresh gown then he fell asleep in the chair. It seemed only minutes went by when he woke again. She sighed and moved before her eyes fluttered and opened.

William sat beside the bed in the chair, stunned to see her misty green pools again. Moving to her side, he took her hand in his, and gently squeezed it. "Cassie."

"William."

"Thank God you are awake." He smoothed away the strands of hair from her eyes, and smiled as she blinked several times.

"Winnington."

"You must not concern yourself with anything Cassie. You have been very sick. Conserve your strength." He patted her hand.

"He is dead." She made the statement without regret in her voice.

"Yes," he said.

"He was mad."

"I am certain he was."

She closed her eyes a moment before they snapped back open and she cried out, "The baby! Oh, William, the baby!" She grabbed his hands and beseeched him with pleading eyes.

His heart nearly broke at seeing her in such distress. "The babe is fine."

She relaxed and fell back on the pillows as tears streamed down her cheeks. "I was so afraid."

"It is over, and you are here, awake, and all will be well."

"I pray you are right. I am so tired," she said.

"Rest."

And she did.

Chapter Twenty

CASSIE FLEW THROUGH THE AIR and landed with a thud in the cold mud. Rain poured over her like a never ending pitcher of water. She coughed, and sputtered, and choked on the taste of mud in her mouth. The sounds of whinnying horses and rumbling thunder tunneled through her ears, as a sharp swath of crackling light crossed her vision.

Winnington's white face appeared and blood gushed from his forehead, then dripped down his cheeks and flowed from his mouth. She screamed, but the sound was lost in the fury of the storm. "Forgive me, my love" echoed in her ears again and again. A crack of thunder shook the ground as the trees whipped in the wind. She lay in the mud, unable to move, or speak. She prayed for life, but expected death.

"Cassie...Cassie." William shook her until her eyes opened.

Alive. She was alive and her baby was still growing within her. She touched her stomach and wondered at the miracle. She closed her eyes and breathed in the scent of roses, and when she opened them she only saw William's blurred face. She blinked until he came into focus, and she could see the concern etched across his face. He looked so tired. She wanted to reach out and comfort him in her arms forever.

William had stayed by her side throughout her illness and filled her room to the brim with vases of flowers. She had vague memories of sitting up in bed, eating soup, and drinking tea. She remembered snatches of conversations, and passages of prose being read to her by the wonderful man she loved.

She wiped away a tear. "I am hungry."

He laughed. "Hungry? I have never heard such exquisite words. Shakespeare himself could not have written a more perfect line. What would you like, my love? You may have anything your heart desires."

My love. The words poured over her like warm honey and dribbled all the way down to her wiggling toes. He loved her. She was sure of it, and no longer did she need to hear the words in order to know. She wanted to tell him she loved him. She wanted to declare her love, and to spend the rest of her life showing him how much she meant the words.

But not yet. Not until she could leave her bed, bathe, change, and look her best. She was certain she would regain her strength soon. As soon as she had something decent to eat. "I would love roast beef and potatoes... and cake. Yes, I would dearly love some cake. I would also like a cup of tea, but not any soup, or at least not broth, but I would not mind some hearty stew."

"I will order a feast, but you must be careful not to overdo it. Dr. Ainsworth said you must slowly introduce food into your diet, or else you will become sick to your stomach."

"Alright then. Stew and cake."

William sent Katie down with the order then came back to sit next to her. Cassie noticed the creased lines in his face along with his disheveled appearance. Had he slept at all? "What day is it? How long have I been in this bed?" She moved to sit up. William helped and gave her plenty of pillows on which to relax.

"It has been four days. Four of the longest days of my life."

"I am sorry you worried over me, but I am fine. I just need to regain my strength, but it looks as if you need sleep. I doubt you have slept a wink since you brought me home. Oh, how did you find me?" The last thing she remembered was lying next to Winnington as he lay dying in the mud. She still ached all over.

"I was on my way to London when Stephen came down the road in his coach. He was coming to visit us, or more precisely, to check up on us. Apparently, Mother was concerned with our quick departure from Town. The missive was false, and the footman was a plant. I believe Winnington was behind it all. He wanted to get me out of the house so he could steal you away."

She nodded her head. "Yes, my thoughts exactly. He was completely irrational. I find it quite disturbing that I nearly married the man. I am such a poor judge of character."

William took Cassie's hands in his. "You could not have known. Winnington acted like a gentleman in the company of others, and only showed his true colors after we were married. Your parents agreed they never would have thought Winnington capable of such acts, and I believe they are as good a judge of character as any."

"My parents?"

"They came right away, and Jocelyn too, and well, the entire Prescott family. We have a house full of guests, my dear."

"Oh, and I must look such a fright." She touched her hair then wiped her hands across her face.

"You are the most lovely creature on God's green earth." He bent down to kiss her, but, before he made it to her lips there was a knock on the door. William lifted his eyes to the ceiling in obvious frustration. "Come."

Katie entered with a loaded tray full of food. Cassie's parents followed, and so did Jocelyn, then Lady Camberley and Anne. They fussed over her, but let her dig into the stew. She savored it as if it were the finest food ever eaten. She finished half the bowl then managed a few bites of cake.

Realizing she was tired, everyone left the room, except her mother, who insisted William get some rest. Cassie agreed and her mother kissed her cheek then hummed a lullaby from her childhood until precious sleep claimed her.

The next morning she awoke stronger and restless. She managed to get down a descent breakfast, then her mother and Katie helped her take a bath, wash her hair, and change into a day dress. All of this took a great deal of effort and left her exhausted, but she refused to stay bed bound. William carried her to the drawing room where she was surrounded by family.

"Cassie dear, it warms my heart to see you up and dressed. We were all so very worried. You gave us quite a scare," said Lady Anne.

Cassie grasped Anne's hands. "I am fine now. The entire ordeal is one I would prefer to forget."

"Yes, of course," said Anne.

"I, for one, cannot believe Mr. Parker, I mean, Lord Winnington, turned out to be such a blackguard. Thank goodness you married Lord William and not that madman. It makes one think twice about marrying a man you hardly know," said Jocelyn.

"I knew Lord Winnington longer than William." said Cassie.

"True enough, but I shall endeavor to know a man well before agreeing to marry," said Jocelyn.

"That sounds like a wise plan. I shall do the same," said Anne.

William appeared at that moment. "I thought you did not want to marry at all. All of my sisters seem quite determined to become lifelong spinsters."

"I never said I did not want to marry, William. I do not want to marry for convenience. I want a love match, and I shall not settle for less." Anne clasped her hands and pursed her lips.

William insisted on carrying Cassie to luncheon. Although she thought it was silly, she secretly enjoyed his attention. She was able to manage a portion of her meal, but must have a looked tired because her family insisted she return to her room to rest.

Once again, William swept her into his arms and carried her to her bedchamber. He helped her out of her gown and into the bed, then he locked the door and undressed. He climbed into the bed and cradled her next to his body. His warmth engulfed her, and she snuggled deeper under the covers to rest her head against his chest.

"Sleep now. You need your rest," he said.

She kissed his chest. "I am tired, but not sleepy."

"Then lay here with me. I just want to hold you."

"William."

"Hmmm."

"I love you."

The only sounds in the room were their heartbeats. He did not have to say the words. She could live without them as long as she lived with his arms wrapped around her.

William rolled her onto her back and came over her. His chocolate eyes shined with love and hope. He palmed her cheek with his hand and bent down to kiss her. She tasted the brandy on his warm lips, then she flicked her tongue across his open mouth and invited more.

He deepened the kiss and touched her tongue with his then explored her whole mouth. Their lips and tongues tangled and danced to a new tune—one of love, trust, and commitment. His lips left her mouth only to begin a trail across her jaw, cheeks, and eyelids.

He lifted away from her and buried his face in her neck. "I want to make love to you, but not until you regain your strength."

He pulled her against him and they both rested. She worried her bottom lip with her teeth, and refused to allow his lack of words to bother her. It was enough he was here holding her. She placed her ear against his heart, and listened to the the slow and steady beat matching her own. William ran a comforting hand along her back. She could stay in the warm and cozy bed snuggled up against her husband forever.

"I am sorry," he said.

Cassie lifted her head and gazed into his sad, worried eyes. "For what?"

"I allowed my own foolish jealousy to override common sense. I accused you of terrible things and treated you horribly. I am ashamed of my actions and my words."

"Oh, William." She reached a hand up to stroke his face.

He held onto her hand. "No, I mean it. By the time I met you I had started to believe that stupid curse. The mirror does not lie, you know. I am not spotted or fat, nor do I have a double jaw, or beady eyes. I thought perhaps I was dull, but truly, I do not think I am."

"You are handsome and witty and charming."

He laughed. "I also have a tendency to make a complete cake of myself. Did you know I proposed marriage to twelve women before I met you, and everyone of them turned me down? I do believe I hold the record."

"I heard, and I am ever so grateful, for if one would have accepted, I would not be lying here with you now." Cassie touched her lips to his. They shared a few tender kisses before she sighed and rested her head against his chest.

"I thought you were in love with Winnington."

"I was in the foolish first blush of love with *Mr. Parker*. I think more than anything that I was in love with the idea of being in love, and married with children. But, he became Lord Winnington, and, with the title came a different man. A man I did not know or even want to know. He was so unlike the man I thought I knew, and terribly frightening. I am so glad I did not marry him."

He kissed the top of her head. "So am I...so am I."

William cradled her in his arms as the one candle in the room flickered out, and the dying embers of the fire became their only light. She would love him forever, even if he did not love her, but, perhaps he would come to love her in time. Hurt hovered over her happiness, for in truth, she hoped he would confess his love, but she would have to make do with what he gave.

She would endeavor to be happy, and perhaps when her child came, he or she would be followed by a house full of children to love. Cassie blinked back moisture that threatened to expose her feelings.

"When I saw you lying in the road, in the mud, pale and broken, I thought you were gone. I thought it was too late to tell you what I feel, but your pulse was strong and steady. Then the long days and nights of waiting for you to awaken, of trying to get your fever down. I have never been so scared in my life."

She said nothing, but kissed his chest and ran her fingers lazily through his dark curls. She only desired to go forward after surviving such an awful ordeal.

"Three small words seems insignificant in comparison to how I feel, but I do not know any other words to express it. I love you, Cassie. I love you with all my heart and soul, and I promise you, I will spend the rest of my life proving it to you."

William tightened his hold and she snuggled deeper against him. He reached down and wiped away her tears and the past.

* * *

"What do you plan to do for the rest of the Season?" Stephen twirled his brandy in his glass.

"We will stay here. Take the time to get to know each, and wait for her lying in." William poured another glass and joined his brother. The study, his own personal sanctuary was one of his favorite rooms in Rosehill Manor.

An evening light beamed through the windows and danced across the mahogany floors. They sat in deep leather chairs grouped informally into a sitting area. Tonight, a celebratory dinner was arranged in Cassie's honor. Tomorrow, all of their relatives would return to their homes.

"Does that mean you have worked things out between you?"

William lived his life under the false impression marriage was easy. He had exemplarily models to watch as he grew up. His parents never hid their affections for each other, or their children, and certainly not from the *ton*. They broke the rules by attending Society events together, dancing with each other more than once in an evening, and smiling and flirting with each other in public.

Now, he knew better. His parents loved each other, and, when two people love each other, they are bound to experience a wealth of emotions such as anger, jealousy, and fear. Marriage required hard work, trust, and compromise; but most importantly, marriage required openness. He could not hide from his wife. From now on, he would face their troubles and talk to his wife when things bothered him.

"We will spend the rest of our lives working things out together, and I, for one, am glad of it. I made the mistake of not letting Cassie in, of not trusting her, or confiding in her. I know better now."

"I am not sure I understand it, but I am glad to hear it. Shall we join the ladies?"

They walked to the drawing room where his family waited for dinner. Cassie looked healthy and flush in her pink silk dinner gown. Her hair was swept high upon her head and surrounded by curls made of sunshine. Her green eyes sparkled with life. Their eyes met and held long enough for him to experience a charge of desire. William swallowed and privately promised to give his valet a raise for selecting the longer dinner jacket.

He started towards his wife when Anne grabbed his arm. "Shall we take a turn around the room brother?"

"Of course."

William would much prefer to go visit with his wife, but he would never purposefully hurt his sister's feelings. He escorted Anne about the perimeter of the drawing room. She looked particularly fetching tonight, dressed in a yellow gown the color of a rose in the evening light. Her fine figure and a lovely face embraced doe eyes, an upturned nose, and a well proportioned mouth. Some gentleman would someday sweep her off her feet.

His sisters avoided the marriage shackles as much as the men of the *ton*, but deep inside, he was quite certain they were romantics at heart, especially Anne. She would marry for nothing less than love. He smiled and waited for her to begin a speaking.

"I know you do not want to hear this, but I feel I must say it. I am convinced Cassie loves you. Leaving her alone has done great harm to her. She wants to make a go of your marriage, but she cannot do it alone. You must meet her halfway."

"Now see here, Anne..." William could say certain things to Stephen, Stephen was his brother, another man, but Anne, she was his sister, his *younger* sister, at that.

"Do not cut me off. Listen and listen well. Women want, no, they *need* romance. Flowers and picnics and random acts of thoughtfulness. Running off to your club all day, and doing, well...I do not know what men do at their clubs exactly, but I do know this is not the way to build a lasting relationship. You must talk to her, William. You have always desired marriage and children above all else. Do not lose your dream because of that silly curse and your foolish jealousy. Winnington is dead. You no longer need to consider him an adversary. Cassie is alive and with child. Go to her. Love her. Be a husband to her."

"Are you quite through?"

"Yes, as a matter of fact, I am." Anne let go of his arm and strode away as if they just shared a private joke.

Sisters! And he was *cursed* with four of them. Thank heavens the other three did not come. He would not know what to do if they decided to lecture him as well. Of course, his mother was just as willing to offer him advice. He headed back towards his and Cassie's families, who sat talking, laughing, and waiting for dinner. Both mothers were deep in conversation. Stephen and his father stood by the hearth, drinking their brandies and laughing. Anne had returned to Cassie and Jocelyn's side.

William hoped for a moment alone with his wife. At least he was able to escort her into dinner, but since they had guests, they sat at opposite ends of the table.

"Have you heard the most shocking *on dit* of the year?" William's mother, a walking gossip column who always knew the most recent London news, which included some of the most secretive and scandalous pieces of gossip.

"Do tell Mother." He knew by the placement of her hand on her heaving bosom that his mother was dying to share.

"The new Duke of Montford is an *American*."

Shocked gasps echoed throughout the room. There was dramatic pause of one, two, three. "Of course, he was not *born* an American, he was simply *raised* as an American."

"He sounds positively fascinating," Anne teased. William laughed at his mother's raised eyebrows and shocked expression.

"Why would a duke raise his son in America?" asked Mr. Chambers.

"Oh, he is not the old duke's son. He is the grandson. Years ago the duke and his son had a fallout, so the son took his family to America. They say the new duke is incredibly handsome."

"I do believe I shall swoon at his feet if we meet." Anne placed the back of her hand on her forehead and pretended to faint as everyone laughed.

William watched his wife enjoy herself. Cassie's beauty entranced him. The rest of the table fell away and it became just the two of them. She lifted her eyes to meet his. She positively glowed in the candlelight.

He had spent each night in her bed since they declared themselves to each other. They did not make love, but, instead, they held each other, shared kisses, and talked long into the night. He wanted to give her time to heal and fully recover from her injuries. Her bruises were gone now, and she was back to her old self—strong, and full of love and laughter.

Tonight.

He would go to her and love her in every way possible. *Damn.* He really should watch his own thoughts at the dinner table. He hardened painfully as everyone talked on.

Their families stayed until they were certain of Cassie's health and recovery. Although William made a point to spend time with his wife during the day, his time alone with her was as rare as a blue rose. Someone was always with her. A mother, or sister, or both, or all of them. He cherished the nights when they all retired to their beds.

He loved his mother and sister, and he respected his mother-in-law and young sister-in-law, but he looked forward to their departures. Yet, he would miss the company of his brother, father, and even his father-in-law. He enjoyed their heated political discussions and late night card games, but if their leaving meant more private time with his wife, he would gladly shake their hands goodbye.

"William. William." His mother's voice broke through his private thoughts.

"Yes, I am sorry. I do believe I was woolgathering. Not well of me at all."

"I asked you if you and Cassie planned to return to London soon."

"No. We have decided to stay at Rosehill Manor for the rest of the Season. The country air is much better for an expectant mother's constitution."

Squeals of delight bounced around the room. Stephen, Anne, and his mother were the only family members who knew their secret. The mothers jumped out of their seats, cried, fussed, and carried on over Cassie's condition. Jocelyn clapped with joy and Mr. Chambers blustered something nonsensical at the news of becoming a grandfather.

"Shame on you two for keeping this a secret. Why did not you tell us?" asked Mrs. Chambers.

"Well, in truth, we wanted to wait until Cassie fully recovered and Dr. Ainsworth could assure us all was well. Cassie was enceinte before the accident."

"Oh, dear heavens!" exclaimed Cassie's mother. "Thank the Good Lord for miracles. You could have lost the child."

He watched Cassie's pink cheeks turn white, and William was immediately incensed at his mother-in-law's insensitive comment. "We would prefer not to think of what could have happened, since it did not. Cassie and the babe are perfectly fine."

"Of course not, it is just that I am her mother. I should have known. She might have needed me."

"I am fine, Mother. I am alive. Our baby is well. Dr. Ainsworth said I can expect a healthy delivery."

Mrs. Chambers dabbed a handkerchief at her eyes. "Yes, dear, I am just so happy for you."

The conversation turned to babies and nurseries until the ladies made their excuses and left the gentlemen to their port.

"Do you have one of those fancy cigars boy?" asked Mr. Chambers.

William smiled. The reverend loved cigars, but he would catch hell for it later. "Are you quite brave enough to smoke one with your wife present?"

"She can fuss all she wants. I am going to be a grandfather. A man only becomes a grandfather for the first time once. A celebration is in order, and a cigar is the perfect way to celebrate."

They laughed, and William sent a footman to fetch cigars. They took their smokes to the veranda off of the study. The cool, night air was exactly what his heated body needed. Seeing his wife flushed in pink beneath the candlelight did more to his lower regions than he thought possible. He could not wait to retire for the evening.

They finished their cigars and joined the ladies in the drawing room. William made his way to Cassie's side, bowed and took her hand. "My lady, may I have a private word with you?"

"Yes, my lord."

They walked arm in arm over to the far end of the room. "You are looking tired, my dear. I do not want to overtire you. I think we should retire early."

Amusement flashed in the deep green pools of her eyes. She playfully slapped him on the arm. "Silly man, I am not the least bit tired. You worry too much."

"Oh, but I am certain you are exhausted. Too much so to stay a moment longer. We should make our excuses, and I should carry you up to *bed*."

Awareness dawned in her eyes. "Oh, yes, I *am* feeling a bit tired, now that you mentioned it. Too much excitement over dinner. Perhaps it would be best if I allowed you to carry me to *bed*." She joyously laughed, and his heart burst with happiness.

They stayed for another quarter of an hour before they made their exit, then practically racing up the stairs, and fell onto the bed laughing, kissing, and tugging at each other's clothes.

Chapter Twenty-One

CASSIE PUSHED AGAINST WILLIAM'S CHEST. "Wait."

"Wait?"

"Yes, wait. We have had precious little time alone. I think we should talk first."

William groaned and Cassie laughed. He was so hard he was near to bursting, and she wanted to talk. They had the rest of their lives to talk. They had all day tomorrow to talk. *Why now?*

He watched her bottom as she sashayed over to a chair and sat down."Poor me a glass of wine, darling."

Wine. She wants wine and talk. He walked over to the sideboard and poured two glasses of wine. Perhaps they could talk fast. He handed Cassie a glass and sat down in the seat opposite of her. "What would you like to *talk* about, sweetings?"

The laughter drained from her face. "You are angry."

"I am frustrated. *Sexually* frustrated."

Cassie's cheeks went from rosy to white then back to rosy. "Oh."

Now it was William's turn to laugh. "I am going to make love to you tonight, Cassie. I plan to explore every inch of you over and over again. You will not get much sleep." William swirled his wine in his glass then took a swallow.

"Oh." She reddened.

His wife looked like an angel. No, she looked like a goddess sitting on the large cushioned green chair with her feet tucked beneath her pink silk gown. Cassie leaned against the arm of the chair, and her bosom pushed over the tops of her bodice. She appeared relaxed and stunning. She took a sip from her glass then licked her lips.

He experienced pain in his lower region, and he worked hard to tamp down his lust. He might need to order a cold bath, or to go take a dip in the lake. She deserved a thorough loving, that was long and slow, and perfect. He would do his damndest to give it to her even if it killed him.

"How will we spend our days here at Rosehill Manor?" she asked.

"Hmm..."

"I am serious."

"I know. We still have several rooms to furnish and decorate, including the nursery. I suppose we will need to interview for a wet nurse and nanny."

"I will nurse my own baby, but I do suppose we need a nanny. I want to decorate the nursery in yellow. A child's room should be bright and cheery."

"Nurse your own child? That is beyond the pale, you know. My mother will have a serious case of the vapors when she finds out."

She laughed and her entire face became animated. He loved her smile. A perfect set of white teeth accompanied her luscious pink lips. *Talk.* She wanted to talk. "And there is estate business. I, I mean, *we*, own a great deal of farm land. We should get to know our tenants, find out their needs, and begin establishing community relationships."

"Oh yes. Times are hard right now. We should take them baskets of food," she said.

"Excellent idea. We can set Margie and her kitchen staff to the task tomorrow." William realized one of the things he loved most about his wife was her kind heart. He expected she would want to be involved in various charity events. She had already taken an active role in helping Anne with her orphan home project. "We should also get to know the local gentry. I have neglected to socialize with my neighbors thus far. I wanted to get the house in order first."

"Perhaps we should hold a dinner party. Lady Moreland called on me before we left London. She wanted to introduce herself to the new lady of Rosehill Manor. I believe she has returned to the country as well. I shall call on her tomorrow and obtain a list of the local gentry whom we must invite."

Cassie needed a sense of purpose, something to do besides sit around and wait for her husband to make an appearance. He neglected her in this. He would work to make amends, and perhaps, his guilt would eventually evaporate. "Besides, decorating and socializing, we will take walks in the gardens together, go on morning and evening rides, and picnic by the lake or in the secret garden. Make love in the secret garden..."

"Outdoors?" she exclaimed. He loved the blush on her cheeks.

"Outdoors. Take down your hair Cassie."

"What?"

"I want to watch you take down your hair." They already *talked* long enough.

She stilled for a moment, her chest heaved, her eyes studied him, and then she sat down her glass and sat upright. She pulled one pin from her hair. A long golden curl dropped down across her bosom. And then she removed the pins slowly, one after the other until each curl dropped and bounced, and every blonde strand of hair lay across her like a golden shroud, a glorious crown on the head of an angel.

"I love your hair."

"I need to brush it now."

"Allow me." He set his glass on the side table, then stood and offered her his hand. They walked through her bedchamber door, and he sat her in front of her vanity table and mirror. He picked up the brush and ran it slowly through her hair, stroking, ever so gently.

William watched Cassie's eyes in the mirror as he reached down, pulled her hair from the nape of her neck, and planted a kiss between her neck and shoulder. Her eyes widened as tremors shook her body. Delighted by her reaction, he kissed a path along her neck and ran his tongue along the outer edge of her ear. Her nipples tightened and pressed wantonly against the pink silk of her dress. The erotic sight set his own skin on fire, and his cock hardened beyond redemption.

William pulled the brush through her silken strands. "I love your hair, so soft, like silk." He put the brush down and ran his fingers through her hair, then he reached up and massaged her scalp. Cassie made a mewling sound from her throat. He pressed a strand of her hair to his nose. "You smell like lemons, like sunshine."

"I bathe in lemon water. Do you like it?" she asked.

"I love it."

She grabbed his hand and kissed his palm. He stepped back and helped her stand. Then she stretched, and pressed her breasts against his chest. She ran her slender fingers through his hair.

"I love your hair too. I hope our son has thick, soft hair like his father."

"I hope our daughter has golden curls like her mother."

William dug his hands into her hair and pulled her in for a kiss. He touched her lips with featherlike kisses then moved across her cheeks and eyes, and to the bridge of her nose. He trailed his way back to her luscious, sweet raspberries and cream mouth. He loved the taste of her, and dived in with his tongue, and explored her depths.

He pressed his desire against her, and she moaned and tightened her hold on his hair. He smiled in their kiss. "What do you want, sweetings?"

She kissed him with everything she was worth. He wrapped his arms around her and lifted her up off the ground. Their mouths merged and their tongues tangled in a sweet dance. He restrained from stripping her clothes from her body, and made a silent promise to love her slow and easy, until she burned with desire, and tipped over the edge.

He kissed her as if they had all the time in the world. Her little sighs made it difficult for him to control himself, but he was determined. He could spend a lifetime exploring the feel of her mouth against his, and indeed, he would do just that. He broke their kiss and leaned his forehead against hers, taking a moment to catch his breath, and to control his building desire to bury himself within her *now*. "I love kissing you."

"I love it when you kiss me." She whispered and wrapped her arms around his neck then plunged her hands into his hair. "Kiss me again?"

"I will do just that after I tell you that you are the most beautiful woman in the world. My very own angel."

"Well done. Now hurry up and kiss me."

And so he did. Breathless, scorching kisses that set their world on fire. He moved his hands down Cassie's back and cupped her bottom, and pressed his aching cock against her. She moaned as he kissed a trail down her neck, and across the swell of her breasts. He suckled a breast through her silk gown. She cried out and held him to her, as he continued to scrape his teeth across the thin fabric. He cupped her round bottom in his hands, and she wiggled beneath him. Not one to leave a job undone, he moved to her other breast and repeated his actions.

"Oh please, William, please," she begged.

William lifted his mouth from hers and pulled away. "Please what, Cassie? Say it."

She stared at him wide eyed, and breathed deeply. "I want you to make love to me."

"Oh, I am. I am."

He ran a finger down her cheek to the tip of her chin, then down her neck and across her breasts until his finger rested on the center of her cleavage. "Turn around." He removed his finger and stepped back.

Cassie eyed him warily, but did as he commanded. He pushed her hair over her shoulder and unfastened her dress, one button at a time. Once her dress was undone, he kissed a trail across her shoulder, then released the silk confection to slither down her body and pool to the floor at her feet. He followed the path with his hands and mouth before he returned to the nape of her neck.

She stood before him in her chemise, stockings, and slippers with her hair down to her waist, as the candlelight bounced off the golden strands. He reminded himself to breathe. His angel stood before him in all of her glory. For such a long time he believed he would never have her in this way. He dropped to his knees before her and wrapped his arms around her waist. He smothered her stomach in kisses through her chemise before he pulled back. "Lay your hands on my shoulders and give me your foot."

She followed his instructions, and he grasped her foot to slide off her slipper. Then he did the same to her other foot. He ran his hands up to the top of her leg, untied her stocking, and rolled the silk down her leg one inch at a time. He kissed and licked her leg above her stocking, all the way down to her ankle, then lifted her foot to remove her stocking completely. He did the same with her other stocking, taking his time, inching the silk down her leg. He followed with his mouth and tongue. She dug her nails into his shoulders as little mewling sounds escaped from her lips. Over and over again, he kissed and licked her leg until she collapsed to her knees.

They crashed to the floor and laughed, overwhelmed with love for each other. He wrapped his arms around her and hugged her tightly to him. He simply embraced her, knee to knee, chest to chest, face to face. "I love you, Cassie. I promise I will spend the rest of my life telling you and showing you how much I love you."

"I love you too. So very much. I will make you a good wife, William, I promise."

William leaned away from her and looked into her eyes. "You are the most wonderful wife a man could have." He wiped away a tear that spilled from her eye, then realized his own eyes were wet. *Good heavens!* He had turned into a watering pot! She caused emotions to surface in him he did not know existed. She wiped away his tear with her hand as he said, "I have not been a good husband thus far, but that changes as of this moment."

"Oh, William. You are a perfect husband. Perfect for me. Everything between us happened so quickly and our emotions were confused. We needed time to come to each other, and now we are here. I suppose marriage is not an easy venture, but if we both work at it, then we can build a strong and happy marriage."

"I suppose you want me to talk to you more," he chuckled.

"Yes, but not now. Now I want you to kiss me again." Cassie put her hands on his shoulders and yanked him against her, until they almost teetered to the floor again.

They laughed as their lips came together. If he were not careful, he would make love to her right here on the floor. Keeping his mouth on hers, he stood, took her hands and brought her to her feet. He wrapped his arms around her once again and kissed her deeply.

Cassie tugged at his cravat until she freed it from around his neck, then made short work of his jacket, before she tackled the buttons of his shirt. He let her have his way and stood back, as she kissed his chest then ripped open the rest of his shirt. Her trail of kisses stopped short of his breeches, and he sucked in a breath as her mouth came so very close to his cock. She trailed her kisses back up to the center of his chest then tugged his shirt out of his breeches and pushed it off of his shoulders.

William swept Cassie up into his arms and carried her to the bed, where he laid her down with complete reverence. He intended to worship every inch of her. Her white chemise barely concealed her dusky nipples and the golden triangle at the apex of her thighs. His eyes drunk in her long legs and dainty feet. He kneeled down before her and massaged her foot from heel to toe, then shocked a moan out of her when he put her large toe in his mouth and sucked.

Cassie set up on her elbows and stared at him with lusty green eyes and gaping lush lips. He lifted his eyes to hers and chuckled. "I suppose no one has ever suckled your toe before."

"Hardly." She giggled and crashed back onto the bed.

"I feel honored to be the first to worship you at your feet." He let down one tiny foot and picked up the other to repeat the performance.

She laughed, grabbed a pillow, and threw it at him, smacking him in the face. He lunged at her, and pressed the entire length of his body against hers. She wrapped her arms around him as bent down for a deep and lingering kiss.

His hands roamed her body, grazed her breasts, stomach, hips, then moved to her thighs and back up again. William rolled off of her and removed his boots and stockings. Then he tugged her chemise from her shoulders, and pushed the silk past her breasts, down her hips and long legs until he yanked the fabric from her and sent it flying across the floor.

William sat up next to Cassie and stared at her perfectly formed body. He lightly touched the soft, rounded curve of her stomach. "I am looking forward to watching you grown round with my child."

"You mean fat."

"I mean perfect," he said as he bent down and trailed kisses across her stomach. "You are perfect. And when you are large and *round* with child, you will still be perfect."

"You say that now..."

"And I will say it then."

"Do you think doing this will harm the child?" Alarm crossed her face.

"No. I confess I asked Dr. Ainsworth if the act of lovemaking was safe. He said it was perfectly safe, unless you become uncomfortable. You will tell me if it ever becomes uncomfortable or painful?"

"Yes, of course."

"Turn over on your stomach."

"What?"

"Trust me."

Cassie did as she was told and William climbed over her to straddle her lower back with his legs. He leaned over and touched the backs of her hands with his hands, and then slowly eased his hands up her arms to her neck where he gently massaged her shoulders.

"Mmm...that feels wonderful."

He continued massaging his way down her back, and moved to her side, until he reached her bottom and massaged it too. She giggled as he made his way down her thighs and calves. Then he returned to one of her hands and kissed the back of it, and kissed and licked his way up one arm. He climbed over her to her other side, and took her other hand and kissed his way up until he reached her shoulder.

William brushed Cassie's hair to the side, as he kissed her neck and shoulders, then trailed kisses across her back. He massaged her with his hands until she was pliant beneath him. "I am not putting you to sleep, am I?"

"Mmmhmm..."

William chuckled and she let out a squeal when he kissed her bottom and ran his tongue in swirls along each cheek. She wiggled beneath him, but he did not stop, and instead, he made his way to the backs of her thighs. He pushed her legs apart in order to find a path down the insides of her legs. He moved past her knees until he reached her calves, then flipped her over and met her smiling eyes with his own.

"Are you going to come into me now?" she asked.

William lifted himself off the bed, undid his breeches, pushed them past his waist, and down to the floor. His hardened cock was proof of his desire for her. He watched her eyes widen and heard a small giggle.

"I think I shall make you wait."

"Wait? I have waited long enough, husband. Please, please come to me." She reached out her arms to him, but he denied her, instead, he went to his knees and kissed her inner thighs.

She twisted on the bed, but he refused to give in. He spread her legs apart and licked her inner thighs, then skipped over her womanhood to make his way to her stomach. He dipped his tongue into her belly button, and burned a path to the underside of her breasts. His hands roamed freely, as her hands explored his shoulders and back. Her nails scraped his skin, lightly marking him. He tongue ran circles around one of her breasts, while he squeezed and flicked the nipple of her other breast. Finally, he took her sweet nipple into his mouth and suckled until she screamed.

William switched positions and moved his mouth to her other breast and his hand to the one he laved with his tongue and mouth. He gave both breasts equal treatment before he lifted his head and grinned at her. "Do you like this, Cassie?"

"Yes, oh, yes." She pushed his head back down. He kissed each perky nipple before he moved down her body and propped her legs over his shoulders.

She lifted her hips to meet his mouth where he stroked her feminine core with his tongue. He dived in and swirled his tongue around and around her cleft. She squirmed beneath him and squealed when he dipped a finger inside her, as he continued to lick and suckle her. Then he added a second finger and mimicked the act of lovemaking by pushing his fingers in and out of her. She lifted her hips and established a rhythm until she finally came.

William lifted himself over her and thrust into her, then stilled as she adjusted to him. He began the motions of pumping into her over and over again. Their bodies smacked together, skin against skin, until he reached the pinnacle of release and sent his seed spilling deep into her body. Her muscles clenched around him as she orgasmed again, and they both cried out into the night before they relaxed into each other's arms.

They breathed heavily, as their sweat and scents mingled into one. It was the most powerful orgasm ever for William. He rested his face into her neck. "You are amazing."

She kissed his cheek, then lifted his head for another kiss and he obliged her. "I have never had such a wonderful experience in my entire life. Can we do it again?"

He laughed and pulled out of her, then rolled off of her. "Absolutely, but let me catch my breath first. I plan to spend my life making love to you, morning, noon, and night." He kissed her on the cheek, and she snuggled into him.

"Morning and noon? I am not sure that is at all proper. Of course, I am not sure what we did is proper either." Her smile lit her face, and he could not resist kissing her again and again.

"We are married. Husband and wife. Everything we do together intimately is perfectly proper. I have not even begun to show you all the ways we can love each other."

She sat up slightly and pressed her hand against his chest. "There is more?"

"Oh, yes, there is more." He kissed her and flung one of her legs over his waist and then entered her.

"Oh my!"

William moved slowly within Cassie until they became a frenzy of one movement. The pressure built and exploded, as they clung to each other to reach another climax. He pressed her bottom with his palms while she ran her hands down his back. She moved her hands to his muscled buttocks, then grasped them and giggled. He chuckled at her innocent gesture and kissed her again before he moved out of her and arranged her until she was draped partially across him.

"That was interesting," she whispered.

"Only interesting?"

"Well, more than interesting. I quite liked it. Are there other ways of completing, the, ah, act?"

"Many more ways."

"Oh my. I suppose we will have to spend a lot of time in bed so you can teach me everything I need to know."

He laughed out loud. "We will spend the rest of our lives learning and practicing together until we get it perfect."

"I thought it was already perfect," she sighed.

"Then we shall *perfect* our perfectness."

She settled her cheek on his chest, and kissed him lightly before going quiet. They rested, and listened to their mingled breathing until they fell fast asleep in each other's arms.

* * *

Sometime in the night, Cassie's eyes fluttered open. She lay in William's arms, completely sated from their lovemaking. Their naked bodies clung together in a tangle. She turned her cheek to kiss his chest.

"I love you," she whispered, although he could not hear her in his sleep. She would tell him again tomorrow when they awoke, and again the next day, and the next, for the rest of their lives.

She placed her hand on her stomach, amazed at the life growing inside of her, then closed her eyes, and breathed in the scents of man and sex and sweat. Whoever thought such smells would intoxicate her? Her body still thrummed and her private place pulsed to life. Wet and desirous, she moved her hand down his chest and stomach, until she reached him *there*. She hid her mouth in his chest to keep from giggling. After they made love, he was shrunken and softened, but when he was ready to go again, he grew long and hard.

Gently, she touched a finger to his hardened sex, then grew bold as it leapt to life beneath her finger. She grasped it and stroked until he caught her hand.

"If you continue to do that you will be on your back again with your legs spread around my waist."

She stroked him in response. He groaned and she delighted in the sound, and the ability to make him want her. Feeling powerful, she sat up and continued to move her hand up and down his length. He grit his teeth and grunted.

"Climb on top of me now, or risk me spilling my seed into your hand."

Cassie climbed on top of him and straddled William. He positioned himself at her entrance, and she sank onto him until he was deep inside of her. She tightened her muscles around him and began to move slowly up and down his shaft. She pressed her hands against his chest and threw back her head.

He squeezed her breasts gently as he let her set the pace of their lovemaking. She trembled with desire as the fullness of his body entered in and out of hers. Cassie wiggled and searched for the perfect friction. When she found it, her entire body burned with heat. They moved faster and faster until she came so close to heaven, she thought she might fall back down to earth before she soared beyond the clouds.

And then it happened.

Her body exploded with his in their own private fireworks show. Their release came together, and they smothered their cries of passion in each other's shoulders. Her body convulsed in wave after wave of exquisite pleasure, until she finally came to rest completely on top of him.

William stilled within Cassie and whispered her name, then told her he loved her. She breathed in his masculine scent, then rolled off him onto her back. She took his hand in hers and kissed it. "I love you. I love you, so much."

"And I love you. Forever."

Chapter Twenty-Two

GOLD AND RED LEAVES FLOATED to the ground at the first signs of autumn. Cassie sat on the swing in the secret garden, and gently pushed her feet back and forth. She was big and round with child. William sat in the grass next to her, and plucked the last bits of green grass from the ground and tossed them at her.

The air was cool, and the flowers in the garden closed up to sleep until next spring. The London Season was over, and the Little Season was about to begin. Most of the *ton* had already made their way to their country homes. Yet, Cassie and William never left Rosehill Manor.

They preferred their quiet time together in the clean country air. Most of the renovations and decor in the house were finished, all except for the final few touches in the nursery. They interviewed dozens of candidates before finally deciding upon a nanny. The baby was not due until Christmas, and now with an aching back and sometimes swollen feet, she was beginning to wish for her pregnancy to be over and done.

"I think we should name our son John Henry after both of our fathers. What do you think?" she asked.

"Hmm...I think we should name our daughter Angel, after her mother."

She laughed. "My name is not Angel, silly man, and this baby is a boy. I am sure of it." It was one argument they playfully continued on a daily basis.

"We shall see. We shall see. I suppose we should return to the house before everyone arrives."

"Probably. As much as I am looking forward to spending the next fortnight with our families, I shall miss our solitude. I have enjoyed our time alone together."

William stood up and offered her his hand, which she took, since she ungracefully wobbled out of the seat of the swing. They walked hand in hand through the hidden door to the secret garden, and then took their time meandering down the twisted pathways through the gardens to the house.

They made it inside just as the first carriage carrying her parents and Jocelyn came rambling up the drive. She pressed her hand to her back and continued to the front door to greet her family. William followed closely behind her.

The Chambers and Jocelyn climbed out of the carriage and made their way up the long steps to the front entrance where the door was flung open in greeting by Scott. Both her parents embraced their daughter, and Jocelyn gaped when she saw Cassie's stomach.

"Close your mouth, Jocelyn. It is undignified. Oh, Cassie, you look positively gorgeous," said her mother.

"You mean fat."

"I mean gorgeous. You carry well. Now, let us go into the drawing room so you may rest your feet. I would love some tea and biscuits. I am quite famished. Perhaps some sandwiches as well."

Cassie laughed and took her mother's arm. Jocelyn came behind them, as well as her father and William. She ordered refreshments and they all settled down, and chatted about ordinary things, such as the weather, her father's parish, the most scandalous Society *on dits*, and the renovations of Rosehill Manor.

"I shall want a tour of the newly decorated rooms. You have always had a fine eye for colors and arrangement, Cassie," said Mrs. Chambers.

"Of course, perhaps this afternoon after you have had a chance to rest from your journey."

"Before you go to your rooms, there is something Cassie and I would like to discuss with you," said William.

"This sounds important. Do tell," said Cassie's father.

"Jocelyn will turn eighteen next Season. We would like to sponsor her into Society with the help of Lady Camberley who has agreed, of course. We would also like to add to her dowry." Cassie watched her parent's reactions, particularly Jocelyn's face whose eyes lit up as she clasped her hands to her chest.

"I do not know what to say. That is quite generous of you William," said Mr. Chambers.

"Say thank you, of course," said Mrs. Chambers. "Oh, Cassie, William, this is so wonderful. The girl's grandmother left them a small pittance of a dowry, and, well, we've tried to add to it over the years, but it is rather meager. And a Season. Oh, Jocelyn, a London Season! How wonderful!"

Jocelyn reached over to hug her sister. "I am so excited. Thank you, Cassie."

"'Tis only the right thing to do. I love you, Jocelyn." Cassie hugged her sister back and they both had to retrieve handkerchiefs to wipe their wet eyes.

Scott arrived at that very moment and announced, "The Marquis and Marchioness of Camberley, the Earl of Shelbrooke, Lord James Prescott, Lady Elizabeth Prescott, Lady Mary Prescott, Lady Anne Prescott, and Lady Jane Prescott have arrived." Scott moved aside as William's entire family burst through the door.

"Such formalities, Scott." Mary kissed Scott on the cheek and laughed when he turned purplish red.

"*Mary.* Must you send poor Scott over the edge with your extreme lack of propriety," scolded William. He grabbed Mary up in a bear hug and swung her around. "Minx."

Mary swatted William's arm. "Do not fret, dear William, Scott and I have an understanding."

"Oh, do you?" William laughed.

Cassie watched the twins exchange greetings, as she greeted his parents and other siblings. Everyone hugged and kissed, then pulled chairs into a large family tableau.

Mary was the last of the Prescotts to greet her sister-in-law. She kissed Cassie on the cheek and then took her arm. "Shall we take a turn about the room, sister?"

Cassie smiled at Mary's use of the word *sister*. Perhaps there was hope for their relationship after all. She loved Anne the best, as they had hit it off right away, and became the best of friends. Elizabeth was always kind, but she had little in common with her. Jane and Jocelyn, closest in age, formed a friendship, for which she was grateful. *But Mary.* William's twin was a challenge, and at best things were strained between them.

Mary spoke softly as they moved away from the family. Only Cassie could hear her words. "We did not get off on the right foot, I believe. I suppose it was mostly my doing. You see, William and I are close. We understand each other in ways only two people born of the same womb can. I am quite protective of William. I was born first, you know. A minute earlier than William, which technically makes him my younger brother. Although, he often forgets and treats me as if *I* am the younger sister."

"I understand, Mary. You love William, and you must believe me when I say I love William too."

"Of course you do. How can you not help but love William?" Mary laughed. "In all honesty, I first thought you married William to save your reputation."

"I suppose I did, but in truth, I was already wildly attracted to him." Cassie glanced at her husband, deep in conversation with his brothers on the far side of the room.

"I thought you were in love with Lord Winnington?" Mary lifted her brow in question.

"Mary, I loved Mr. Parker, or so I thought. I was betrothed to him and expected to spend my life with him, but I am ever so grateful I did not make it to Gretna Green. When Mr. Parker became Lord Winnington, I am afraid he became a different man, and I must admit I never saw the darker side of him. My feelings were confused at first, but now I am completely and totally in love with your brother." Cassie stopped and looked Mary directly in the eye.

Mary hesitated for a small moment then lit up in a brilliant smile as she hugged Cassie. "I am so glad. I only wanted William's happiness. You are truly a love match. I see that now. And I cannot wait to call your babe niece or nephew, or perhaps both."

"Both?"

"Twins do run in the family, you know."

Cassie touched her stomach. "Oh my. I never considered."

Mary laughed and they both walked back over to join the rest of the family. Anne met them halfway with a smile on her face, as she flashed a warning smile towards Mary. *Oh dear.* Cassie hoped the sisters were not at odds because of her.

"You two appear happy." Anne's statement sounded a bit more like a question.

"We are indeed. I think Cassie is ready to get off of her feet and rest awhile." Mary led Cassie to the settee where she sank down gratefully.

William came over and pushed a footstool under her legs to prop her feet. "You look tired Cassie. Perhaps you should rest awhile in your bedchamber?"

"I am fine for now, but an afternoon nap will do me some good. I want to visit awhile longer."

"Stop fussing over her William. She is not the first woman to become enceinte, and I dare say, she will not be the last. Women are tougher than you think," said Lady Camberley.

"Tough does not begin to describe it. Can you imagine if men carried babies and gave birth? I do believe the world would come to an end." Mrs. Chambers caused a storm of laughter to blow through the room.

"Mother, please." Cassie rolled her eyes at her mother, but did not bother to contain her laughter. In secret, she enjoyed William's lavish attention.

The families spent the next hour talking and catching up with each other's lives. Content, but tired, Cassie allowed William to escort her to her bedchamber for a nap. They held hands as he helped her navigate the stairs. His hand in hers warmed her from the inside out.

"Do you think you are up to entertaining for the next few days?"

"Oh, of course. They are just family, after all. I am looking forward to spending time with everyone, and to getting to know your family better. It is not as if we have formal entertainments planned. Everything is quite relaxed and informal."

When they reached her bedchamber, William commanded Cassie to turn around. He undid the buttons on her dress and helped her out of it. He wrapped his arms around her from behind and rested his hands on her large belly.

The baby moved and they both laughed as they watched a bump run across the length of her stomach. Now, the babe kicked furiously.

"She wants out," said William.

"You mean *he* wants out," said Cassie. "Or, perhaps, they *both* want out."

"Both?" William drew back and looked at Cassie with a startled expression in his eyes.

"Mary suggested I might be carrying twins. She claims twins run in your family, and I am over large, so I suppose it is not an impossibility."

"Twins?" William chuckled. "A son and a daughter, or two daughters."

"Or two sons," said Cassie.

"Perhaps we should purchase another cradle. Just in case," he said.

"I think that might be going a bit overboard."

William came around to her front and knelt down on his knees. He touched her stomach, and moved his hands over the round protrusion. He kissed her midsection and looked up, a definite twinkle in his eyes. "Just as a precaution. And it is not as if an extra cradle would go to waste. I suspect we could use it in the future."

Cassie ran her fingers through William's hair. "Silly man. Our next baby can use the same cradle."

"Oh no! That will never do. Each child should have a cradle of his own. I always hated wearing Stephen's breeches or inheriting his toys. You would think we were poor as church mice when we were children for all of the sharing we had to do. No. My children shall have their own cradle, clothes, toys, and books." William stood and kissed the tip of Cassie's nose.

"You will spoil them rotten," said Cassie.

"But not nearly as rotten as I shall spoil their mother." William planted his mouth firmly against hers. She cradled his face with her hands, and gave back his kisses with kisses of her own.

"Have I told you today that I love you?" she asked.

"Hmm...I do not believe you have."

"I love you. You are my one true love, you know."

"Just as you are mine." William kissed her again before he slipped from his clothes, and joined her in bed for an afternoon nap, or bed play, as it so often turned out to be.

THE END

About the Author

Lisa Follett reads, writes, and loves all things Regency. She is married to her one true love, and the mother of two beautiful children.

Visit Lisa Follett's Blog
http://lisafollett.blogspot.com

Follow Lisa Follett on Twitter
@lisafollett

If you enjoyed *One True Love*, please consider leaving a review on Amazon.

www.ingramcontent.com/pod-product-compliance
Lightning Source LLC
Chambersburg PA
CBHW070442260626
47161CB00004B/1179